ADVANCE PRAISE FOR
THE SWEETNESS IN THE LIME

"A frank story of romance not only between cultures, but across the First World–Third World divide, with all the inherent economic tensions and frustrations, where the poor will risk everything for greener grasses and the rich won't understand their own wealth. Skeptical yet tender and generous, this is a tense, honest, and moving tale of latter-life love in the time of post-colonial globalization. You won't want to put it down."

–Chris Benjamin,
author of *Boy With A Problem*

"Vividly drawn, intriguing, lyrical, funny, and always entertaining, *The Sweetness in the Lime* is a story about home, friendship, loss, and new beginnings; about second chances and the power of loyalty and abiding love."

–Carmen Rodríguez,
author of *and a body to remember with*
and *Retribution*

"A terrific read and a beautifully crafted novel, with lots of twists and turns in the central plot. It is both a tender love story and a moving, insightful glimpse into the world of people moving in, and between, two different cultures—Canadian and Cuban. The portrayal of Cuba and her people is both authentic and insightful, and the character portrayals real and convincing. I found it hard to put down."

–John Kirk, Professor of Latin American Studies
at Dalhousie University

"Part love story, part mystery, this engrossing tale of Cuban–Canadian connections avoids clichés and gets to the heart of what can happen when we cross borders."

–Karen Dubinsky,
author of *Cuba Beyond the Beach: Stories of Life in Havana*

PRAISE FOR STEPHEN KIMBER

WHAT LIES ACROSS THE WATER: THE REAL STORY OF THE CUBAN FIVE

WINNER, Evelyn Richardson Prize for Nonfiction
LONGLISTED, Libris Award for Canadian Nonfiction Book of the Year

"In this remarkable piece of investigative journalism, Kimber has unearthed a riveting story at the very heart of why there is little hope of political reconciliation between Cuba and the United States—until there is justice for the Cuban Five."

—Judges' Citation, Evelyn Richardson Prize for Nonfiction

"An invaluable and informative account of the last chapter of the Cold War between Cuba and the United States—a story that is alternatively bizarre, surreal, and ever suspenseful."

Ann Louise Bardach, author, *Without Fidel* and *Cuba Confidential*

REPARATIONS

"Stephen Kimber has woven a difficult story about racism and power politics in Nova Scotia with exceptional skill and sensitivity...an important literary voyage into a largely unexplored region of the Canadian experience...reads as fiction...resonates as history."

—Linden MacIntyre,
Giller Prize–winning author of *The Bishop's Man* and *The Wake*

"Canadians have waited too long for an entertaining, ambitous, multi-layered novel about the historic black community of Africville, but they need wait no longer...an entertaining, provocative legal thriller about power and race relations in Nova Scotia...bold, outrageous, and dangerous."

—Lawrence Hill, Governor General's Award–winning author of
The Book of Negroes

THE SWEETNESS IN THE LIME

A NOVEL

STEPHEN KIMBER

Vagrant Press is an imprint of
Nimbus Publishing Limited
3660 Strawberry Hill St, Halifax, NS, B3K 5A9
(902) 455-4286 nimbus.ca

Printed and bound in Canada

NB1465

This story is a work of fiction. Names characters, incidents, and places, including organizations and institutions, either are the product of the author's imagination or are used fictitiously.

Editor: Elizabeth Eve
Editor for the press: Whitney Moran
Cover design: Jenn Embree
Interior design: Rudi Tusek

Library and Archives Canada Cataloguing in Publication

Title: The sweetness in the lime : a novel / Stephen Kimber.
Names: Kimber, Stephen, author.
Identifiers: Canadiana (print) 20200264222 | Canadiana (ebook) 20200264257 | ISBN 9781771089135 (softcover) ISBN 9781771089142 (EPUB)
Classification: LCC PS8621.I5448 S94 2020 | DDC C813/.6—dc23

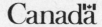  

Nimbus Publishing acknowledges the financial support for its publishing activities from the Government of Canada, the Canada Council for the Arts, and from the Province of Nova Scotia. We are pleased to work in partnership with the Province of Nova Scotia to develop and promote our creative industries for the benefit of all Nova Scotians.

"What's Love Got to Do with It?"
—Tina Turner, 1984

CONTENTS

FLOTSAM

There must have been a storm, but it has passed. Nothing remains
but a yawning silent void, a mist-shrouded, blue-black-grey sea
that extends to the horizon in all directions—to the beginning of sky,
to the end of hope. She scans the mirror of flat-calm water, pocked here
and there by scattered bits of flotsam—mismatched planks and pieces
of metal, broken hunks of white Styrofoam, multi-patched inner tubes,
forty-five-gallon steel barrels, a tattered bedsheet sail still snagged by
one corner to its mast.

She knew Roberto and his cousin Delfín had been building a raft
inside his uncle's shed out of those very same pieces. It was supposed to
be a secret. But everyone knew. The neighbours would come to watch,
and gossip. No one told the authorities. Sometimes, other men offered a
hand with the construction.

Alex had offered. *Why are you helping them?* Mariela had asked
her husband.

Roberto's my friend, that's all. She'd believed him. She'd been
wrong. About that. And much more.

Now, the bloated bodies finally sharpen into her focus among the
remnants of the raft. They are all face down in the water, their arms
and legs akimbo in a kind of studied repose, as if they'd been snorkelling
and come upon a particularly beautiful expanse of coral. She can't see
their faces, but she recognizes Alex's balding head, burned red now by
the sun. How long had they been at sea? How far had they gotten? How
close had they come?

She senses movement, a sound, an intense whooshing, like something breaking the surface of the water, breaking the silence, just beside her or maybe behind her, somewhere beyond her field of vision. She turns toward the sound. He bubbles up out of that still sea, a tiny head turning toward her, smiling.

Tonito! Tonito is alive!

He shakes his little head like a puppy, water flying away from his hair in slow motion. His hair is a raven's black like hers. He will be such a handsome man one day. She watches those tiny droplets fly through the air, feels them splash her face. She opens her mouth, tastes the saltiness. As soon as Tonito sees her, he smiles his big, goofy, gap-toothed smile.

"Mami!" he yells, delighted but not delirious like her, as if this was any other day, as if she had just arrived home from work and he was waiting by the door to greet her. She flings open her arms, reaches out to embrace him, and—

She awoke with a start, twisted up in her bed sheet, clammy with sweat. Alone. Still. The electricity must have gone out overnight. The fan had stopped working. The alarm had not sounded. She did not want to get up, to endure the cold dribble of the broken shower, to navigate her way past the broken elevator, climb down that makeshift ladder into the blackened stairwell and out into a morning that didn't know and didn't care.

She wanted only to curl back into herself, to drift back into that place and time where Tonito was smiling, where she could reach out and touch him...to the place and time that had never been.

MANY SADNESSES

HAVANA, 2017

Tony waits for me by his classroom door. My wiry little bundle of energy, dressed in his standard-issue kindergarten white shirt, red shorts, and blue scarf, bounces from foot to foot as if the floor beneath him is burning. While his body moves, apparently independently of his arms and legs, his eyes remain laser focused on an amused Señorita Isabella as he earnestly explains something to her in a rapid-fire Spanish I can admire but not completely comprehend.

"Ah, Señor Cooper," his teacher interrupts when she sees me. "It is so good to see you. How are you today?" She says each word precisely, carefully. She likes to practise her English on me. I try not to betray my continuing ignorance of Spanish to her.

"*Estoy bien. Muy bien.*" Careful too. And precise, I hope.

Tony notices me then, grins, runs up, wraps his tiny arms around my leg. "Papi, papi!" he yells. "Can we go down to the sea? Count the boats?"

"If they're there today." Like everyone else of every age here, Tony's favourite new game is sighting the gleaming white American cruise ships in the Bay of Havana. Last week, we spotted three. Tony doesn't wait, just grabs me by my hand and push-pulls me toward our destination. I shrug my goodbyes back toward Señorita Isabella, who smiles and waves.

This is our time, his and mine, but mostly his. While Tony is in school, I take care of the daily business of our *casa*. After the guests have departed and the rooms are re-set for the next guests, I head over to the Parque Central hotel, settle into my favourite couch in the lobby, order my second *cafecito*, and respond to email inquiries from potential guests. When I have finished my duty correspondence, I check the news sites. Once a newspaper editor, always.... The internet is still painfully slow here, but faster than when I arrived. I don't linger, not just because connectivity still costs by the hour, but also because the news is never good, and it mostly just repeats itself. Besides, I have better things to do with my afternoons now. Like spend them with Tony.

"Papi, you know Olaf?" I do know Olaf. How could I not? Tony and I watch *Frozen* at least once a week, more often so long as he promises not to tell his mother. I don't like the movie because it takes me inside places in my head I don't want to know. But Tony loves it, and I love Tony. And that's enough. We discovered *Frozen* last year on a *Paquete Semanal,* the thumb drive filled with Hollywood movies and popular TV series a courier hand-delivers to our door each week. The packet is illegal but, as I've learned in Cuba, "No one cares...unless they do."

For reasons that make no sense to me—we are in sunny, never-snow Cuba, after all—Tony has become obsessed with Olaf, the snowman character in the Disney movie. "Olaf is made of snow, right Papi?"

"Right."

"What's snow made of?"

Suddenly and for no reason, a memory I try to keep flash-frozen inside my head flashes hot and flares in front of my eyes. It's my father, his face bloated, mottled, and blue-ish, covered by the lightest dusting of snow, staring up at me through dead eyes. Imagined? Real? I force myself not to tighten my grip on Tony's delicate hand.

"Water," I tell him. "Think of raindrops. Imagine the drops get so cold they turn white and stick together. Like Olaf."

"I like water. Papi, do you like water?"

Water never used to terrify me. I grew up in a harbour city. Now I live in another one, on an island, and I've become an aquaphobe.

Was that Mariela's doing? Or the stories I have invented to replace the ones Dad never told me? No matter. I must not pass my panic on to my son. I must let him create his own phobias.

"Of course I like water," I answer. "Who doesn't?"

We have reached the Malecón. I lift Tony up and set him down on the concrete wall overlooking the bay. His brown legs dangle over the edge. I admire his brown skin, that black hair, and, most of all, those green eyes. Where am I in Tony? Perhaps that small dimple on his chin? Perhaps not. I wrap my arm around his tiny waist, root my own feet to the sidewalk, force myself not to imagine what Mariela imagines—wading into the Bay. Deeper, deeper, deeper, gone.

There are no cruise ships today, just a few small fishing boats bobbing in the distance. On the rocks to the right of us, an old man casts his rod into the water, fishing for his supper. In the tidal pool beneath, half a dozen teenaged boys shout and splash and swim.

"Papi, can you learn me to swim?"

"Someday," I tell him. "When you're older."

"With Mami?"

"Of course."

"We can swim together." No, we can't. I will not even mention this conversation to her. Mariela still has her...what did David call it so many years ago? "Many sadnesses."

WE'LL MEET AGAIN

McGlashlen told me that his rim fell off after his car
plopped into one of to many among the popping potholes along North Barrington that motorists must now
manoeuvre in order to reach the downtown of Halifx...

THIRTY-SEVEN ILL-CHOSEN WORDS STUFFED INTO ONE UNSUSPECTING
sentence! Where to begin? McGlashlen? So obviously mis-
spelled. But who had the time, what with this week's new publisher-
mandated hourly tweets for twits, to check the mangled spelling of
one lonely proper name? Let tomorrow's city editor field the out-
raged, can't-you-guys-get-anything-right phone calls and write the
day-after-space-filler, regret-the-error correction. *Told me?* Who
told these kids to insert themselves into news stories? *His rim fell
off....* His what? Off what? His hat? His head? A car wheel? Not to
mention—don't mention—*to* many? Or all that artsy alliteration.
Plopped, popping, potholes.... Was this what they taught them in
journalism school?

As the *Tribune*'s foreign news editor, I should have been over-
seeing a "World" section. But with ad sales tracking well below even
their usual mid-February blahs, the publisher last week ordered

another reduction in the paper's page count, which the higher-ups had then translated into—surprise—two fewer pages for foreign news. My section had shrunk to however many briefs I could squeeze onto one tabloid page, minus the two columns reserved for bill-paying advertisements.

"The Taliban claims responsibility for a suicide bombing that killed thirty-eight Afghan civilians and injured four Canadian soldiers...." Six graphs. Wounded Canadians in the lede, of course. "American Democratic presidential hopeful Barack Obama makes it ten primary wins in a row...." Five graphs. "Fidel Castro resigns...." Resigns? Didn't he die already? Washington rejoices. Three graphs. "The fallout from the British government's nationalization of the Northern Rock Bank." No room. Pawned off on the business section. I did find space, however, for the earth-shattering news that formerly famous (for what I can't recall) actress Kirstie Alley was no longer the official spokesperson for Jenny Craig. She had started her own weight-loss brand. Give that one six graphs, same as the suicide bombing. That should please the publisher ("We need more stories people give a fuck about"), if not the entertainment editor, who would bitch—again—I was poaching her material.

It took less than an hour to injudiciously slash and burn those once information-packed, grammatically correct international news-that-mattered stories into the pulpy gruel required to fill my allotted space. So I had no excuse when Liv tagged me to handle tonight's late local copy.

Liv was the *Trib*'s night news editor. For eight hours a day, from five in the afternoon until one in the morning, Liv sat staring at an over-sized computer screen, her taut body leaning back at a forty-five-degree angle with only her shoulder blades and butt touching the edges of her chair while she directed copy, edited copy, checked, re-checked, approved, and then dispatched final electronic pages into the production ether, soon to reappear as your ink-on-paper morning miracle of a newspaper.

In the harsh fluorescent glow of the newsroom at night, Liv's overgrown forest of grey-flecked red hair crowded her face and spilled over her shoulders in limp ringlets. She was too thin, too pale for my liking. But I liked her anyway. I tried to remember her—full makeup, bouncy curls, too-short red dress—at the company Christmas party. I did remember her later that same night—makeup messed, slobbery drunk, too-short red dress pushed up above her waist in the back seat of her car outside my father's house. Was that the last time? There was so much I couldn't conjure anymore.

"Eli? You get Wendy," Liv had called out then, adding, unnecessarily, "She's late. Again." Wendy Wagner—no wonder she was so fond of alliteration—was the *Trib*'s newest, youngest reporter. A formerly undistinguished J-School intern, she had been hired by Gibson, apparently for her cheerful can-do attitude even when she couldn't, which was most of the time.

Wendy's story wasn't just abysmally written. It was, more importantly at this late hour, too long, spilling over its allotted text-box space on the page on my screen by fourteen lines. I squinted at the digital clock on the wall opposite my workstation. Four-and-a-half minutes to the paper's production deadline. No problem. I started, as usual, zapping all her story's unnecessary "thats," which inevitably meant all of them. I have a thing about thats. Search. Check. Select. Delete. Next. There were fourteen thats in Wendy Wagner's 436 ill-chosen words, none necessary to make more sense of her senseless story. Not that I cared about that. My job now was simply to make her words fit on the screen, on the page. I scanned again—I'd cut five lines by eliminating thats—and began zeroing in on all those one-word widows dangling at the end of paragraphs. If you eliminated even a single other word within a paragraph, I'd learned long ago, you could often save a full line as the type reflowed. Done. The story was still crap, but now the crap fit. I looked back up at the clock. Thirty-three seconds to spare. Not bad. I hit Done.

"Back at ya," I called to Liv. She smiled, gave me her I-knew-you-could thumbs up, and turned her attention back to her screen.

I leaned back then, scanned the emptied newsroom. The glassed-in managers' offices at the far end of the newsroom had been lights out and empty since six o'clock. Most of our diminishing pool of local reporters had filed their stories hours before and headed off to wherever they went. Even the chairs at the workstations around the editing rim—so recently occupied by the entertainment editor, life editor, business editor, early news editor—were empty. Only Liv, the sports guy still sneaking in results from west coast games, and I remained at our posts.

Oh, and Peggy Aylward. She sat alone at her desk in the reporters' section. Peggy was our marquee reporter, justly famous for a decade-old exposé that had driven the mayor from the city. The awards she'd won for the paper used to earn her slack from the bosses. No longer. After the fresh crop of new owners arrived last year, one Toronto Suit began charting "content output," establishing specific weekly word quotas each "content provider" must fill. Peggy's output, Toronto Suit recently reported gravely to Gibson, who confided to Peggy, who blabbed in righteous indignation to the entire newsroom, was "well below average." She was given one month to get her numbers up to the publishing chain's metrics of 7.4 stories per week, averaging 360 words per content unit. Otherwise, Toronto Suit said, "There are plenty of other content providers in the ether." Or words to that effect.

So Peggy was still at her desk, probably polishing her résumé for the next government flacking job ahead of what everyone knew would be another round of newsroom cuts. Perhaps I should do that too. I'd heard talk the chain was considering outsourcing all its page preparation functions to a private contractor in Shanghai, or Singapore, or someplace not here. Or maybe to an algorithm.

I glanced back at Peggy, who was now engaged in an animated conversation with Wendy Wagner. They were discussing a printout Peggy held in her hands. My edit of Wendy's copy? Was Peggy mentoring Wendy? Why wasn't I? Wendy, dressed, as was her wont, in black—black turtleneck top, short, form-fitting black pencil skirt, black tights with requisite run above the knee, black mid-calf boots—had draped herself across the end of Peggy's workstation, her head resting on her folded hands, looking up in seeming supplication at the older, wiser woman. My Wendy rant, which I luckily hadn't ranted aloud, had been unfair. I was simply channelling my collective curmudgeon Ghost of Editor Past, the one who lamented that kids these days don't already know what we probably didn't know either at their age (but have now conveniently forgotten we didn't know). I once told myself I would quit when I began sounding like the ghost of Editor Past. I should quit. But what else would I do?

"I'm sorry. I really am." I looked up, startled. How had Wendy ended up in front of me when she was?... I stole a glance at Peggy's cubicle. Peggy was putting on her coat. Wendy stared at me, apologetic. "I just can't help myself," she explained. "I want to write the best story I can, so I just keep playing with the words, like, trying to make it as perfect as I can. Anyway, sorry I was so late. And thanks for making it read so much better."

"No worries," I mumbled. I had never been good at actual conversation.

"Maybe tomorrow, we can go over my story and you can tell me how I could have made it better."

"Sure."

She brightened. "Peggy and I are going over to the Shoe. Wanna come?" The Shoe was the Shoe Shop, a trendy downtown bar I rarely frequented. I don't like crowds.

"Uh, thanks, really, but I—"

"Our Eli has more important things to do." It was Liv to my rescue, calling out from behind her desk as she wiped the evening's electronic detritus from her terminal. "While you girls party the night away, Eli will be home hunched over his computer, writing his great Canadian novel, won't you, Eli?"

Thank you, Liv.

Wendy flashed me a look. Admiration? Respect?

I shrugged helplessly. There was no novel. Perhaps there had been once. Was it the novel based—not loosely enough—on my own life, the one that, like my actual life, had depressed, then bored me into submission? Or maybe it was my stillborn memoir? I was going to call it *Father Knows Nothing: And I Know Nothing About My Father.* I never got past the title.

"Next time," Wendy offered, her face betraying neither disappointment nor relief. My presence, or absence, didn't really matter.

And then Wendy and Peggy were gone.

"Want a drive?" Liv asked. I was never sure with Liv. Sometimes, a drive meant a drive home, sometimes it meant a quick fuck in the back of her car outside my father's house. Don't give me that look. She would have described it that way too. We were work friends. We talked about the news, and the news behind the news. We bitched about the bosses and gossiped about our co-workers. Occasionally we had wild, utilitarian sex that signified nothing more than the obvious. I liked Liv, and she liked me too, I think. "You're a good-looking guy," she would tell me whenever she thought I needed a talking-to. "No, really, my friend. You are. You're just too hard on yourself. You have to get out there and meet someone."

Sometime. Someone. But I wasn't in the mood tonight.

"No thanks. I think I'll walk."

"OK." Like Wendy, Liv's face betrayed neither disappointment nor relief. My presence, or absence, didn't really matter.

* * * *

My father waltzed around the kitchen table, deftly navigating obstacles like the couple-resembling chair, smiling at some secret memory, eyes squeezed shut, leaning in now, savouring, perhaps, an imagined whiff of perfume, hugging the broom closer, cheek to broom bristle, humming along while Vera Lynn sang "We'll Meet Again" yet again.

Standing in the kitchen doorway, a tumbler of Bacardi Black in my hand, I considered the father I'd never really known, not growing up, and certainly not now that his mind had faded like one of those old photographs, the image never properly fixed in the darkroom. Who knew Dad would be obsessed with Vera Lynn? No, not Vera Lynn. Vera Lynn singing "We'll Meet Again." Just that.

It had started one night after I'd returned from work and neither of us could sleep. I flipped on the TV and found a channel showing *Dr. Strangelove,* the sixties satire about a nuclear holocaust, which ended with Peter Sellers, as a wheelchair-bound former Nazi scientist named Dr. Strangelove, rising from his chair and shouting, "Mein Führer, I can walk!" The scene then dissolved into a montage of nuclear explosions, accompanied by Vera Lynn singing ironically how they'd all meet again some sunny day.

"Again," my father said as the credits rolled. "Again." For days after, he would point to the TV and simply say, "Again," again and again. I finally rented a VHS copy. My father stared blankly at the screen until the end when Lynn began to sing. Then he turned to me, smiled, and nodded enthusiastically. Rewind. Play. Rewind. Play.

It had seemed as good a time as any to ask him about his war, to segue into the black hole of his life before mine. "What do you remember about that time?" I asked, all innocence and curiosity.

"Nothing!" he barked. "I didn't do nothing in the war! Stop asking me that!" So I did.

Eventually, I downloaded a copy of Lynn's best-of album to my iPod. But my father wasn't interested in Lynn's other World War II songs. He'd shake his head, stomp his feet until "We'll Meet Again," the last song on the album, came on. After a few days, I put it on continuous repeat, which made my father happy. Except—

"Fucking cunt!" My father would suddenly scream at the broom for no apparent reason, throw it to the floor, and put his hands over his ears to block out the music. He did this randomly, yet more and more often. His nightmares were becoming more frequent, less random too. He'd wake me from a deep sleep, babbling incoherently. "Ping...Ping... Got you!...Not this time, you bastard...No clean sweep for you." And then there'd be a pause, followed by a plaintive howl and an almost eerie declaration. "I killed them! I killed them all! It was me!"

"It's not unusual," my father's doctor explained when I expressed concern. "People with dementia often lose their traditional inhibitions, begin acting in ways opposite to what we have been conditioned to expect from them." The doctor prescribed an antidepressant he said was popular among seniors. "It'll take a few weeks, but, after that, he'll settle down...." The doctor stopped, switched gears, launched into the spiel I now knew as well as the lyrics to "We'll Meet Again."

"But Mr. Cooper, you really should consider—"

The doctor said so. Sarah said so too. Our father needed to be in a home where professionals could care for him twenty-four hours a day. "And you," my sister said, "you need the freedom to live your own life again. It'll be better for everyone."

So why did I resist? Perhaps because I knew Sarah wanted me to do what she knew—she *always* knew—would be better for everyone. Smart Sarah, the older, wiser sister who'd long since escaped the stultifying confines of our upbringing. "What's wrong with you?" she'd chided me before our mother died, when leaving still seemed possible. "You're smart." But Sarah won the scholarship to the law school on the other coast. Sarah hooked up with the smartest guy in her first-year law class, married, settled in Calgary, gave birth to the requisite one boy and one girl, and then made partner in some downtown law firm specializing in something well-paying to do with oil and gas. So it had been Sarah who'd lived happily ever after somewhere other than here. And I had become the child left behind to care for my demented dad.

Each summer, Sarah would fly home with the children (*sans* husband since "Saul's too busy at the firm") for her dutiful-daughter visit. She would stay in a downtown hotel, stopping by the house once or twice to see our father who—surprise—no longer recognized her. While he sat on the couch, puzzling out who she might be and what she was doing in his living room, Sarah pretended he wasn't sitting across from her, puzzling out who she might be and what she was doing in his living room. Instead, she would re-board the endless train of her complaints. At some point, she would criticize me—again—for not having renovated our parents' kitchen as she'd suggested. "How do you expect to get a decent price if you don't fix it up. I told you I'd contribute." That was her signal to segue—again—to what to do with our father other than the nothing I was already doing so well.

"It's not fair to you," she'd insisted. "You're what? Fifty-five?"

"Fifty-four. I'm fifty-four."

"You could be travelling—"

"There's nowhere I want to go."

"You know what I mean." I did. Sarah wanted me to be normal, to be like her, with a husband and kids and a mortgage. That ship had sunk long ago.

"And it's not right for him either. The locks...." She'd noticed—couldn't help but notice—the new locks I'd had installed on the basement door to keep our father from falling down the stairs, and on all the kitchen doors to keep him from forgetting to turn off a burner and setting the house on fire while I was at work.

"What about when you're at work?" she asked. "What then?"

Doris, I could have answered, but Sarah already knew that answer and it didn't satisfy her. Doris, a neighbour, was my father's part-time caregiver and companion, not to forget our very occasional house cleaner. I suspected Doris and my father spent most of their time together watching TV, companionably filling in the hours until I returned from work. It was not an ideal living situation, but—

"I called the woman at Sunset." Sarah was relentless. "She says they have an opening, a sunny, south-facing room in the dementia unit. I'll pay."

"It's OK. We're fine."

Why hadn't I just said yes, thank you very much? My own guilt at having nothing else to do with my life that made more sense than what I was doing? Inertia? My father picked up the broom again, resumed dancing as if nothing had happened. Vera had never stopped singing.

"Hungry?" I asked. "Want me to make you some more of those squished peas with maple syrup? You like those."

My father smiled his goofy, whatever-you-say, whoever-you-are smile. Why would I even consider putting my father in a home?

I KNEW THE PHONE WAS RINGING, KNEW THE TELEPHONE WAS ON THE TELEPHONE table in the hallway, knew I would have to get out of bed to answer it, knew the linoleum floor would be ice cold, knew no one ever called. It must be a telemarketer. I vowed to wait out my caller—we had no answering machine—hoped the ringing would stop. It didn't. Finally, I opened my eyes.

My father was hovering beside the bed, naked, wisps of white pubic hair staring me in the face at my eye level. He was holding two pairs of identical black jogging pants, one in each hand. How long had he been standing there? Seeing I was awake, my father held out one pair, and then the other, as if to ask, which one should I wear?

"In a minute," I said, pushing back the covers, hauling myself into a sitting position. I looked at the alarm clock on my bedside table. Seven in the morning! I navigated past my father, who turned and followed me through the bedroom door. The telephone table was at the far end of the second-floor hallway, outside what had been my parents' bedroom, where it had been since I was a kid. It was a big black rotary handset. No colour, no punch digits, no caller ID. It must be the oldest telephone on the planet. Not that it mattered. No one ever called.

"Hello?" It was more question than answer.

"Good morning, sunshine!" Liv. Chipper, chirpy, like a bird. I said nothing. "Did I wake you?... I woke you. That's all right. Gibson woke me. All hands on deck." My father was standing close now, still holding out one pair of pants and then the other, waiting for an answer. "It's something big. I don't know what, and neither does Gibson, or he isn't telling me. Just that he got the word from above. High above. An all-staff meeting in the newsroom at eight o'clock. Be there or be square."

"What—" I paused, tried to process, couldn't. "What's going on?"

"Who knows? But I do know you could use a coffee. I'll have one waiting."

"Is it bad?"

She laughed. "Maybe they're going to give us the Christmas bonus they forgot this year." She paused, but I didn't respond. "Oh, and Eli? No walking to work this morning. Take a cab. You won't have time. There's going to be a mother of a storm this afternoon. And it's fucking freezing already."

She hung up. I put down the receiver, looked at my father. "Those," I said, pointing to the pair of pants in his right hand. "Wear those."

* * * *

"I'll need to see some ID, sir." The guy was security. It said so on the gold plastic pin on his lapel, but I would have known. He was one of those shaved-headed twentysomethings who popped steroids and pressed benches. All that exercising and power-shaking had puffed up his body until he was too bulky for his clothes. His blue sports jacket bunched uncomfortably at his armpits. His grey slacks bunched even more uncomfortably at his crotch. That must hurt, I thought. Why, I wondered in the middle of thinking that, did I bother to note such irrelevancies?

"Your ID, sir," Security Guy said again, still polite if unsmiling, but with a sharpening edge to his voice. He was not used to being ignored. "I can't let you in until I examine your photo identification." Long silence. "If you'll step aside, sir, there are people waiting."

While I stood in front of Security Guy, catatonic, Peggy Aylward waited behind me, holding her press card, the one with the photo that identified her as a reporter for the *Tribune*. I stepped aside. She handed the card to Security Guy. He handed it back. "Sorry, ma'am," he said. "It needs to be government-issued with your photo on it. Like your driver's licence." I was surprised Peggy did not say *I'm a fucking reporter for this fucking newspaper. That's my picture on the goddamned press card, so let me fucking pass now, asshole.* Instead, she meekly took the card back, handed him her driver's licence. She must be in shock. Security Guy let her through. As the door opened, I could hear the thrum of confused conversation in what should be—at this early hour—a somnolent newsroom.

"Thank you, sir," Security Guy said, still sir-ing, still unsmiling, handing me back my own government-issued identity card, the one that wasn't a driver's licence because I had never learned to drive, the one I apparently had handed over without realizing it. "You may enter now, sir."

Too many strangers crowded into my newsroom. There were reporters and editors from dayside I rarely encountered, columnists whose faces I recognized from their headshots but who filed their screeds electronically and never actually appeared in the newsroom, and wary guys from the state of sales who understood they were unwelcome in the church of the newsroom. There were managers, even editor Gibson, who now stood alone, adrift, without anyone to manage, not to forget all the civilian non-combatants, the secretaries, clerks, and accountants who toiled in the business office and were essential to the running of the newspaper but whose names and life stories I had never learned.

"We're fucked," Liv declared, sidling up beside me, handing me a Starbucks. "It's over."

I was about to ask what she meant when a flying wedge swept past us. Half-a-dozen lookalike Security Guys surrounding one small, grey-faced, grey-haired man in a grey suit who ran to keep pace. They came to a sudden halt in front of the editing rim. Two Security Guys lifted Nervous Man up on to the tabletop.

"Hey, that's my desk you're standing on," I wanted to shout at him. I didn't.

Nervous Man turned to face the suddenly silent gathering. The six Security Guys turned too, folded their arms, stared menacingly outward. *Don't fuck with us.*

"Good morning!" Nervous Man shouted as if he expected to be shouted down. He did not introduce himself. "Global Communicators International will issue a media release later this morning, but the board has asked me to inform you of its contents in advance." He paused, took a sheet of paper from his inside jacket pocket, unfolded it, began to read. "The board is pleased to announce it has partnered with one of Germany's most successful information technology companies to launch a global chain of interdependent, free daily information publications and websites to meet the needs and desires of busy urban commuters." *What the hell?* "The first Canadian test site for this exciting new venture will be right here in Halifax." He paused. It was an applause line. There was none. He resumed. "The first edition of *Morning Hi Halifax*"—gasps, a few guffaws—"will appear on local newsstands Monday." Mumbles, murmurs. Was this good news, or bad news, or just more corporate bafflegab? Security Guys, sniffing danger, edged closer together, puffed themselves up even more. Nervous Man cleared his throat. "In order to capitalize on these exciting new opportunities, the board has had to make some painful strategic restructuring decisions in the interest of corporate sustainability. Effectively immediately, the company is suspending publication of the *Tribune*."

Now there was pandemonium. Gasps, shouts, cries, inchoate rage. "Motherfuckers...."

Then Nervous Man again, no longer nervous, shouting over the rabble. "You must immediately return all company cellphones, laptops, and any other company devices and property to the security desk at the rear door. Any company equipment not returned by 6 P.M. will be considered yours and charged back to you at full replacement value and reflected in your final paycheque, which will be mailed to the address we have on file within two weeks. You must exit the building immediately. If you have personal belongings, you will need to leave your name and contact information at the security desk. You will be contacted to pick up any personal materials."

Fewer and fewer people paid attention. They were hugging, crying, commiserating, milling about.

Security Guys herded, prodded everyone toward the door, the elevator, the world beyond. No one wanted to leave.

"Hey everybody! Listen up!" It was Liv, standing on the rim, reclaiming her turf. "I just got off the phone with Victor at the Shoe. He'll open the bar for us. We can drown our sorrows, celebrate who we are and what we did!" Liv held her cellphone above her shoulders, as if in a toast. "Fuck Global! Fuck global capitalism!"

Everyone—even the sales guys, who all considered themselves capitalists—roared approval.

Security Guys eyed each other apprehensively. Had the revolution really begun?

* * * *

I knew should have gone straight home. My father must have been confused by this disruption in our daily routine. Our routine? Who was I kidding? I usually slept until noon while my father sat, alone, in the plush brown La-Z-Boy recliner in his bedroom, staring out the window. After I awoke, I would make us both breakfast, usually cereal, occasionally French toast on raisin bread, my father's favourite. Sometimes I'd feed him, not because he couldn't feed himself but because, otherwise, he'd forget to eat. Later, we'd sit together on the sofa. I'd read him stories from the morning paper and tell him some of the stories behind them. Today—before the call that had changed everything—I'd planned to tell him about Wendy and the potholes. My father appeared to listen intently to all my stories, though he never responded. He was happiest after Doris arrived and turned on the TV soap operas.

At least I'd remembered to call Doris before the taxi arrived and left a message on her machine. I told her about the newsroom meeting, asked if she could stop by early to check on my father. I said I'd be back soon. I wasn't. I should find a pay phone, make sure she was there, ask her to stay until...whenever.

At least my father had something worth staring at today. A snowstorm blanketed the city, shutting down schools and businesses.

The police advised everyone who didn't need to be on the road to stay home...or inside. I was inside. At the Shoe. *Cheers to that.* I'd ensconced myself on a stool at the far end of the bar—my own personal un-workstation—from which I could observe the universe unfolding, without having to be part of it. I preferred to watch. There was much to watch.

Liv led everyone in toast after toast, whose defiant revolutionary fervour only increased with each empty glass. Peggy arrived, clutching her framed journalism awards, which she had liberated from the boardroom under the surprisingly un-watchful eyes of Security Guys, and passed them around for everyone to admire. Everyone did. Editor Gibson wandered in, but only stayed a few awkward minutes. This was not a party for bosses. He stood off to the side, raised his glass to Liv's "Fuck 'em all!" then slipped out into the snow.

A prim woman from marketing, who'd handed out don't-drink-and-drive taxi chits during the staff Christmas party a few months earlier, strolled purposefully through the bar, handing out more of the same. She put several chits in my hand. "Use them before the motherfuckers know we have them," she said with a wink. The bartender yelled out that reporters from our rival-no-more daily had called to say the next round was on them.

"Bacardi Black, neat." I raised my empty glass to the bartender. "And make it a double if those fuckers are paying." Old rivalries died hard.

I would need to offload before I on-loaded any more alcohol. I set down my glass, stood up. I navigated as decorously as possible around the bar, found a hallway that led to the washrooms. Damn! Wendy Wagner was standing outside the closed door to the women's. Beyond it, the door to the men's was open.

"I have to pee," Wendy declared when she saw me. "I really, really have to pee." Leaning against the wall, ankles crossed, jittery, I could see she did. I could see too she'd been crying. Her mascara smeared around her eyes, her nose was red.

"You go ahead." I pointed to the unoccupied men's room. "I'll watch the door."

"Really? You're so sweet, Eli. I know I never told you, but you are. Sweet. Sweet Eli."

I urged her through the open door, closed it behind her. I only hoped she would be quick.

"Don't go away," she called from inside the bathroom. "I have something to ask you, something really, really important."

"Don't worry, I'm not going anywhere."

But then the door to the women's washroom opened. It was Liv. She stood on her tiptoes, stuck a wobbly pointer finger in my face. "This isn't over," she said with drunkard's intensity. "We're going to start our own fucking newspaper, show those fuckers. You in?"

"I'm in," I replied, but without enthusiasm. Liv didn't notice. "I'll let you know when and where. Be there or be square." And then she disappeared, back into the bar, back into the raised glasses.

I debated with myself for less than a second before entering the women's washroom. When I came back out, Wendy was waiting. "I just want to say how much I love all of you, I really do," she began without preamble. She was standing in the middle of the narrow hallway, blocking my way back to the bar. "You've all taught me so much. And I just respect you so much, Eli. That's why I need you to tell me what I should do." She'd washed the makeup smudges from around her eyes. She looked better without makeup. I wanted to tell her that, wanted to tell her she should go back to school, learn a trade, find a job that pays overtime, double time on holidays. Before it was too late.

"Don't do anything hasty," I said, trying my best to sound sober and wise. "Give it a few days and then—"

"But I'm meeting with Hitchcock in the morning."

Hitchcock? Who—?

"The new publisher of *Hi*. From Toronto. He came up to me after...you know. He offered me a job with the new paper."

"Uh, congratulations." I tried to sound enthusiastic, or at least unsurprised. Global must have decided to pluck the lowest-paid fruit from the newsroom tree to staff its new daily information blah blahs. "Good for you, Wendy, good for you."

"But won't everybody be, you know, mad at me for—"

"It's not your fault, Wendy. No one—"

"But do you think I'm, like, you know, ready to be the editor?" *The—?!*

"Mr. Hitchcock says they've had their eye on me for a while, that they have confidence—"

"And he's right, Wendy," I cut her off. Before I laughed. Or cried. "You'll be fine. Just fine." Was I being perverse? Editor? Wendy?

"Do you really think so, Eli? I mean, I really respect you. I really, really do. You've helped me so much. Thank you, thank you, thank you!" She wrapped her arms around me. She was taller than I'd realized, almost as tall as I was. She kissed me, first on the cheek and then full on the mouth. Teeth to teeth. I could smell and taste hot alcohol breath. Hers? Mine? *No!* My eyes darted down the hall toward the bar. There was no one. I needed to stop this, needed to.... She pulled her face back, inadvertently pressing her crotch against mine. *Something!* In spite of myself, I felt something stir. Did she feel it? I pushed my butt back, away from her crotch, hoping she wouldn't notice. She looked at me. Her cheeks were wet again.

"I love you, Eli Cooper." *No, you don't. You don't. You're drunk.* The words trapped inside my head, stayed there. She edged forward now, arms still wrapped around me. Suddenly, we were inside the bathroom. My arm reached out, closed the door. *Don't!* I was too old, too unattractive, too...*Eli.* I must be fantasizing. Time to go back to the bar. My drink would be waiting for me. This was not a fantasy. But it was wrong. Wendy was drunk, too drunk. Was I drunk? Not *that* drunk. It was up to me to say something, save her from herself, stop her from— The last time I'd had sex in a bathroom had been in high school. After my senior prom...with...I closed my eyes. I was no longer here. I was there. Again.

And then it was over. Back to reality. To this bathroom. To Wendy. "Look, Wendy, I'm sorry. I shouldn't have. I didn't mean—"

She shushed me with a finger to her mouth. "It's OK," she said. She placed her finger on my lips. "It's OK."

But my fantasy bubble had burst. Doubt and recrimination sloshed around my brain, mixed with the alcohol. *What the fuck had I just done?* How old was she? How old was *I*? Was it rape? Not rape. But she was drunk. She never said yes. But she'd been the one to come on to me. She was drunk. Would she accuse me? Of what? Sexual harassment? I wasn't her boss, just a lowly copy editor. I couldn't have hired or fired her, even before.... Fuck, at this very moment, I didn't have a job—and Wendy Wagner did.

"We should get back," she said. She had already rearranged her clothes. She gave me a quick, demure peck on the cheek. "Thank you."

Thank you?

Numbly, I followed her out the door. I heard Liv's voice from down the hall. *Shit.* "He's probably gone home already," she was explaining to someone behind her. "He was pretty drunk. But this is where he was when I last—Eli?" Liv noticed Wendy first, then me behind her, saw the door we'd just come out of, understood what we'd been doing behind it. I looked down to see my shirt hanging over my pants. Liv gave me a brief, disgusted flash. "Here he is," she said to the two men standing behind her. "He's all yours." And she turned and headed back to the bar. Wendy, looking embarrassed, gave me a brief smile and followed.

"Eli Cooper?" I nodded. "Sergeant Wilson. Halifax Regional Police. This is Father Tupper." Wilson acknowledged the man standing beside him, who nodded gravely at me. Neither of them wore a uniform. "Could we have a word?"

They led me into an empty kitchen, found three mismatched chairs, arranged them in a semicircle, beckoned for me to sit in the middle.

"Mr. Cooper, do you live at 3106 Union Street?" It was Wilson. He seemed to be in charge.

"Yes."

"Who else lives in that dwelling?" Why were they asking? I couldn't believe I didn't interrupt Wilson, didn't ask what the hell was going on. Instead, I obediently answered, "My father. Just me and my father."

"That would be...Arthur Cooper?"

"Yes."

"Your father have any issues?"

Issues? "I guess. I mean, he has dementia. What's wrong? Is he OK?"

Wilson paused, looked over at Tupper, back at me. "I'm sorry to have to tell you, Mr. Cooper, but we found your father this morning up in Needham Park."

Jesus. Hadn't Doris gotten my message? I should have called her again. I should have had my own cellphone. I should have called from the bar phone. "I'm sorry," I told the officer. "It's my fault. Is he home now? I'll go right now. I'm sorry, I should have—"

"Mr. Cooper." Wilson held up his hand, stopped me. "Your father was deceased when our officers found him. They immediately called paramedics, who did everything they could to revive him. But it was too late." *Deceased? Dead? My father!* Father Tupper reached out, placed a hand gently, tentatively, on my shoulder. *Father* Tupper. Now I knew why he was here.

"We won't know for sure until we hear from the medical examiner's office later in the week, but we believe he froze to death," Wilson continued. "At this point, we don't suspect foul play. But just for the record, you say you took a cab. To your job?" I nodded, told them about the message I'd left on Doris's machine, didn't tell them I hadn't followed up. "My understanding was there was some sort of announcement at work this morning." Another nod. "And then you came...here. And you've been here ever since. Is that right?" Yes. "We'll need the name of the cab company. Just to confirm the time. Just routine, you understand."

The chaplain arranged to go with me to identify my father's body, and then offered to accompany me back to the house. I demurred. "If you need anything," the chaplain said as I got into another cab, "don't hesitate to call."

"I won't." I would. Back at the house, the front door was wide open still. Snow had blown into the hallway, piled against the wall. Vera Lynn was still singing, inviting everyone to keep smiling through, just as they always did until those blue skies made the dark clouds go away. Until we meet again. We wouldn't. Ever.

I found my father's broom, tried and failed to push all the snow out the door, got down on my knees, scooped out the rest with my bare hands. I grabbed a handful of wet, cold snow and pressed it to my face, held it there, let it sting my cheek, imagined what my father felt in the moments before he stopped feeling? My father, whose nightmares always ended the same way—"I killed them! I killed them all!" Now, it seemed I had killed him, killed my father. Had I? This would not be a nightmare from which I could wake up.

I looked at my watch. Four o'clock. I should have been starting my shift at the *Trib*. How my world had changed in just twenty-four hours. I no longer had a job. The newspaper for which I'd worked almost half my life no longer existed. My father had died. I hadn't killed him, not really, but I was responsible. And, oh yes, I'd fucked the new editor of *Morning Hi Halifax*. And the day was far from over.

I needed to call Sarah, tell her our father was dead and I was responsible. I needed a drink first.

Cooper, Arthur (Art) Elijah, DSM, 88, of Halifax, passed away suddenly on February 21, 2008. Born on January 28, 1920, he was the son of the late Albert and Inez (MacDonald) Cooper of Halifax. A quiet man, he rarely spoke of the "gallantry and devotion to duty," which earned him Canada's Distinguished Service Medal in 1945. Art went on to serve the public for 35 years as a records clerk in the provincial Department of Motor Vehicles until his retirement in 1985. He was predeceased by his sister, Abigail, and his wife, Elizabeth. He is survived by his daughter, Sarah (Saul Cohen), a lawyer in Calgary, son, Elijah, a journalist in Halifax, and his grandchildren, Samuel and Amy. Visitation will take place on Sunday, February 24, 2008, 6 – 8 p.m. in Snow's Funeral Home, Windsor Street. No funeral service by request. Cremation has already taken place. Memorial donations may be made to the charity of your choice.

DSM? FOR A JOURNALIST, I HAD BEEN CURIOUSLY UNCURIOUS ABOUT MY father's existence before I'd become part of said existence. Distinguished Service Medal? I hadn't even known what the initials stood for, let alone that he'd won one. The morning after my father died, while waiting for Sarah to call back to tell me when her flight was arriving, I'd riffled through my father's bureau searching vainly for his will. Instead, I stumbled across a lumpy brown envelope underneath a pile of mismatched socks. "On His Majesty's Service" appeared in the space at the top left-hand corner of the envelope where a return address would typically have been. His Majesty apparently didn't need a return address. Surprisingly—though it didn't register that way in the moment—the envelope was addressed to my mother. From inside the envelope, I pulled out a small silver medallion mounted on a blue-white-blue ribbon with a fine dark blue stripe running down the centre of the white. On one side, there was an image of King George VI, and on the other, the words "For Distinguished Service." Below that were engraved my father's name, service number, and rank. After a brief internet search, I discovered the DSM was one of the country's highest military honours for non-commissioned personnel who "set an example of gallantry and devotion to duty under fire."

Sarah and I immediately agreed our father's newly discovered medal should highlight his obituary. That had helped me, the obituary writer—"You're the journalist," Sarah had said, delegating responsibility—since there was little else to enliven the he-was-born-he-lived-he-died blandness of what I knew of his existence. Or make up for the lack of concrete information.

"He had a sister?" I had to ask.

"Aunt Abigail," Sarah repeated. "They had some sort of falling out, and she refused to have anything to do with us. Mum told me about her."

"You're sure she's dead?"

"I asked Dad when I was preparing his will after mum died, back before, you know," she explained. I knew. So Sarah had prepared his will. "Dad told me she died back in the 1960s."

But Aunt Abigail wasn't dead. She was, in fact, the only person, living or dead, to show up for our father's visitation.

"What happened to all your co-workers?" Sarah demanded an hour into our lonely vigil. "I can't believe not one of them showed up." Sarah had ordered tea and sandwiches in anticipation of a crowd. I had to remind her again I no longer had co-workers, and the co-workers I used to have were too busy looking for new jobs, or fomenting revolution, or becoming the editor of some new giveaway rag to take time out from reconstructing their formerly busy lives to browse the obituaries, especially those that appeared in the *Herald*.

Did they also still hate the other paper—I could barely bring myself to think its name—as much as I did? Irrational as it was, especially now, it had pained me to phone in my father's obituary to the *Herald*. That the bored woman at the other end of the line didn't bother to connect the dots to the police report of the elderly man who'd frozen to death in Needham Park and pursue its story possibilities both disappointed and also relieved me. I instructed the woman to spell out each of the obituary's proper names twice just to be sure she was no Wendy Wagner. But I'd been the one responsible for the error.

When Sarah first saw the older woman, probably in her late seventies or early eighties and dressed for church, enter our too-large visiting cubicle, she jumped instantly into hostess mode, extending her hand. "I'm Arthur's daughter, Sarah Cohen," she said. "And this is my brother, Eli." The woman, who was thin and appeared frail, took Sarah's hand, but she didn't introduce herself.

"And you would be?" Sarah finally had to ask.

"I'm your 'late' Aunt Abigail. I was so sorry to read that I'd died too." She said it deadpan, then broke into a full-throated laugh that reminded me of a laugh my memory could almost place. My father? Had my father ever laughed like that? "When you get to my age," she confided, "you don't take living for granted."

Although I could discern family resemblance—the deeply dimpled chin I myself had inherited—Aunt Abigail seemed a creature from a different planet. Outgoing, charming, funny, witty. "Oh, you should have known your father back in the day," she replied when Sarah made the too-obvious comparison between our dour father and this woman standing in front of us. "He was a different person before the war. Before his...what do they call that now? Post troubles syndrome?" Post-traumatic stress disorder? "I have to say I was surprised when I saw the reference to Arty's medal in the paper," she continued. "You know he tried to send it back?" We hadn't. "From what I understood from your mother, bless her soul, it gave him nightmares."

As my aunt unfolded the story in fits and starts between sips of weak tea and bites from another of the too-many crust-less sandwiches Sarah had ordered, we discovered that our father's "gallantry and devotion to duty under fire" had changed his life. He had, in fact, sent back the medal, declared himself not a hero but a murderer. A murderer! Jesus! *His nightmares!* "I killed them. I killed them all...." And I'd bragged in his obituary about a medal my father returned!

"Your mother came to me after she found out what he'd done, and I helped her write a letter to the admiral. He managed to retrieve it and mailed it back to her for when Arty felt better again." So that was why the envelope was addressed to my mother. Was the admiral's letter buried in one of the drawers? "But Arty never really felt better again. And when he found out I'd helped your mother write the letter, he cut me off completely. Told me never to darken their door again. Even when things got a little better, after you were born—" she nodded toward Sarah— "Arty never changed his mind, never spoke to me again. Arty was stubborn that way. Always was. And now...." I could see her tears welling up, felt my own.

* * * *

"Are you OK?"

"I am."

"About Dad, I mean? About what happened?"

About which what happened? About the fact I'd let my father wander away to die in a snowdrift? About the fact my father was obsessed with the notion he'd killed all those other people? He hadn't, of course. Not really. Not if I understood what Aunt Abigail told us. In fact, he'd saved the lives of his fellow crew members on board his destroyer that night. They would have all been killed if not for my father. The others? The young Germans on the sub? The ones who did die? Not my father's fault. He was no murderer. But what would he say if he knew I'd celebrated what he considered his shame in the last words written about him? What would he say now if he was in his right mind, here, in our kitchen?

"I'm fine," I said.

"You're sure?"

"Of course I'm sure." I wasn't sure. And I wasn't fine.

After the visitation—no one else visited—Sarah and I returned to our father's house. We drank coffee, picked at the leftover sandwich triangles, picked at the comfortable, comforting conversational crumbs.

"Aunt Abigail's dimple?"

"Yes, yes, I thought so too. Exactly like Dad's."

"And her laugh? Did that sound like...?"

"Yes, it did."

I tried not to pick at those other wounds that had not yet scabbed over, the ones Sarah wanted me to rip off.

I'm not good at feelings, worse at expressing them. That's not to say I don't feel. I do. I felt a white-hot, cold-sweat, nauseous, flash-flood sweep through my entire body the moment the cop said, "Your father was deceased." I felt a bilious volcanic bile in my gut the moment the chaplain pulled back the sheet in the morgue. "Is that your father?" My father in his black jogging pants, no top. Why hadn't I chosen a shirt? His face blue. "Yes, that's him." And later, and worse, at home, alone, standing in the hallway seeing the snow that wouldn't melt, hearing the wind that wouldn't calm, and the door I couldn't bring myself to close. In case? In case this was a dream from which a ringing telephone could wake me. I knew it wasn't. At that moment I felt an unbearable pain-dagger plunge into my eye and through my brain and out the other side.

That was how I felt, but how did it make me feel? Guilt, of course. I should never have left my father alone, should have told Liv I couldn't go to that stupid staff meeting, to call me after and tell me what happened. My presence there would not have changed the outcome. My absence changed my father's forever. I should have called Doris again from the newsroom, from the bar. I should never have gone to the bar.

Dad's death made me feel anger, at myself of course, but also at the world. At Global, for deciding to shut down the newspaper and triggering every other rotten event that day. At Doris, for sleeping through my call and not checking her messages when she woke up, then not realizing (how would she?) I would be at the bar, and therefore not calling me (because I don't have a cellphone) after she found the door open and no one home. And at the snowstorm, and everything and anyone that was not me until I could no longer pretend it did not all inevitably come back to me.

His death made me feel regret too, an unfillable emptiness at not having been that curious, caring son when I still had a sentient father to care for and be curious about. I regretted having refused to accept I could no longer provide him with what he needed and finding him a place to live with professional caregivers who would have made sure he didn't wander off in a snowstorm and die, and mostly I felt remorse for not being with him at the end.

My father's demise also made me feel, I have to confess, relief. Now that his death had commuted our shared life sentence, I felt the weight of a burden I hadn't known I was carrying slip away, replaced by an airy, unknowableness of promise and possibility. Relief.

Feeling that, of course, only made me feel guilty again, and so the circle—guilt, anger, rage, regret, relief, guilt again—circled round and round in my head, unbroken.

"I worry about you," Sarah said into the silence. "I mean, I have Saul and the kids. What about you? Do you have someone? Someone special?"

"I'm OK."

"I know you are. I just realized—and I know this is my fault—I've been away so long I don't know any of your friends. Or your girlfriends." She laughed. "The last one I remember was that one from high school, the girl you had that huge crush on. What was her name? Ellen."

Eleanor. Her name was Eleanor.

"You know, I thought I saw her once," Sarah filled in the silence. "Maybe ten years ago. On the street. In Portland. Oregon. Saul and I went there for a conference and this woman, the one who looked like she could have been her, walked right past us. She was with a young girl, a teenager. By the time I realized she might have been the one you knew and turned around to say something, she was gone."

Eleanor! With a girl? A teenager? It made no sense and yet, maybe, it did. I wanted to ask more, but then the moment—like Eleanor and the girl, like the memory of our last time together—was gone.

"I'm going to try to do a better job of being part of your life," Sarah said. "Now that Dad's gone, there's just the two of us. And I do worry about you."

Me too.

* * * *

Between the mains and desserts, Sarah slid an envelope across the table. I picked it up, looked at her quizzically.

"I knew if I asked, you'd say no," she said.

I would have. I'd never been to a beach resort. I didn't think I'd like it. But then, I'd never been to Jane's on the Common either. And I liked it well enough. Sarah had suggested the restaurant. "You can never go wrong with their daily special," she said. I hadn't. She told me Jane's was her favourite restaurant in Halifax. I tried to think whether I had a favourite. I didn't. I worked nights. And then there'd been my father. I was still coming to terms with the sudden absence of everything I had known, and with the newfound presence of possibilities I had never considered. And with Sarah.

It was as if our father's death had freed Sarah, too, though I couldn't be sure from what. Regret at having written herself out of our family's life so many years before? Guilt at having left me with the burden of caring for our father? Sarah was still the all-knowing older sister, of course—she couldn't help herself—but she'd also emerged, butterfly-like, as my all-protective, all mother-father-older-sister-lawyer friend.

She'd accompanied me to the police station for my follow-up interview. After Sergeant Wilson hinted I could be charged with negligence causing death, Sarah cut him off, threatened to call her friend, Chester Rose, one of the city's top criminal lawyers.

"No need for that, ma'am," Wilson said quickly. "We're just talking hypotheticals here."

"I'd suggest, hypothetically, you stop trying to bully my client," she replied sharply. When had I become her client? "And, not so hypothetically, that you have no grounds on which to charge him with anything."

Later that day, Wilson called to say Dad's death had officially been ruled accidental, and the investigation was closed.

Sarah also explained to me the terms of our father's will, which she'd drawn up in 1987 after our mother died, and about which I'd never been told or bothered to ask. "You get everything," she said, handing me the document. What? Why? "I just didn't want anything to do with it," she told me. "Not then. And not now either. Saul and I both do very well. I thought you might need it more. Officially, I'm the executor of the estate," she continued. "I'm the lawyer, so that seemed to make sense at the time. But I'm in Calgary and you're here, so you do what you think is right. I'll sign off on whatever you decide."

Not that she didn't have suggestions about what I should decide. "You should sell the house. Fix it up first—put in a new kitchen, a new bathroom, get rid of those goddamned jailhouse locks—and sell it. You'll do all right, and you'll be able to start fresh."

She'd offered to return in the spring to help me clear out our family's accumulation of lived life and lost memories. Our mother's clothes still hung in the closet in my parents' bedroom. In the attic, there were boxes of photos, toys and books, tablecloths and old shoes. And, in the basement, boxes of jam jars, tools, skates, bicycle wheels, and other rusty, dusty debris.

Sarah also invited me to visit Calgary in the summer "when the weather's better" so I could spend time with her and Saul, get to know their kids. "They're not kids anymore, you know," she said. "Jacob's twenty-four. Still living at home." She shook her head. "He's a rap singer. A white Jewish rap singer!" I'd forgotten Sarah converted to Judaism after she married Saul. Did that make their kids Jewish too?

"There are lots of white rap singers," I responded helpfully. "Like Eminem." I'd edited that piece for the entertainment section. Eminem had apparently become a depressive, pill-popping, overweight, Elvis-like recluse, so his mother had written a tell-all book to save Eminem from himself, or cash in on his fame, whichever came first.

"Jacob will be fine," Sarah said definitively, brushing past Eminem. "He'll grow out of it." Subject shuttered. Switched. "Amy's in her third year at UBC. She's already studying for her LSATs. She's talking about doing her law degree in the US, maybe at Harvard or Yale. You'd like her." I'd probably like Jacob better, I thought.

That was when she'd taken the envelope out of her purse, slid it across the table in my direction. "Cuba!" She smiled, as if she'd invented the place. "Two weeks! You deserve a break after your job, after Dad, after this winter you've been through. Take some time, Eli. Forget it all. Hang out on the beach. Drink some drinks. Relax. Figure out what you want to do next."

And so it was settled.

PHANTOM

*M*ariela sensed Alex hovering over her, a phantom disturbing her sleep, rearranging her dreams. Finally, he slipped into the bed beside her, the strange yet familiar scent of some other woman's perfume invading her nostrils, reminding her of where he'd been, what he'd done. And then, suddenly, he was on top of her, his hot, alcohol-fumed mouth hungry on hers, the stale, slick stink of their commingled sweat and salt and sex assaulting her, his arousal rousing and arousing her.

She didn't want to. Not now. Not like this. But then she did. Some part of her must have. She had missed the sweetness of the boy-man he had once been, the Alex she had fallen in love with. She wanted that boy-man back.

"Condom," she whispered in his ear. She made him wear a condom when they had sex, partly because she worried what he might be bringing home from the resort on his penis, partly because she wasn't ready to bring a child into their world. Not now. Not while they still lived here with her family.

"Condom." She said it again, more urgent this time. She heard him sigh, sensed his frustration, his anger, felt him shift his weight above her, his arm reaching across to the night table.

"No, not those," she told him. She didn't trust the Chinese condoms the government handed out like candy. "Don't you have any?" Alex often returned home with packages of fancy European condoms in his pocket. He'd claim some "gentleman" gave them to him as a tip. She didn't believe him. But she trusted those condoms.

"No," he grunted. And he was back on top of her, his drunken fingers fumbling with the Chinese packaging. Finally, she took it from him, deftly

freed its contents, reached down and rolled the condom over his erection with her fingers. Which was when she discovered that tear in the latex....
        "No, not yet!" she said. But it was already too late. He was inside her.

And that was when she woke up. Every time. It had happened. All of it. And then it replayed, over and over, imagined but not. She wished it had never happened. She was so glad it had.

SENIORS' SPECIAL

HAVANA, 2017

"WE'RE LOOKING FOR SOMETHING SPECIAL," THE MAN EXPLAINS. "Because it's our last night. And because...well, you know." I do.

We are sitting on the second-floor balcony of the casa, companionably sipping *cafecitos* while savouring the scents and sounds and sensibilities that waft up from the streets of Centro Habana below. Mariela is still at work, showing another group of tourists her city. Tony is doing his homework.

The man, whose name is Charles, is a retired carpenter from Bayonne, New Jersey. He and his wife, Sandra, who is back in their bedroom now, resting from their day's adventures in Havana, had decided they must do "do Cuba" before it's too late.

"Now that that Trump bastard's in the White House, who knows what will happen?" I do. Our American bookings for this year are already down by half, and everyone I know in the business says it is only going to get worse.

Charles and Sandra had spent the first four days of their package tour at a beach resort in Varadero, sandwiching in this two-day whirlwind visit to Cuba's capital before returning to Varadero and catching a flight home to the US. They'd found us on Tripadvisor, where we are highly rated. "Beautifully restored accommodation, centrally located, close to Old Havana," gushed one reviewer. "Eli, who runs the casa, knows Havana well and speaks excellent English. Highly, highly recommended." She'd signed her review, "Sarah from Halifax." *Sarah!* Imagine that.

"I only wish I'd known," Charles confides. "What a city! If I'd realized, we would have spent all our time in Havana." I wish he'd known too. Four more days of even one paying customer would have been a nice buffer against what I know is to come.

So what should I suggest Charles and his wife do on their last night in the city that might earn me yet another five-star rating on Tripadvisor? I'd already endeared myself to Charles by hooking him up with my friend David for his architect's tour of Havana. I'd met David back in 2008 during my first wonderful, awful, wonderfully awful, awfully wonderful trip to Cuba. In the beginning, I thought David was...and then I learned.... It's strange how wrong a person can be. I'm still not sure I understand what motivates David's boss, Lío, who remains an enigma. Schemer? Samaritan? No matter. David and I are now friends. Lío too, I think. Whenever I can, I send our guests David's way. He's an excellent guide. But today, David had trumped even himself, arranging for Charles and Sandra to visit *La Escuela Taller Gaspar Melchor de Jovellanos*, an innovative vocational school in Old Havana that trains young Cubans in the traditional crafts required to rescue and restore the old city's significant but crumbling buildings, monuments, and infrastructure.

"It was amazing," Charles the Carpenter gushed after they returned to the casa last night. "Just amazing."

I was amazed too. At the absurdity anyone would ask my advice on what to do on their last night in Havana.

"*San Cristóbal*," I suggest finally.

"What's that?" Charles asks.

"A paladar, a restaurant in a private house. It's near here," I explain. "Serves excellent Cuban dishes with a little Spanish flavouring. The Obamas ate there. So did Jay Z and Beyoncé." Mariela and I—full disclosure—have eaten there twice, though I don't mention that to Charles.

Charles laughs, rubs his thumb and forefinger together. "I'm a retired carpenter, buddy, not a millionaire."

I try to explain. While paladars like San Cristóbal might well be beyond the financial reach of ordinary salary-paid Cubans, a complete meal there, with drinks and dessert, would probably cost Charles and Sandra much less than a much worse dinner at Ruby Tuesdays in Bayonne.

"With the seniors' discount?" he asks.

"With the seniors' discount," I reply.

"Sold."

WELCOME
TO
CUBA

"**G**OOD EVENING, SEÑOR COOPER." MY SURPRISE MUST HAVE BEEN obvious. "I'm good with names," the man said. He was. I wasn't. The bell captain had introduced himself (René? Ricky? Roberto?...some "R" name) when he'd grabbed my bag at the registration desk three days earlier and delivered it to my pool-view room.

This vacation had been a mistake. I should have known that on that middle-of-the-night morning when I found myself stranded, solo, in the Halifax airport, surrounded by bleary-eyed, winter-wilted couples, all dressed incongruously in summer shorts or pedal pushers, sandals or flip-flops, each shielded from the airport waiting room's fluorescent glare by their Ray-Bans, and/or straw hats. I had dressed in sensible winter overcoat and boots. Because it was winter! I'd unceremoniously stuffed my beachwear—an old bathing suit I wasn't sure still fit, a pair of cut-off blue-jean shorts, a few never-worn *Trib* T-shirts, two pairs of greying white socks, and a pair of rarely worn sandals—into my checked duffel.

When the sign-waving tour representatives greeted us at Varadero airport, I discovered I was the only un-coupled passenger on the bus to Jibacoa. Halfway between Varadero and Havana, Jibacoa was an adults-only resort Sarah had chosen for my forget-it-all two weeks. It had been easier than I'd expected to forget it all, or at least those parts to do with my father and with the job that was no longer mine. It was far more difficult not to notice how alone I was. On the beach. At the buffet. At the bars. At the evening cabaret. Even the couples who looked unhappy in each other's company—and many did—had each other's company. That any of this should have bothered me surprised—and bothered—me. I had understood aloneness to be my natural, desired state.

By the end of the second day, I'd finished all the books I brought with me—Graham Greene's *Our Man in Havana*, which I remembered reading years before and liking, but couldn't now recall why, Ernest Hemingway's *The Old Man and the Sea*, which had been on the syllabus for an English course I'd enrolled in at university but never attended, and Elmore Leonard's *Cuba Libre,* which I'd picked up on a whim at a used bookstore the day before my flight, and which turned out to be, as the clerk advertised, a "great beach book."

After I read them all, I visited the resort's gift shop looking for more diversionary reading, only to discover I was not just in a different country but a different reality. There were no John Grishams, no James Pattersons. All the books were political, most in Spanish. For some reason, neither *Guerrilla Warfare: The Authorized Edition* by Ernesto "Ché" Guevara, nor *Capitalism in Crisis: Globalization and World Politics Today* by Fidel Castro—both available in English—seemed much like a beach read. Not that I normally read beach books. But what else was there to do at a beach resort?

Drink. "It's an all-inclusive," my sister told me, "so you won't need cash." I didn't. Except for tips. "No need," Luis, the bartender at the piano bar, said, holding up his hand when I tried to give him one of my few remaining Canadian five-dollar bills. But he'd taken it anyway. Luis had more than earned his tip with an erudite explanation of why the bar didn't stock my usual rum of choice.

"Not Cuban."

"Really?" I had always assumed Bacardi was Cuban.

"They were," Luis confided. "But they ran away to Miami after the Revolution. Now they make their rum in Puerto Rico. It's not the same, not as good." He reached under the counter, took out a bottle of fifteen-year-old Havana Club. "*Auténtico*! This is real Cuban rum," he said, pouring a double shot into a snifter, swirling it around in the glass, placing his nose above the glass, inhaling, smiling, and handing it to me like an especially good joint.

I took a sip.

"Better than Bacardi?" Luis asked.

"Better than Bacardi," I answered. I wasn't sure. I was a rum drinker, not a connoisseur, but when in Cuba…. On second sip, I thought I could taste something caramel and warm. I'd seen Havana Club bottles in the gift shop for less than ten CUCs. CUCs—pronounced "kooks"—seemed to be a peculiarly Cuban currency designed for use by tourists, its value pegged to the American dollar. I needed to find a banking machine, get some "kooks."

More importantly, I needed to escape this stultifying, coupled resort in which I was uncoupled, unmoored. I had considered signing up for an off-resort day trip, but none of the destinations appealed to me—except Havana. But the weekly Havana bus adventure had already departed and returned before I knew it existed.

"Try registration," one of the excursion coordinators suggested. "Someone there may be able to find you a ride."

Which was what brought me to the bell captain. "No problem, Mr. Cooper," René-Ricky-Roberto said. "How long you stay?"

"I don't know." I didn't know.

"Place to stay? Hotel? Casa?"

"No thanks. I'll figure it out when I get there."

"OK." The bellhop looked skeptical. "Drive back?"

"I'll find one."

"No problem, Mr. Cooper. I have a friend, Virgilio. He travels to Havana all the time. I'll call him for you. Tomorrow afternoon, after lunch, he'll meet you. Just go outside the entrance, turn left and walk along the highway. Keep walking and Virgilio will pick you up."

I must have looked skeptical. "Don't worry, Mr. Cooper." He winked conspiratorially. "It's just how we do things in Cuba."

* * * *

I did as the bellhop instructed. I turned left up the narrow country highway and began walking. How long before the bellhop's friend would pick me up? Would he? Was there a friend? How long had I been walking? I should have put on sunscreen. "Cooper?" Lost in my own interior monologue, I'd failed to notice a lime-green-and-white, nineteen-fifty-something Cadillac materialize beside me.

"Vir-gee-ill—?" I tried.

"Virgilio. You call me Lío," the man in the car said. He was dark-skinned, bald-headed, of indeterminate age, wearing mirrored, wraparound sunglasses and a broad smile that showcased a gold front tooth. He reached behind himself to open the car's rear door. There was no handle on the door's exterior. I slid into the back seat and felt the strangely familiar, stick-to-your-skin, fitted clear plastic seat coverings. My father had had the same ones when I was a kid! That's when I noticed someone else in the car, a woman in the front passenger seat. She was young, late twenties, early thirties maybe, her long black hair parted in the middle, pulled back.

"My niece, Mariela," the driver said. "Give her ride to Havana. OK?"

"Sure."

The woman turned and flashed me the briefest of white-toothed smiles. She had thin, lightly glossed pink lips, smooth olive skin, and thick, sharply defined black eyebrows that showcased the most stunning emerald green eyes. They reminded me of that famous *National Geographic* cover of the Afghan woman whose eyes seem to glow. I would have stared, but she'd immediately turned her head back toward the highway.

"Where from?" Lío asked.

"Canada."

"Oh, Canada! Many friends in Canada. Toronto? Vancouver?"

"Halifax," I answered before he ran out of place names he knew. "East coast."

"Cold?" Lío simulated a shiver.

"Yes."

"First time in Cuba?"

"Yes."

"You like?"

"Very much," I lied. Then I remembered the question I'd for-gotten to ask the bellhop. "How much?" I asked. "The ride? How much?"

"One hundred CUCs." Lío said it confidently, matter of fact. I thought the bartender at the piano bar said it should cost no more than eighty. Not that it mattered. I didn't have any cash, Canadian or CUCs.

"I'll need to stop at a banking machine when we get to Havana," I said.

Lío looked back. "No cash?"

"No. But I have money. I just need to find a machine."

"No easy in Cuba," Lío told me. "What kind of card?"

"MasterCard."

"Maybe...depends...."

As we drove in silence, my attention focused on the verdant swaths of rolling green between the highway and the azure waters of whatever body of water. Was Florida beyond the horizon? We passed an incongruous oil derrick near the shoreline. Did Cuba produce oil? I could have asked Lío, but I didn't. How could I have ever imagined myself a journalist if I couldn't even articulate my own curiosity?

"See," Lío said, pointing at the derrick, answering the question I hadn't asked. "Canada company. Forget name. Joint venture. All joint venture." We passed a town. "Santa Cruz del Norte," Lío con-tinued his random guided tour. "Many lives here. Work in resort.... Also, Havana Club factory. Make dark rum. You have?" He mimicked putting a glass to his lips.

"Yes."

"Is good?"

"Yes. Good."

"But not best, Cooper. Ron Santiago is best. I get you some?"

"Sounds good." Was Lío trying to sell me rum? I should have said I was fine, thanks.

"Reynaldo say you spend few days in Havana, see real Havana?"

Reynaldo! So that was his name. "I do."

"Where you stay?"

"No place yet. I was thinking of the Hotel Nacional...."

"Yes, yes. Good choice. Mafia! Meyer Lansky! *Godfather*! Bang. Bang." Had Lío seen the movie?

"They take credit cards, right?" I was still trying to wrap my mind around Lío's doubts. Who didn't accept credit cards these days?

"Credit card? Not probably. But CADECA in basement. I show you." CUCs...CADECA...suddenly, the woman reached across, touched Lío on the shoulder, nodded in the direction of the road ahead.

"Sí," he said, turning his head back toward me. "Cooper. Need you stay down back seat. For minute."

I did as I was told, not knowing why. I sensed the car slowing down, then picking up speed.

"OK, Cooper." I realized Lío must think Cooper was my first name. "Up now."

I looked around. Nothing seemed untoward. I turned my head back in the direction from which we'd come. I saw a sign over the highway, a man in a uniform beside the highway.

"Checkpoint is all," Lío explained cheerfully. "No legal me have you in car." He tugged on his non-existent beard. "Just rule. No one care...Unless they do. And then trouble. But me, not you. You OK."

The woman turned to me. "There'll be a few more before we get to Havana. But I'll try to let you know sooner," she said. She spoke better English than Lío—maybe better than me.

"So what you want do in Havana?" It was Lío again.

"I don't know. I'll just wander around, see the city."

"Havana interesting, but can be confusing if you no know," Lío said, then smiled as if an idea had just struck him. "Need tour guide? Mariela best tour guide in Havana. Show you what you want. Anything."

Mariela looked back at me, embarrassed.

"No, no, that's OK," I answered. I wasn't sure whether Lío was trying to be helpful, or setting me up for a scam, or if he had just offered his niece for sale.

"Yes, Cooper, of course. Understand." Had I unfairly assumed the worst of the man?

"We're coming up to another checkpoint," Mariela said, smiling back at me. Why hadn't I said yes to her as my guide. "You'll need to duck your head."

After she gave me the all-clear again, Lío and Mariela drifted into an easy conversation in a rapid Spanish I couldn't begin to understand. I was surprised at how smoothly Mariela had slipped from one language to the other. When I was in high school, I'd taken Spanish for a semester but never got beyond, *Me llamo Eli...encantado de conocerte.* Was I too old to learn now?

Lío drove on, past what looked like a highway toll booth—this one with no toll takers, no police, no ducking my head, no slowing down—and disappeared down into a tunnel that swallowed up Lío's car. We must have crossed under a body of water and, just as suddenly, were spit out into Old Havana. After an hour and a half of nothing but empty highways, vacant green, and endless blue, emerging from the tunnel's subterranean darkness into Havana's bright, noisy, late afternoon urban other world, filled with vintage American cars, stinking exhaust, honking horns, people of all shades and hues, beautiful, crumbling Spanish architecture...seemed like some sort of revelation. But what had been revealed?

"Welcome to Havana," Mariela said.

"**D**ECIDE," Lío INSTRUCTED GRANDLY, FILLING ONE SHOT GLASS WITH A last gulp from a bottle of Havana Club Añejo Reserva and plunking it down on the kitchen table beside a second small tumbler already filled to the rim from the bottle of Santiago de Cuba Ron Añejo Lío had carried in from his car. "Keep with me always," he joked.

"So, Cooper," my even newer best friend, Esteban, instructed, "you decide which is best. Lío's Ron Santiago? Or my Havana Club?"

I wasn't sure I could drink any more rum. I'd already polished off three mojitos since we'd burst into Esteban's kitchen, unannounced but apparently expected, a few hours earlier. "My friend Esteban," Lío had said, by way of cryptic introduction. "Make best mojitos in all Havana."

It turned out—as best I could understand from a Spanglish conversation I couldn't really understand—Esteban worked for Havana Club in some sort of marketing capacity. That explained his kitchen full of Havana Club paraphernalia—shot glasses, bottle openers, T-shirts, ball caps—and the shelf filled with Havana Club rum bottles of many colours and ages. He handed me a red Havana Club baseball cap to officially welcome me to Havana.

Esteban opened another bottle then, generously sprinkled some of its contents in a corner on the kitchen floor. "For the gods," he said to me. "Santería tradition."

"Let the gods clean it up then," Esteban's wife, Silvia, responded, smiling, mock-angry, reaching for a mop.

But I'm getting ahead of myself.

* * * *

After Lío dropped off Mariela outside a sketchy-looking building downtown, I had finally seen the rest of her and was impressed. We then drove along the Malecón, the highway that runs alongside the Bay of Havana, to the imposing, turreted Hotel Nacional. We parked on a street nearby and walked up the long driveway toward the hotel. After Lío engaged an official-looking man at the hotel entrance in a brief, businesslike conversation, Lío led me down a back staircase to the basement and a small, glass-fronted kiosk with a sign that read CADECA, which I learned later was short for *casa de cambio,* which was Spanish for where you exchange your money. I was catching on.

"Show card," Lío instructed. I did, sliding my MasterCard through the opening.

"Cuánto?" the bored woman behind the glass asked.

"How much?" Lío translated.

"Five hundred. CUCs." When in Cuba.

While the woman went about her business, Lío quizzed me about my life in Canada, why I had chosen Cuba, why I was travelling alone. I offered my best non-answers. I had a job with a newspaper, I explained, without explaining the nuances of "had." Having decided I needed a vacation from winter, I had picked Cuba because it seemed interesting, leaving out the dead father–generous sister wrinkle. I was here alone because I wasn't in a relationship at the moment, a moment, I also failed to mention, that had lasted more than thirty-five years.

"Want woman?" Lío asked solicitously. "Can get. Very nice." His arms traced a shapely woman's figure.

"No. No thanks. I'm OK." Did he mean his niece? Perhaps I should not have been so hasty.

"Man?" Lío tried again. "OK too."

"No, no one. Really, I'll be fine." I just needed to get some cash, check into the hotel, order room service—

"Declina." It was the woman behind the glass. She said it without judgement, without inflection, without interest. She slid the card back through the opening.

"But I have money," I protested. I did. I didn't live lavishly, or even well. For the last twenty years, I had lived in my father's house, rent- and expense-free, in exchange for providing care and companionship. Until I'd failed to provide either. I had no idea how much money was in my account, but it was significantly more than whatever denomination the money changer had declined.

"Try again," I asked, sliding the card back at the woman. She did. My MasterCard wasn't even really a credit card. It was a cash card tarted up to look like a credit card. It should work as long as there was cash—

"Declina."

"Other card?" Lío suggested. My panic increasing, I dug through my wallet. I gave the woman my credit union client card, then my father's Royal Bank Visa card, which he'd rarely used, but for which I still had signing authority. *Declina. Declina.*

"I don't understand." My eyes darted from the woman behind the glass to Lío and back again, frustration mingling with fear and helplessness. Why hadn't I brought cash? Why hadn't I just stayed on the resort? Why had I come to Cuba at all?

"Welcome to Cuba." I had not noticed the man standing behind me in a line of customers that had not existed when Lío and I began our non-business here a few minutes ago. The man was tall, tanned, dapperly dressed, undoubtedly a guest-in-good-standing at the hotel. He smiled at me with an air of detached, been-there bemusement. "It's a mistake we all make—once," the man said. He was holding a wad of Canadian cash in his right hand, his passport in his left. "The mistake is imagining Cuba is like any other place you've ever been. It isn't. It's not the Cubans' fault. And it's not even your bank's fault...or at least not directly. Blame it on Uncle Jesse." I didn't mean to look puzzled. But I was. "Jesse Helms," the man continued. "The Republican Senator? Helms-Burton? No?" Vague recollections of stories I'd edited. "Anyway, it's an American law, part of the US embargo against Cuba. The Cubans call it the blockade, *el bloqueo*. It's illegal for American companies to do business with Cuba—"

"But it's a Canadian credit card—"

"So you'd like to believe." The man smiled, a smug, knowing smile. "But I'll bet if you dig deep enough, you'll find your Canadian credit card company at some point subcontracted processing credit card transactions to some huge American-based multinational that can do it far cheaper than your bank in Canada. So when the nice lady here tries to process your transaction, a light on some computer somewhere in Mississippi or Tennessee flashes 'No.' So, even though it may be a Canadian credit card, the American company won't process it because the US Government would fine the bejesus out of them for 'trading with the enemy.'"

The man held up the Canadian dollars in his hand, his smile broadening even more. "Next time, remember to bring cash, lots of cash."

"But what—"

"Your best bet? Get someone back in Canada to wire you cash but get them to do it right away. Nothing happens that fast down here." With that, the man stepped past me and handed his dollars and passport to the woman. "Room 610. Whatever this is in CUCs, my dear."

"No worry," Lío reassured me. "I help." He knew a couple, he said, who ran a *casa particular*, which sounded like a Cuban version of a bed and breakfast. I could stay with them until my money arrived. Once we got to the casa, Lío explained, I could call Canada and have someone there send me money. "Tomorrow, take you Asistur. Sign papers. Few days, get money."

I had only the slightest idea what Lío was talking about. Asistur? Papers? A few days? Should I trust this person who'd picked me up just a few hours ago on a country road in the middle of nowhere, whose last name I didn't know? Was this all an elaborate scam? Were they all in on it? But what choice did I have?

We drove in silence back toward the downtown where Lío had dropped off Mariela. Lío stopped on a narrow street outside a three-storey apartment-like building, which looked like every other down-at-the-heels building on the block. Lío snatched my duffel from my hand, pushed open a paint-peeled door with no sign I could see to advertise its purpose, and waved me inside. "Up," he said. The door closed behind us and, as my eyes adjusted to the lack of light, I could barely discern a long, crumbling stone staircase with random chunks of missing concrete. The walls were unpainted, and exposed wiring hung from the ceiling. At the top of the first set of stairs there was a landing, and then yet another flight of equally uninviting stairs leading to a third floor, which appeared to be guarded by a wrought iron gate. When we got to the top, Lío reached past me and unhooked the latch, pushed the gate open and....

We entered a different world. Suddenly I was in a brightly lit hallway with freshly painted powder blue walls complementing intricate blue and gold mosaic floor tiles. Directly in front of me, I could see what looked like a huge dining–living room filled with antique furnishings that opened onto a balcony overlooking the street. Lío guided me to the left and down a long hallway. To my right, there were a series of doors, behind which, I would learn later, were the casa's guest bedrooms. On the left a half-wall opened to the sky above and an interior courtyard below. At the end of the hallway, there was a small kitchen that resembled a set for a 1950s-style family sitcom—Formica counter tops, a round chrome kitchen table and vinyl covered chairs, a clunky fridge and stove.

In this delightful setting, Lío introduced me to Esteban and Silvia. They were both small and round and welcoming. They hugged me, kissed me on the cheek like a long-lost friend. Silvia had prepared a plate of sliced meats and fruits.

"You must be hungry," she said, urging me to eat. "Lío called to tell us about your troubles at the hotel." She shook her head in disgust. "*El bloqueo*," she said.

I can't remember when Esteban began making mojitos.

"We grow the mint in a garden on the roof," he explained proudly. "Not just any mint. To make best mojitos, you start with *yerba buena*, special Cuban mint." He snipped leaves from the base of a stem. "Never rip them," he showed me. "You want to hold the flavour inside." He then added a dozen leaves to each glass's base of freshly squeezed lime juice and cane sugar. "A mojito is like life," he continued expansively. "You must find the sweetness in the lime." He paused, picked up the bottle. "Then you add your white rum... always Havana Club," he said, looking at Lío and smiling. "The best."

Somewhere between the second and third mojitos, I finally remembered to call Sarah. Silvia led me to the living room where she placed the call from a cordless phone. "

I'm sorry for all the trouble," I told Silvia. "But I'm good for it, I really am. I'll pay you back as soon as—"

She placed her fingers on my lips. "I know you will. No problem. You're a friend of Lío's. You're a friend of ours. It's ringing." She handed me the phone.

"Sarah? Hi, Sarah. It's Eli."

"What's wrong? Are you OK?" Did I sound drunk?

"No, no, I'm fine. It's just that I'm in Havana—"

"What are you doing in Havana? You're supposed to be—"

I tried to explain—about the resort, the bellhop, Lío, the Nacional, the credit cards, the bloqueo—embargo, the casa, Esteban and Silvia.

"You're sure you're OK? You sound funny. And there's a lot of noise in the background."

There was. Others had apparently joined Lío's and Esteban's kitchen party. They were, I would discover over breakfast the next morning, a young Australian couple backpacking through Cuba. They had been staying at the *casa* for the last few days while they explored Havana and planned to spend their last night in Cuba at a jazz club on La Rampa.

"I have the money," I explained to Sarah when we'd finally sorted through the preliminaries, and I was able to ask her to wire me cash. "I just can't get it at it. You were the one who said I wouldn't need cash."

"You wouldn't have if you'd stayed on the resort the way you were supposed to." We were bickering like siblings.

"It doesn't matter," she said finally. "I'll send you the money. What's the address again?"

"Asistur, A-S-I-S-T-U-R," I began reading from the note Silvia had prepared for me. "Paseo de Martí—"

"Are you sure this is OK?"

I wasn't. I had no idea what Asistur was, or why she should wire me money there. "I am," I answered. "Absolutely."

By the time I got back to the kitchen, Silvia had retired for the night, the Australians had gone, and Esteban and Lío were deep into their debate about the relative merits of their favourite rums. It was probably not the first time they'd asked a stranger to decide.

I lifted the shot glass of Havana Club Lío had proffered, pretended to savour the aroma, and swallowed it in one gulp. The alcohol burned my throat. I then picked up the glass of Lío's Ron Santiago, did the same. It burned my throat too.

"I don't know," I said, smiling, drunk. "Maybe we need to do it again." My two new friends laughed, clapped me on the back.

"Again!" Lío said, picking up his bottle.

***

The next morning, Lío drove me to the Asistur offices, which were located beside a boulevard that separated Old Havana from Central Havana. Lío had explained that Asistur was a government-owned company—"Every company government company," he said simply—that assisted unlucky visitors with everything from lost luggage, to travel documents, to unexpected medical needs, to bail bonds ("Cooper no need!" Lío had laughed at his own joke), to acting as a conduit and money-skimmer for cash sent from abroad ("Cooper need").

Lío not only drove me to the office but also accompanied me inside and interpreted for me. I still couldn't decide whether Lío was genuinely helpful or just making sure I didn't skip out on what I owed him. Or both. Regardless, I was grateful.

While Lío spoke to the woman at the reception desk, I read the typewritten notice in English on the wall behind her. "Serving customers since 1991," it said. "To do so requires the disposal of a highly-qualified personnel…." Maybe I could land a job translating

Cuban English into comprehensible English. When Lío finished, the woman appeared to appraise us both carefully.

"Nationality?" she asked me in English.

"Canadian."

"Sit," she said, pointing to two red leather chairs. We sat. And waited. Eventually, the woman picked up a telephone and spoke to someone. When she hung up, she looked at me, pointed to a staircase. "Second floor. Wait for Vivian."

As Lío and I headed for the stairs, the woman held up her hand. "Only Canada." Lío shrugged. Upstairs, I sat alone in a hot, empty, airless waiting room for what seemed like forever. Finally, a woman—Vivian?—emerged, looked around at the empty room and asked, "Canada?"

I followed her back into her office. "Passport?" I handed it over and the woman disappeared down a long hallway. She returned five minutes later with my passport and a sheaf of forms for me to fill out and sign.

"When?" I asked as I slid the last signed page back across the desk. "The money? When?" I realized how rude—and Neanderthal-like—I must sound. I wanted to tell her I really could speak in full, rich sentences with subjects, verbs, objects, sub-clauses, adjectives, even occasional metaphor and simile, and that I understood she probably could too, but we were trapped into word-grunts because I couldn't speak Spanish. It was all my fault. "Sorry...please."

She smiled for the first time, as if she'd heard what I hadn't said. "Is OK. Understand.... Money? Depends. One day...a few days. All depend." I wasn't sure what anything depended on, but I thanked her anyway. "I call casa when cash come."

"YOU HAVE MONEY IN YOUR ROOM?"

"Yes." I did. My cash had finally arrived, but by the time Sarah's wired $2,000 Canadian had passed through all its various curious currency conversions, mysterious fees, inevitable taxes, and invisible hands, my share was just 1,274.70 CUCs. After I paid Lío his one hundred, plus another fifty for all his help, I'd put the remainder in the bottom of my duffel in my room at the casa, all except for twenty CUCs. That should have been more than enough to cover the cover plus a few drinks at the jazz club Esteban had recommended. And it would have been. Except—

"You get money," the man said. "Bring here. Sixty CUCs. We wait."

"OK."

How had I ended up here in the back seat of this Lada outside Esteban's and Silvia's casa, squeezed between a skinny, menacing young man on my right demanding my cash, and a now silent woman-girl on my left who hadn't earned it?

Menace Man opened the car door, got out, waited while I struggled to my feet. "Remember," he said, "we find you."

"Yes."

I'd found the jazz club Lío had recommended. It was in a large, low-ceilinged room in the basement of a building on La Rampa. Perhaps a dozen tables—I wasn't counting—circled a dance floor. Beyond, there was a small raised stage with a single stool and a microphone. I took a seat to the side, near the bar, ordered a Cuba Libre.

"*Música?*" I'd asked when the waiter brought my drink. My Spanish was clearly improving. "When?" I pointed to my watch.

"Soon," the waiter said. I waited. It was not soon. In fact, I never heard the música. After a while, a slight, dark-skinned young woman in a low-cut white top and blue-jean mini skirt came into the room and sat down, alone, at the table beside me. She smiled at me. I smiled back. She smiled again. She nodded then, beckoning me over with her eyes. Why not? I sat down at her table. She smiled. I smiled.

"English?" I asked.

She shook her head. "Español?" she asked.

"No, unfortunately not," I said, then pointed a finger at my chest. "Eli."

"Gertrudes," she said, placing her open hand across her chest. "Trudes." I tried not to stare. Though she seemed to understand I couldn't understand, she spoke to me earnestly in Spanish anyway. I tried to catch a word or phrase I understood. Finally, I called the waiter over.

"Can you help?" I asked. "Translate?"

He spoke to the woman in Spanish, but it was clear he already knew what she'd said, where this was headed. "She wants to know if you want to have a wonderful night?"

"Maybe...no...OK. But not sex." I imagined, ever so briefly, an interview with the woman, neglecting to account for the fact neither of us could speak the other's language. The waiter apparently failed to note my caveat while translating my words. The woman stood up, put her arm in mine, led me to the exit. As we passed a Cuban couple near the door, I caught the look of disgust on the woman's face. *No, I wanted to tell her, it's not what you think. I just want to talk to her. I'm a journalist....*

Like a fish at the end of a line, the woman kept my hand in hers as she led me to a side street where two young men stood beside a black Lada, smoking and talking. A taxi? There was no sign. The men barely acknowledged either of us as Trudes opened the car's back door, pushed me in, closed the door, hurried around to the other side of the car, and slid in beside me. The two men casually butted their cigarettes on the street and got into the front seats, still talking about whatever it was they'd been talking about, and drove off. They had not exchanged a word with the woman, with me. Who were they? Where were they taking us? I could feel my heart race, my mouth was dry. I'd come to Havana seeking adventure, craving something more interesting than the resort. Was this it?

They drove in silence through darkened streets for what could have been ten minutes, seemed like an hour.

"Where are we?" I asked finally. "Where are we going?" Trudes didn't answer. Did she understand anything I'd said? She just smiled and kept my hand in her clammy one. I was not a journalist. I was a dumb-as-dirt foreigner. I wanted to ask if we could go back to the club now, have a do-over.

The Lada finally came to a stop in front of a building in what seemed a much more suburban residential neighbourhood than any I'd seen so far. The one who would become Menace Man got out of the passenger seat and opened the back door. The woman kept her hand in mine as she crawled out after me. We followed the man into what turned out to be a ground-floor apartment. A family watched television in the living room. One man exchanged a nod with Menace Man, but no one else even acknowledged our presence. Menace Man stepped aside then, and Trudes took over, leading me down a long hallway to a small bedroom with a single bed. She'd obviously been here before. It was a girl's bedroom, pink, with dolls neatly lined up on a bureau, girl's clothes hanging from the closet. Did the room belong to a little girl who was now sitting in the living room watching TV with her family?

Trudes had given up on any talk, small or otherwise. She handed me a condom from a bowl on the night table—the little girl's night table!—shucked her top and began to undo the button on her skirt.

"No," I said, putting the condom back in the bowl.

She looked at me, tried to puzzle out what I meant, slipped off her skirt anyway. She stood in front of me in her bra and panties, looking at me expectantly, waiting for me to make the next move.

She was young. How young? Not the little girl whose room this was. But young, too young.

"No," I said again.

"No?" she replied.

"No." We stood and looked at each other for what seemed forever. Finally, she held up her hand to indicate I should wait here. She slipped her clothes back on, left the room. I should leave, get the hell out. But to where? I didn't have a clue where I was.

She finally returned with the man who was now Menace Man.

"What?" he said, menacing.

"No sex," I replied tentatively. "I don't want to have sex with her. I didn't intend—"

"No sex," the man repeated.

"No, I just—"

"You pay." It was not a suggestion.

"How much?"

"Sixty CUC."

"Sixty?"

The man nodded. If I spoke the language better, I might have pointed out Trudes and I hadn't actually had sex, that this was all an unfortunate misunderstanding, that I would be happy to pay for their gas and perhaps a ten CUC tip if.... The man did not look amenable to a discussion in any language.

"I don't have sixty CUC," I said, smiling hopefully, patting my pants pocket. "Not with me. Not here." I didn't.

"You have money?"

"Back at my casa." My mistake.

"Go to casa. Get money."

"Uh, OK." What else was there to say? We drove in silence, Menace Man seated in the back beside me, menacing, Trudes on the other side of him, silent, no longer smiling, no longer holding my hand.

And now, standing at the bottom of the inky-black stairwell of Esteban's and Silvia's casa, I briefly considered what might happen if I didn't come back down with the money. Would Menace Man come up? What would he say to Esteban? What would Esteban say to him? How would I ever explain my stupidity to Esteban and Silvia? I wouldn't. I couldn't. I didn't. Luckily, everyone was asleep. I went to my room, took three twenty CUC bills out of my duffel and returned to the street where Menace Man and his friend were waiting. Trudes was no longer with them. Was she back at the jazz club, scoping out her next score, someone who actually wanted to have sex?

I handed the CUCs through the car window to Menace Man, who smiled at me for the first time. "Sorry," he said as he pocketed the money. Sorry? Sorry for what? Did he think I had been unable to perform? Was that why...I wanted to tell him, no, it was all just a misunderstanding, I'm a journalist, I just wanted to talk. I tried to find words. It was useless.

"No," I said. "It's OK. Thank you." *Thank you!?*

"OK. Ciao, man. Ciao." He waved at me as the car drove off.

I HAD DESIGNATED TODAY—THE DAY AFTER MY DISASTROUS NIGHT BEFORE—
as my self-directed Ernest Hemingway Appreciation Day. I'd envisioned a solo morning walking tour of Hemingway's Old Havana
haunts followed by an afternoon taxi ride to *Finca Vigía*, the plan-
tation-farm-lookout on the outskirts of Havana where Hemingway
spent his last years in Cuba and which was now Cuba's official
museum-veneration of the Nobel prize—winning author.

So far, I'd only gotten as far as *La Bodeguita del Medio* in Old
Havana, the first stop on my tour. La Bodeguita was famous for a
handwritten sign above the bar, "My mojito in La Bodeguita, My
daiquiri in El Floridita. (Signed) Ernest Hemingway." I wasn't sure
how long I'd sat at this bar stool in front of the sign, mesmerized,
while the bartender, all doctor business-like in his white guayabera,
carefully lined up yet another assembly line of Havana Club glasses
for mojito making. How many had I drunk? I wanted to stand up,
wander around this tiny, overcrowded, come-in, drink-your-drink,
be-gone tourist bar and examine the names of the famous and the
obscure who'd hand-scrawled or carved their signatures on its walls.
Gabriel García Márquez, Pablo Neruda.... I would liked to have found
their signatures. But I did not get up. I did not inspect the walls. I did
not want to lose my seat. I did not want to have to remember where
I'd planned to go next. Or puzzle out how to get there.

At breakfast this morning, Silvia had offered to arrange a taxi
to take me to the Hemingway museum, which was in the suburbs

near Cojímar, but I'd declined with thanks. "I'll find a cab when I'm ready," I told her. "That way, I can go at my own pace."

What pace? I'd assumed I could uncover Hemingway—and Havana—for myself. I'd walk Old Havana's narrow, cobblestoned streets, navigate its soccer-playing boys and shitting dogs, sit on its plaza park benches and watch beautiful Cuban women parading past for my personal pleasure. And somehow, I presumed, Hemingway himself would emerge, magically, from behind a backdrop of who-knew-what combination of crumbling Cuban baroque-neoclassical-Moorish architectural wonder of the world.

That was the problem. I certainly didn't know. I needed a guide! I should have taken Lío up on his offer to line me up with his daughter...his niece? Whatever. Beautiful Green Eyes! "Best tour guide in Havana. Show you what you want. Anything." I rolled "anything" around in my imaginings. I could use a little anything about now. I imagined her, her life beyond those few hours in Lío's car.... Stop. I just needed a tour guide. Perhaps I would ask Silvia tonight to ask Lío if she might still be available to show me around.

But if not a tour guide for today, perhaps a tour book. At some point, I remembered I'd passed a bazaar-like plaza in Old Havana, which was ringed by stalls where Cubans peddled all manner of used books. Surely, one of them must offer a Havana tour guide. In English. Or even just one with pictures. Could I find the plaza again? I would try. I slid off my bar stool—

Her! Beautiful, beautiful Green Eyes. Standing near the entrance. She was dressed today in official-looking blue—powder-blue blouse open to reveal a hint of cleavage, a dark blue skirt that landed just above her knee. She wore those fishnet stockings Cuban women seemed to favour. She looked like a tour guide. "Maria!" I called over the cacophony of music and noise, waved. She didn't respond. Had she heard me? Was that even her name? Maria?... Marina?... Her name was..."Mariela!"

The pale man beside her—who the hell was he and what was he doing with her?—noticed me, gently touched Mariela's arm, pointed in my direction. I smiled at her...goofy, drunk, hey.... She looked my way. Blank. She didn't recognize me. But then she slowly rearranged her expression, not so much recognizing me as knowing she should, trying to frame my face to some experience, to some time, or place, or person. She remembered. She smiled back. Recognition? Relief? Something. I couldn't tell.

"Cooper!" So she did remember. "How are you enjoying your visit to Havana, my friend?" she shouted across to me.

I walked toward her, unsteady, following the beam of those luminous green eyes. "Great! Love it! Really great!" What the fuck kind of stupid was I? I needed to sober up.

"Cooper, meet my friends Ellen and Hank." Ellen! That must mean Ellen was with Hank, so Hank wasn't with Mariela. Thank god for Ellen. "Cooper here is visiting from Canada, right?" I nodded, oddly, giddily gratified she remembered. "Hank and Ellen are—" Mariela paused suddenly, as if not sure what to say next.

"We're from the United States," Ellen cut in, casting a dismissive look toward Hank. "We're just pretending we're not."

Mariela caught the eye of a waiter carrying a tray filled with mojitos, held up two fingers.

"No," Hank said, pointing toward the waiter, holding up three fingers. "You deserve one too," he gestured toward Mariela, "for putting up with us." Then he remembered me. Did he recognize something in my hangdog-hopeful expression, some pathetic eagerness not to be banished from her presence?

"And Cooper? Can I buy you one as well?"

I needed to say no. I was drunk, and it wasn't even noon. "Sure, thanks," I said.

"Canada, eh!" Ellen took a long pull from her straw, giggled. "That's where we are right now. In Toronto. Not Havana. Right, honey?" Hank did not look amused.

Mariela tried to change the subject. "So, Cooper, what have you seen so far?"

"A little." Should I tell her the truth, or just some shade of it? "Mostly, I've been walking around...." I wanted to crawl into those eyes. "But it's hard when you don't always know what you're looking at, or for." I was too drunk to be casual, too me to be suave. "Are you available—?" I asked. There were thoughts there, perhaps intended but not to be spoken. "As a guide, I mean," I added quickly. "Your?... Lío. I remember, he said you were the best. Would you be able to show me around sometime?"

"When were you thinking?"

"Now. Today. Whenever."

She laughed. I wished I could think of ways to keep her laughing. Was that the mojitos talking?

"I'm sorry, Cooper," she said, sounding sorry. "Maybe another day. Today, I am busy with my friends—"

"Look, don't worry about us," Hank cut her off. "We were thinking about hanging out at the pool at the hotel."

"We were?" Ellen needled. There was stuff going on between these two, I thought. If I hadn't been so drunk, I might even care. "Sure," she said, resigned. "I'd love to hang out at the pool, cover myself in sunblock...."

I ignored the undertones, didn't wait for Mariela to object. I clinked my glass with my new best friend Hank. "So," I said, "that's it then."

5

"**C**AN I ASK YOU A QUESTION?"

"Certainly."

Will you sleep with me? Will you marry me? Will you have my children? These were just a few of the inappropriate questions neon-dancing around my sun-baked, rum-addled brain. I wanted to ask Mariela but couldn't, shouldn't, wouldn't/didn't. Not yet. Maybe never. "Do you love...Hemingway?" I asked instead.

We'd spent a Hemingway afternoon. I'd learned things I didn't know. La Bodeguita del Medio, for example, was not Hemingway's favourite bar. He only ever visited it a few times, Mariela told me, but the bar's founder asked him to write those famous words on a note, which he then shamelessly hung above the bar to promote his business. And that other famous Hemingway-Cuba tourist tale, the one about Hemingway writing *For Whom the Bell Tolls* in Room 511 of the Ambos Mundos Hotel in Old Havana? Not true either, at least not according to Mariela. By the time Hemingway wrote that book, she said, he was already so famous he maintained the room at the Ambos for public show, but actually wrote in a secret hideaway at the Sevilla-Biltmore Hotel a few blocks away. "I can show you." *Who knew? How did she know? Did she?*

Still, we visited Room 511 in the Ambos Mundos, which had been carefully preserved by the Cuban government in its Hemingway state, and paid our two CUCs to stand where Hemingway himself supposedly once stood.

"You still must see the room," Mariela told me, "so you can tell your friends you were there, and that Mr. Hemingway was not."

Her smile crinkled the skin around the corners of her eyes. I did not tell Mariela I had no actual friends to whom I could tell this story. Instead, I admired the single bed with its red bedspread where Papa had slept. I marvelled at his stand-up, sit-down desk and the glass-encased typewriter where he wrote (or didn't). Whatever. The important point was that I now possessed secret knowledge unknown to ordinary Hemingway tourists—unless, of course, Mariela told everyone the same story. Did she? Was I just another client?

After we'd completed our pilgrimage to Room 511, Mariela suggested we take the hotel's wheezing gated lift up to the rooftop bar—where Hemingway had indeed held court, she assured me—so I could enjoy an end-of-tour drink. I wasn't ready for the tour to end.

On the roof, Mariela showed me the city's skyline, pointing out historic Old Havana landmarks and, beyond them, the harbour, El Morro, the castle, and the Christ of Havana statue that watched over the city. Though we could not see the detail from our distance, Mariela assured me the Christ figure had no eyes so he could see, and be seen to see, nothing and nowhere, yet everything and everywhere. That made no sense to me. Nothing made any sense to me. And I was fine with that.

"Your place, the place where Lío dropped you off that night...." I was finding my geographic bearings, but it was still a question. "It's around here somewhere? Right?"

"Somewhere," she said. It was a non-answer answer that did not invite further questions.

I wished I'd brought my camera, not to take photos of the views, but to ask our waiter to take a picture of Mariela and me standing together with the Havana evening skyline at our backs, or sitting together at a table, drinks in front of us, smiling for the camera. I wanted to document this moment and send the results to Sarah. "See, I did have a good time. See, I am normal." Or perhaps I wanted to prove to myself that this—whatever this was—had really happened.

"Sir?" It was our waiter. "Something to drink?"

"You go ahead," I said to Mariela.

She looked at me, uncertain. "Nothing," she told the waiter. "I'm fine."

I suddenly realized I'd put her in an awkward position. "My treat," I told her. "To thank you. This has been a great afternoon. I've had a wonderful time." I looked at the waiter, held up two fingers. "Dos mojitos."

"Thank you," she said simply. "You are my guest."

Her guest? We hadn't discussed her fee, or anything beyond the bubble in which we existed. On the taxi ride back to Old Havana from Finca Vigía, I had belatedly asked, "How did you become a tour guide?"

"Uncle Lío," she said simply. "After Fidel opened our country to tourism during the nineties, Uncle Lío created his own business. He was a professor of economics at the university in Matanzas, but he quit his job and became a tour guide—"

"Wait a minute! Your uncle was a professor of economics, and he gave that up to become a tour guide?"

"You have to understand, Cuba is not like other places," she told me. "Amigo?" She reached out, touched our taxi driver on the shoulder, asked him something in Spanish. The man laughed, shook his head, replied. Mariela turned back to me. "Our driver was an engineer. He drives a taxi to feed his family."

I wasn't listening, wasn't hearing, certainly wasn't understanding. I had disappeared again deep into the dark portals in the centres of her eyes. If I sold my father's house, withdrew all the cash I'd been hoarding for no good reason, cashed in whatever meagre pension I'd accumulated in too many years at the *Trib*, I could move to Cuba, rent an apartment, marry Mariela, live happily ever after....

This was ridiculous. I was ridiculous. It was the rum shouting crazy-think in my brain. Or maybe it was a wishful response to all the self-shaking moments I'd endured these past few weeks. My job was still gone. My father was still dead. Dad? I saw him everywhere, even here in Havana. A look, a gesture, a way of walking. This morning, I followed a man two blocks along Neptuno in the wrong direction simply because his hunched-over shoulders, bobbing head, and loping stride reminded me of Dad's ungainly gait. Following him had made me happy, then deeply sad. I would never see my father walk again. There was nothing to go back home for.

"There is a joke in my country," Mariela was still explaining as the exhaust-spewing taxi stuttered its way back to Old Havana. I tried to plug back in, catch up. "Or maybe it's a Miami joke we tell tourists. But everybody knows it, even those who support the Revolution. 'What are the Revolution's three greatest successes?' someone asks. 'Health, education, and baseball,' comes the answer. 'So what are the Revolution's three greatest failures?' ...'Breakfast, lunch, and dinner.'" She laughed. The driver laughed. I laughed. But I wasn't listening.

"So Lío decided to call himself a tour guide," Mariela picked up the thread of her story. He hung around outside the resorts in Varadero offering to show guests the *real* Cuba. "But he wasn't very good at it," she said, partly because he only spoke Spanish, and partly because he wasn't willing to learn the kinds of information tourists wanted to know.

"Like the fact the Bodeguita wasn't really Hemingway's favourite bar?" I said.

"Like that, and many other things. If you're going to be a successful tour guide here, you must know everything there is to know, everything someone might ask you. The little things like Hemingway's favourite bar, yes, and the big things like the architectural style and history of particular buildings. I spent months at the National Library, studying Cuban history, arts, culture—just like the official guides."

"Official?"

"Licensed by the government. You're supposed to be licensed to be a tour guide."

"Which means...."

"I'm not legal."

"If you get caught?"

She shrugged. "A fine, probably. Jail if they catch me too many times."

"And have they?"

"No. It's like Uncle Lío says. It's just a rule. Nobody cares. Unless they do. I've been lucky."

While Lío didn't have the language skills to be a tour guide, she continued, he clearly understood how to organize his own economy. He'd moved to Havana and assembled a sprawling network of bell-hops, front-desk clerks, bartenders, even maids, at all the city's best tourist hotels. He agreed to pay small but significant fees to anyone who connected him with guests seeking guides. As the middleman, Lío pocketed fifty per cent of whatever the tourists paid his guides.

"So how did you become one of Lío's guides?"

"That is a much longer, more complicated story I won't bore you with today." Today? Would there be a tomorrow? "The brief version is that I studied languages at university. I specialized in English." That much was clear. "And then I became a teacher back in Cárdenas where I was born."

"Cárdenas?"

"Not far from the resort where you were staying. You must have heard of Elián? Elián González, the little boy whose mother drowned in the raft on the way to Florida?" Of course I remembered. When his story dominated international headlines in 2000, I'd included at least one story about Elián every day for what seemed like months.

"Elián is also from Cárdenas," Mariela told me. She insisted on telling me the Cuban version of his story. Elián was a "sweet five-year-old boy" whose mother "stole him" from his father, then tried to smuggle him "illegally" into the United States aboard a raft with her boyfriend. The mother and the boyfriend drowned, but Elián survived. The little boy ended up in an international tug-of-war between his father, who "naturally wanted his son raised with his family in his homeland," and the boy's Miami relatives, who "kidnapped him" so he could be "saved from the evils of communism and visit Mickey Mouse every weekend." Fidel became involved. Fidel won, she said with obvious pride. What were her politics, I wondered? Was this even about politics?

"I was there the day Elián came back to school!" Mariela exclaimed in a voice that sounded almost rapturous. "September 1,

2000. It was my first day as a teacher. Fidel was there too. He shook my hand, thanked me for being a teacher."

"Did you know him—Elián, I mean? His family? It sounds like you did."

"No," she replied, suddenly formal. "I did not know them personally." I wanted to ask why Elián's story seemed to touch her so deeply, so personally, but she didn't give me time. "You asked how I became a tour guide. Like every Cuban, I could not make enough money to survive in my profession. So after a few years as a teacher, I decided I wanted to do...something else with my life, to live...somewhere else. I asked Uncle Lío, and he brought me to Havana, and I've been here ever since."

I sensed this was a truncated version of a story she wasn't ready to tell. Not yet. Or at least not to me. The little hiccup hesitations in her sentences. *Do something else...be somewhere else.*

"So do you like it? Being a guide, I mean."

"Of course," she said, smiling. "I meet all sorts of interesting people. Like you."

Even I understood she didn't mean that. Did she? Could she?

"Or maybe like..." I parried, testing now, "what were their names? Hank? And...."

"Ellen. Hank and Ellen." She laughed. "No, not like them."

Mariela sketched in what she knew of the empty rooms of their lives. Ellen and Hank were a childless couple from Michigan. He was a lawyer, she a university professor. They'd driven from Ann Arbor to Toronto, explained to officials at the border they were meeting old friends in Canada. There, they boarded a flight to Havana instead. When they returned, they would tell border officials they'd spent their entire vacation in Canada.

Mariela had met Hank and Ellen this morning in the lobby of the hotel. Hank had arranged it through Lío and apparently suggested the rendezvous point—a small table behind the grand staircase near the entrance to the men's room—so he could keep a watchful eye on...who knew? "I wouldn't be concerned," he'd explained to Mariela at one point, "except I'm a lawyer back home, and we're not even supposed to be here. If someone sees me—"

"They'll think you're an asshole," Ellen had cut him off flatly, rolling her eyes at Mariela. "Which you are." Before they left the hotel, Hank insisted Ellen slather on an extra layer of sunblock in case customs agents at the US-Canada border demanded to know how she'd gotten a tan vacationing in Canada in the middle of winter.

We'd laughed. Together. As one. *Stupid tourists. Stupid Americans.* Would she laugh later with her friends about me? Was I too obvious? Too ridiculous? A pathetic old man hitting on a...how old was she anyway? Older than Wendy Wagner. Old enough. Was I really hitting on her? Was she indulging in my harmless fantasy? Was I old? Was I harmless? This was certainly a fantasy.

"That's why I was so happy when I saw you in the bar," she said. No, you weren't, I thought. You didn't even remember who I was. Mariela raised her glass. "Thank you for rescuing me from Hank and Ellen."

I raised my glass, clinked. "You're welcome."

"How much do I owe you?" I finally remembered to ask. "For this afternoon, I mean." Part of me understood these delusions had tumbled around in my brain far too long. I needed to close the eyes on my what-if fantasies before I said or did something I could not take back.

"Whatever you think is fair." I had no idea what was fair. Would I offer too little, and risk insulting her, and therefore never see her again? Or too much and be seen as an easy mark.

"What about Hank and Ellen? How much did they pay you?"

She seemed reticent to reply with an actual number. She told me instead about the Cuban economy, that the Cuban pesos Cubans used as cash were worth one-twentieth of a CUC, about the real costs of goods in Cuba today, about—

"You don't seem to want to answer my question," I said finally.

"I don't," she laughed. "I want you to decide what it was worth to you."

Now there was a question. "Will you have to pay any of it to Lío?"

She thought for a moment. "No, he was not involved. This is just between you and me."

I reached into my wallet, took out five twenty-CUC bills, slid them across the table to her.

"No, no. That is much too much." She put her hand over mine. It was soft, her palm damp with sweat, the tips of her elegant fingers shooting flashes of electricity into the back of my hand. "It was my pleasure. Really." She tried to push my hand back across the table toward my body. I held my ground.

"You asked me to decide how much it was worth to me. I've decided."

She shrugged finally, let go of my hand, accepted the bills. "Thank you."

Which was when I'd asked her about Hemingway. That way, I wouldn't ask her something I would regret.

"Do I love Hemingway?" Mariela repeated my question. "Do you want the truth?"

"Of course."

"The only book of his I have read all the way through was *The Old Man and the Sea*—and only because it's about Cuba and because the tourists always ask."

"Did you like it?"

She laughed. "Not really."

"Me neither," I confessed. "All those short, choppy, man's-man sentences."

She looked puzzled. "So why then—"

"Hemingway's a writer. I'm a writer, sort of...." I shrugged. "I didn't plan this trip very well. I hadn't intended to come to Havana at all, so I didn't even consider what I might want to see. And now I'm here, and—"

"There are many things to see and do in Havana besides Mr. Hemingway, my friend." Was that an invitation?

"Would you be willing to show me?"

"Of course."

"Tomorrow morning?"

"Not in the morning. There's...something I must do first." That hiccup hesitation again.

"The afternoon then?"

"Of course." *Of course.*

THIS ONE? THAT ONE, PERHAPS? WAS THE FACADE PASTEL BLUE, OR PERHAPS pink or, more likely, the dull-grey, weathered concrete of all the other buildings on this block? Had Mariela entered through an actual door, or was there a wrought iron gate that opened into a ground-floor apartment, an interior courtyard? How many storeys? Two? Three? More? Balconies? No balconies? Had I even looked up? So many questions.

Perhaps I was asking myself all these peripheral questions to avoid the central questions I was not asking. For starters, what the hell was I doing here this morning, obsessively walking up and down Havana Centro's dusty, narrow streets, staring at buildings, trying to identify the one where Lío had dropped off Mariela? And then, of course, there was that other central question I was not asking: What would I do if I did find her building, or what I thought was her building? Knock on a door, ring a bell? "Does Mariela live here?" "Can Mariela come out and play?"

None of this seemed logical, even to me. We'd already agreed to meet later outside the Habana Libre Hotel in Vedado.

During our afternoon and evening yesterday, I hadn't told Mariela anything important about my own life history—why spoil with reality whatever illusions I might have conjured?—and she had shared almost nothing meaningful from her own. I knew where she was born, but not how old she was. I knew she'd been a teacher and was now a tour guide, but not what happened in between. I didn't even know her last name? She still thought my last name was my first name. Did she have a husband or a boyfriend, family she lived with here in Havana, family back in…where was it, Cárdenas?

I'd offered to walk her home. She'd demurred.

What had we talked about—besides Mr. Hemingway, of course? We hadn't kissed. We'd barely touched fingers. And yet I was in love. I knew I was in love because it had happened to me before. Once. Long ago. I had vowed to myself never to let it happen again.

"You look like you're lost, my friend." I looked around. There was no one on the street. Then I noticed wisps of smoke leaking out from behind a gated entrance. I stepped closer and looked in. A shirtless man with milky café-con-leche skin was sprawled on a couch in what appeared to be a cavernous empty space, smoking a cigarette. There were no windows, so the only light came from the entrance where I stood. I could make out the outline of what looked like a concrete staircase off to my right. There were no railings.

"Are you looking for someone?" he asked in a deep, resonant English as impeccable as Mariela's. How did he guess I spoke English?

"No, no," I replied, too quickly. "I'm just looking…at the buildings."

"Ah, the buildings," he said. He rose from the couch, walked toward me. I could see now he was younger than his voice. Late twenties? Thirties? Younger than me. He was handsome too, with a strangely languid, loose-limbed athleticism about him. He boasted remarkably detailed tattoos on his arms just below both shoulder joints, iconic images of Ché Guevara on the left, Fidel Castro on the right. "The buildings in Havana are worth looking at, my friend. So many different eras, so many different styles, even in this neigh-bourhood, even in its state of disrepair," he said, opening his arms to envelop the neighbourhood. "David," he added, pronouncing it Dah-veed, introducing himself, extending his hand through the opening. I shook it.

"Eli," I said.

"I'm an architect. I'm also a tour guide. Would you like me to show you our city's architectural wonders?"

"No," I said more sharply than I'd intended. Silvia had already warned me several times to avoid the jineteros, Havana's street hustlers offering fake tours, cigars, *chicas*....

"I have to go."

"No problem, my friend." He reached into his blue jeans pocket, his movements still measured—was it the heat?—pulled out a business card, handed it to me. "David Ramírez, arquitecto," it said, and then, in English below, "Your Guide to Havana."

"Thanks," I said, pocketing the card. "But I need to go." And I walked away, suddenly purposeful. At least I hope I looked that way.

"Have a great day, my friend," he said to my back.

* * * *

Forty-five minutes later, I found myself on the Malecón a few blocks west of the Hotel Nacional, putting in time, staring through a forest of noisy, flapping-in-the-sea-breeze black flags toward a stark concrete and glass edifice known as the United States Interests Section. I remembered spending hours in a previous lifetime sorting through wire service photos of anti-American protests here to determine which would best illustrate the latest blade-twist in the neverending knife fight between Washington and Havana. The Havana my mind's eye had conjured then—an oppressive, vaguely threatening police state full of force-marched automatons hectored into obeisance by armies of bearded Fidels—seemed to bear no resemblance to the reality I was now living. Not that I was sure I understood whatever reality I was now living.

In fifteen minutes, I was supposed to meet Mariela outside the Habana Libre.

"I'll treat you to a real Cuban ice cream at Coppelia and then I will find some nice things for you to see," she'd said. "No more Mr. Hemingway, I promise!"

I decided to circle round the building once more and head back toward the hotel. That's when I noticed Mariela herself coming out of the Interests Section.

"Mariela!" I shouted, loudly enough that the sentries in the guard houses outside the entrance started nervously, tensing themselves until they determined I posed no threat. "Mariela," I called again, more calmly. She saw me but pretended she hadn't. She looked away, brushed a hand across her cheek. She was crying.

"Are you OK?"

"I'm fine," she said. But I could see she wasn't.

"What's wrong?"

"Nothing."

Without thinking, I extended my arms, inviting a hug—an awkward, out of character gesture for me. Was this an act of spontaneous compassion? A suitor's calibrated calculation? Not that it mattered. She ignored my proffer, straightened, stared bleakly out to sea as if to situate herself. Finally, as my arms slumped, defeated, to my sides, she spoke. "Why don't we get a drink, talk about what you'd like to see this afternoon?" She said it as if none of what had just happened, happened. "I know a place."

She did. It was, almost literally, a hole in the wall near the Hotel Nacional. I hadn't noticed it before, perhaps because there was no sign to advertise its purpose, perhaps because its purpose did not include tourists. Beyond the hole, a narrow hallway led into a courtyard, in the middle of which stood a makeshift bar surrounded by a dozen card tables ringed by mismatched chairs, almost all occupied. Men played dominoes, women gossiped, and everyone seemed to know everyone's name. It was *Cheers* with a Cuban cast. Bruno, a stout, balding man, was the bartender. Though he wore a stained white chef's apron, he didn't offer us a menu, didn't ask what we wanted to eat or drink. He simply plunked two plastic cups filled with a clear liquid in front of us.

"Be careful, Cooper," Mariela said as she clopped her cup against mine. "This is not Esteban's Havana Club." She put the cup to her lips, leaned her head back, and swallowed it in a single gulp. Her entire body shivered, then she made a face, breaking into a smile.

I tried to do the same. But the harsh liquid—was it rum?—set off a blast-furnace inferno inside my mouth, constricted my throat. I sputtered, gagged. She laughed. So did Bruno. So did the people at the tables around us. They must have guessed I wasn't from here.

"Más?" Bruno asked, looking at Mariela.

"Dos," she said, still smiling, "Before you return to Canada, Cooper, my friend, we will make you a real Cuban."

She began to talk—more quickly, more earnestly than the subjects seemed to require—about the sites we would visit this afternoon, like Coppelia. "Fidel loves ice cream, so Cuba has the best ice cream in the world. Many flavours. More than Howard Johnson. We'll get in the Cuban line. It's longer than the foreign line, but the ice cream is better, and we can pay in Cuban pesos. My treat this time." The *Cementerio de Cristóbal Colón*. "Cuba's most famous cemetery. More than a million people are buried there." She sounded like she was delivering her tour guide's monologue. "Alberto Korda, the photographer who took that famous picture of Ché, the one on the T-shirts? I will show you where he is buried. And then—"

"What happened back there?" I said, cutting off her monologue. "At the Interests Section. You looked, well, upset...."

"I'm sorry," she said after another hiccup pause, as if she were sorting out what, or how much, to tell me. "I didn't intend for you to witness that. It's just that it is all so frustrating. All of it. All of them."

The story, or those parts she was prepared to share, tumbled out in fits and starts, between squeezed-dry tears and shots of what I would later discover was bootleg rum. The rum went down more easily the more you drank.

Mariela had gone to the US Interests Section for an interview with an American foreign service officer, the final step to get a visitor's visa so she could legally enter the United States as a tourist. She had been trying to get one for more than a year. "It is just so unfair." I could see her eyes—those eyes—begin to spill over again. "The American government can't get along with the Cuban government. The Cuban government can't get along with the American. So the Cuban people suffer. I suffer." That seemed to explain it all.

Mariela then led me on a guided tour through the convoluted visa process. First, she told me, she'd had to pay the equivalent of fifty-five CUCs—"Nearly three months' wages for a salaried Cuban"— to the Cuban government to get two official stamps to attach to her passport application. "That's just so you can apply." Then she had to fork over six months' more salary for the passport itself. Even then, she couldn't use her new passport to go to the United States until she'd received an official letter of invitation from some person in the United States who would agree to sponsor her visit, and then both the US Interests Section and the Cuban government would need to sign off.

Since Mariela knew no one she could contact in the United States, Lío had asked one of his friends in Miami, who agreed to write a letter of invitation and even get it notarized—for two hundred American dollars. So, Uncle Lío was a scam artist, or...I was still undecided. But Mr. Miami had been as good as his word—and Mariela's money. His letter, written in English and officially notarized at the Cuban Interests Section in Washington, had arrived at the Cuban Office of International Legal Consultancy in Havana three months ago.

Mariela then had to wait until today to get an appointment to present her documents at the Interests Section and be interviewed by a foreign service officer, who would say yes or no to her plan to visit the United States. The foreign service officer had casually leafed through her file while she sat in front of him.

"He said to me, 'You have no living husband, no children....'"

Yes! I now had the answer to the question I had not figured out how to ask.

"He seemed friendly. He asked me about the man from Miami. 'Is he a blood relative?' I said no. What should I have said? Then he asked if he was my boyfriend? He wasn't, but I didn't know the answer he wanted, so I took a chance. 'Sí, my boyfriend,' I told him. And then his whole attitude changed. He closed the file, looked at me, unfriendly. 'You have no ties here, and a boyfriend there,' he said. 'Chances are you'll try to stay in the United States once your visa expires. Application denied.' Hypocrites! All of them."

I knew I shouldn't, knew it was not the right response, but I couldn't stop my mind from tripping back over Mariela's admission—declaration?—that there was no husband. Which meant there was still a chance. For me. A voice in my head—the voice of reason—told me there were things she wasn't telling me, or things I wasn't hearing, or most likely both. This was the moment I needed to snuff out the flame of her before it consumed me. Lick the ice cream, admire the dead, buy the T-shirt, and then get the hell back to the resort, get on the plane back home.

Bruno brought us another round.

"Maybe I should find someone with a raft," Mariela said bitterly, staring hard into her cup. "Like Elián's mother."

"That sounds...dangerous." And stupid. Don't leave me now.

"Do you know that if a Cuban can get to United States territory by air, by land, or even on a raft, the Americans will let that person stay. Forever. Automatically. They call it wet foot, dry foot. You don't have to fill out any forms, you don't have to pay any fees. Just, 'Bienvenido a los Estados Unidos.... Welcome to America.' But me, an honest Cuban citizen who fills out the forms, pays all the fees, stands in all the lines...'Application denied.' They are all such hypocrites. All of them."

I raised my plastic cup. "Fuck hypocrites," I said. "Fuck them all."

"I'll drink to that, Cooper, my friend. I'll drink to that."

This was the wrong time, but there seemed no right time. "Cooper's my last name," I told her. "My first name is Elijah, but everyone calls me Eli."

"Well, then, I will call you that too." She waved her cup in Bruno's direction. "It is a pleasure to meet you, Mr. Eli Cooper!"

The pleasure was all mine.

THE BEACH HAD BEEN SILVIA'S IDEA. "YOU SHOULD VISIT AT LEAST ONE beach where real Habaneros go," she said. In the short time I'd been in Havana, Esteban and Silvia had adopted me. I'm not sure why. They said it was just because I was alone, but perhaps they meant adrift. They were hospitable, and I felt like the most pampered guest in the casa. So, late on my last Sunday morning in Havana, we had gathered together— Esteban and Silvia, Lío, Mariela, and me—for the drive to the beach at Santa María del Mar. Mariela wore a white, gauzy dress over a modest blue one-piece swimsuit, and flip-flops. I was dressed in what had turned out to be my too-tight bathing suit and too-big *Trib* T-shirt that, thankfully, covered my too-much belly.

"Where's David?" Silvia asked.

Mariela shrugged, offered what seemed like a more fulsome explanation in Spanish to Silvia before offering me the précis. "My friend David can't get out of bed until after he's had his first ciga-rette. He told me not to wait. But he'll be here by the time everyone has finished breakfast."

I rewound that sentence, parsed it. If David—"my friend," whatever that meant—couldn't get out of bed before he'd had his first cigarette, and if he'd told Mariela not to wait for him, then it followed logically she had been in the bedroom with him at the time he said that, probably in his bed. She wasn't married, she'd told me that. But a current boyfriend? Why hadn't I considered that?

David finally bounded into the apartment just as Silvia finished serving everyone a second espresso. David! David, the arquitecto! Lithe, athletic, languid David, still tattooed, still handsome, still shirtless. This was worse than I had imagined. He proceeded around the kitchen table, cheek-kissing each person in turn. I tried to read their emotions as he bussed Mariela. Lover? Friend? Acquaintance?

"And you. You must be the Canadian," he said as he leaned in to kiss my cheek. He pulled his head back, looked at my face again, realized what I had already realized. "Not just any Canadian, but the Canadian fascinated by our Havana buildings."

"David is one of Havana's best young architects," Silvia bragged.

"That's what she always says," David said to me. "Which is why I love her. But she's never seen a building I've built. Because I never have."

"I've seen plans," Silvia retorted.

"Plans, dreams. There's no money to build dreams, no money to build anything in Cuba. Which is why I am—" he paused, bowed in my direction—"your guide to Havana."

"A very excellent guide," Lío chimed in. "One of mine."

"It's not too late, my friend," David said with a smile. "Tomorrow, I'll be guiding a group of architects from Toronto. They want to explore the buildings of Old Havana. It will be very interesting. You should join us."

"Thanks," I said, looking at Mariela, hoping for some sign we would be together tomorrow. There was none. "Let me think about it."

"*¡Vámonos!*" Silvia cut in. To me, "Otherwise, there'll be no place for us on the beach."

Silvia insisted that, as their honoured guest, I sit up front with Lío for the half-hour drive to Santa María del Mar. She and Esteban sat side-by-side in the back seat on the driver's side, and David sat directly behind me on the passenger side, Mariela on his lap. I listened distractedly while Lío explained in stuttering English mixed with some Spanish and much pointing to the many features he'd added to the car, in particular the after-market *sistema de aire acondicionado* an Italian friend had brought into the country for him, and which he had personally installed with some help from a neighbourhood mechanic. Also, the AM/FM/mp3/CD player with 250-watt *altavoces* another friend had smuggled in from Miami by way of Mexico.

"*¿Te gusta?*" he said, cranking up the volume. "*Sí*," I told him. I'd have preferred to overhear what Mariela and David were saying to one another. Not that I would have understood. They were talking, whispering, giggling in rapid Spanish.

The atmosphere at the beach at Santa María del Mar was definitely different from the one I remembered at Jibacoa. For starters, there were many more people of many more colours and ages—all of them Cuban—and they were noisier. A middle-aged man in a bathing suit tossed high fly-balls into the air for a gaggle of kids, who deftly navigated among the beach chairs and bodies. Other children splashed noisily in the waves at the water's edge. Teenagers clustered together away from the kids, away from the adults, away from the water, shouting to be heard above the thumping bass music from a boom box. Servers from a bar beyond the dunes scurried about selling litre bottles (bottles, not glasses!) of white rum.

While Silvia claimed a table far from the crowd, I went with Lío to rent five plastic chairs and a table umbrella. There was an unspoken understanding that I, the rich-in-Cuba foreigner, would pay. I understood. I paid again when we ordered food and drinks from a young woman who wandered from table to table carrying a small wooden fan, which she splayed open in her hand to display the available food and drink items, each one written in marker on the leaf of her fan. Cuba was endlessly confounding. The beachgoers appeared to be Cuban, yet all of the prices were in CUCs, which I'd understood Cubans weren't supposed to use or possess, and yet sales were brisk. How did that work?

After lunch, Silvia announced something to the others in a Spanish I couldn't begin to translate. She then turned to me. "Last one in the water!" she shouted, turned and ran toward the waves. Lío and Esteban, ensconced in their chairs with a bottle of rum between them, had already waved her off. I stood up, turned toward where Mariela and David were seated, pointedly ignored David, spoke directly to Mariela. "Care to join me?" She looked at me, looked at the water, looked away. Was that the briefest flicker of fear in her eyes? "Mariela and I are going for a walk." David interjected, answered for both of them.

They did not invite me to join them. In fact, Mariela had barely acknowledged me—or anyone else—since we'd arrived. She and David seemed lost in some earnest, whispered conversation to which I had no access.

After I watched them head off, hand in hand, I reluctantly joined Silvia at the water's edge. "You should take off your T-shirt," Silvia said as we dipped our toes into the warm water, allowing the shrinking tail of the waves to deposit its sand pebbles over our feet, between our toes. "Get some sun."

"I'll be fine," I told her. I did not tell Silvia I did not want to risk exposing my loose white belly in case Mariela should return and compare my body to David's.

"Are Mariela and David...?" I asked as we waded up to our knees in the warm Caribbean waters.

She laughed, shook her head as if to say...as if to say what? No? Don't ask? And then she turned away from me, laughing, racing, her legs pumping as she pushed deeper into the ocean, up to her hips, and then, in one fluid motion, stretching her arms out in front of her in an arc, plunged into and under an onrushing wave.

I watched the water, waited for her to surface. "Cooper!" Silvia shouted from behind me. How had she gotten there? Standing waist-deep, her hair soaked, rivulets running down her body, laughing, shouting like the mischievous little girl she had once been. "Time for you to get wet!" And with that, she scooped handfuls of the ocean in my direction. There was no escape so, finally, I gave myself up to it, let my body sink beneath the surface, my face, my hair, all the way down, and paused for a moment, almost weightless, on the ocean's sandy bottom. Free. Perhaps that was what I needed to do now. Let go. Forget the past. Plunge into the future, whatever it might be. I sat there, letting the water's buoyancy bring me back up to the surface.

Back at our table, Lío and Esteban had been drinking rum and plotting the rest of our day. First, we would go back to Lío's place in Cerro. "Very nice," Lío bragged about his house. "Fix up. Nice."

Soon after Lío had moved to Havana in the late 1990s, Silvia told me, he'd acquired a dilapidated house in a neighbourhood south of Vedado near the baseball stadium. Rich Cubans used to own summer cottages there before the Revolution. For a few years, Lío shared the place with the original occupants while they plotted their escape to Miami, after which Lío became the acknowledged lord of the manor he wished to create. "Every year, Lío has a new project," Silvia said. "Last year, he put in a new kitchen. Just like in a real restaurant. You will see. I wish it was my kitchen."

While we gathered our stuff for the drive to Lío's, Mariela returned. I looked around but saw no sign of David.

"David?" I said, trying to sound casual.

"He met up with a friend and they went to Mi Cayito," Mariela answered, matter of fact. That was good. "He said to say he would find us later." I did my best to keep my own regret unapparent.

Lío's house turned out to be a flat-roofed, two-storey structure painted a stunning lime-green with orange sherbet trim that highlighted the outlines of the second-floor balcony, as well as all the doors, windows, and even a street-side concrete block privacy wall. On a small street of modest, muted one-storey homes, Lío's stood out.

"All myself," Lío declared with obvious pride. "I show." And he did. We began in the living room where there was a large framed "before" photo of the house's exterior. Back then, Lío's house had looked like all the others on the street. One storey, unpainted, no privacy wall. The smaller, framed pre-renovation interior photos artfully arranged around the larger picture, were even more monochromatic and empty, with only occasional scattered pieces of furniture dotting the rooms. In the here and now, however, there was barely a square foot of brightly tiled floor without a colourful couch or chair or table. The fact none of them seemed to fit together seemed to fit perfectly.

"Come," he said as he led me down a hallway so I could admire the staircase leading to the second floor. "Marble, best marble," he said pointing up, smiling and rubbing his thumb and his fingers together. *"Mucho dinero."*

"And many friends," said Silvia, who'd come up behind us, holding out glasses of rum. "Lío knows everyone. He knows how to get cement when there is none, tiles that don't exist for the rest of us. When we were fixing up our casa, we had money from my uncle in Miami, but we couldn't get the tiles we needed...until Lío got them for us."

Lío beamed. "Friends," he said. "Know what on trucks. Know what not be missed." He smiled enigmatically, gestured with his thumb and fingers again. "Have many friends...."

The tour ended in the kitchen. It was, as Silvia had suggested, a large, gleaming, modern affair filled with stainless steel appliances, expensive-looking food processors, blenders, hanging pots and pans, a preparation island with butcher block and sink. Beyond the kitchen, I could see a small pig that had been roasting all day on a spit in the backyard barbecue pit.

"Porky say hi," Lío said, lifting his glass in my direction.

"Porky says bye-bye," I answered, holding up my glass in response. "Where's Mariela?" I didn't want to appear anxious, or obvious, or proprietary, but I was. All of the above.

Esteban shrugged. "A friend lives near here. She went to visit. But she be back soon."

"A friend?" I quizzed, as if somehow Mariela could have had a friend I wouldn't have known about, as if friend might—worse—be a euphemism for David. No one answered me. Had I even asked that aloud? And where was David anyway? Was she with him again?

I needed a drink. Another one. Now. This was the part I'd hated most so many never-forgotten years ago when I might have once been in love—the tortured, self-inflicted uncertainty of the love-torn. But that was not this, I had to remind myself. We were not in love, or at least Mariela was not in love with me. Otherwise, why would she have gone off with David, or disappeared with a "friend" without saying a word to me? Was I in love with her? I was not. I had just been through "stuff", including the job, my father, finding myself disconnected from everything I had ever known in a place where I had no connection to anything or anyone. It was only natural to grab for the nearest life buoy, the unattainable illusion that was Mariela. I needed to go home, deal with all the realities I'd been holding at bay. Just three more days. I was ready to go home. Or, at least, I needed to believe I was ready to go home. I picked up Lío's bottle of rum from the counter, filled my glass to the rim, took a long swallow.

"She'll be back. Don't worry," Silvia said as she cut wedges from a watermelon before declaring the obvious. "You have feelings for Mariela."

"I don't know. It's just—I *do* worry about her," I said, trying to recast my complicated feelings as platonic concern for her well-being. "She seemed upset yesterday when I ran into her at the Interests Section."

"She was," Silvia replied matter of factly. "Americans. You can never trust them."

I wasn't sure. Based on what Mariela had told me, it didn't seem the Americans were solely to blame. But I let that pass.

"Does she have family in the United States? Is that why she wants to go so badly?"

"Every Cuban has family in the US. Mariela? It's complicated. I can't say. She will explain when she's ready."

"And David?"

"She helps him, he helps her. They are friends." She laughed. "You have nothing to worry about, Cooper, nada."

"But what about—?" If I had nothing to worry about from David—and I was not yet convinced of that—what about all the other issues, impediments? "I'm...you know...and she's—"

"Age difference is not so important here," Silvia answered the obvious question I hadn't managed to make myself ask. "Not between Cubans and foreigners. You see that all the time." Somehow, I was not reassured at the notion I might become one of *those* foreigners.

By the time Mariela returned from wherever she had been, four hours and too many more rums had passed. The rest of us we were seated in the backyard at a table under a matching orange-and-white awning, eating the most succulent pork I have ever tasted.

"OK?" Silvia asked Mariela, without apparently needing to expand further.

"OK," Mariela answered, without apparently needing to explain further.

Over a dessert of flan—Where had that come from? Who made it?—Mariela announced David was expecting me to join him tomorrow for his architecture tour with the group from Canada. "They're staying at the Saratoga, so you should meet him in the lobby at ten."

So she had been with David!

"Cooper, my friend," Esteban cut in, interrupting further questioning. "Have you been to a Cuban baseball game? You must. My *Industriales* are playing Matanzas later at the *Estadio Latinoamericano*. Very near here. We will all go and cheer on the best team in Cuba."

Lío snorted. "You must mean my Matanzas *Cocodrilos*—"

"The worst team in all the world," Esteban teased.

Silvia shook her head. "Havana Club...Ron Santiago.... Those two. They never stop."

We all laughed.

Except Mariela. She seemed to be watching me, considering. Considering what?

* * * *

I stared at him. He was laughing at me. Had I missed something? Body language? Gestures? Or was there anything there to miss? If there was nothing, how was anyone—how was I—supposed to know?

David had brought me to the Inglaterra Hotel's rooftop bar for lunch. "It has the best views," he'd told me in the elevator.

"Better than the Ambos Mundos?"

"Much better." To prove it, he'd taken me on a guided tour around the bar's outer edges. He pointed out the *Capitolio* ("Inspired not by the Capitol Building in Washington, as many imperialist Americans prefer to imagine, but by the Pantheon in Paris..."), the ornate *Gran Teatro de la Habana* across the street ("Originally built as a social centre for Spanish immigrants from Galicia, opened in 1915.... See those sculptures on the exterior...ninety-seven altogether...each one telling a story full of hidden meanings about theatre, or education, or benevolence. Ah, those benevolent Spaniards."), and, of course, Parque Central across the street with the white marble statue of José Martí. "They say it was the first monument ever erected in his honour. Now they are everywhere—public squares, schools, even in many Cuban homes. We love our Martí. Even more than Fidel. Well, maybe not that much. You went to the baseball game?" he asked, seeming to segue suddenly.

"Yes."

"Recognize anyone? Over there, near the statue?" I saw clusters of men standing, sitting, finger-pointing, gesticulating, hand-waving at each other, shouting words I couldn't hear. "That's called the *Esquina Caliente*, the Hot Corner. It is where Habaneros come day and night to argue about baseball. They do that because there is no point in arguing about other things. I will confess to you, but to no one else, I've never understood why Cubans care so passionately about grown men running around hitting a little ball with a stick. Do you?"

I shrugged. I didn't. Not really. But I had revelled in the sense of occasion at yesterday's game, so different from anything I experienced at any game I'd ever attended in Canada. No overpriced beer, no undercooked hotdogs, no orchestrated, desultory rah-rah-rah for the home team. Instead, Cubans ate candies by the paper cupful, got sugar-high, and then yelled at each other with gusto—for their team, against their opponents, against the umpires, sometimes against their own players if they failed to live up to expectations. It never became nasty. Although I couldn't understand most of what they were yelling, I noted the laughter and hoots of appreciation from the other team's supporters when one of their opposite number made a particularly telling insult.

"Do you realize?" It was David again with yet another tour-guider's history lesson. "If this was 1913, we'd be sitting in air right now. The Inglaterra's fourth storey was only added in 1914." He raised his glass of Cristal beer. "To the fourth floor," he said.

"Long may it stand," I replied.

"In all its neoclassical glory," he added. How could I explain to David I wasn't really interested in architectural styles, or buildings at all, only in that one building I'd been trying, for reasons I should not be explaining to him, to identify, and which had turned out, if I understood what I understood correctly, a building he shared with Mariela, along with whatever else he shared with her?

Like Mariela, David knew everything about anything Havana. Especially about architecture. He'd dazzled the Canadian architects in our group this morning. They had come to Havana for some sort of convention and wanted to explore its historic wonders.

"Havana," he told them, "is a vast architectural library, a living museum of African, European, American styles, much of it crusted and covered in dust but still very much alive."

They'd oohed and aahed as he guided them from this Colonial, to that Moorish, to that Art Deco, to that Art Nouveau building, pointing out along the way various cornices and valances and balustrades and other gewgaws, about which I knew nothing. And cared less.

Although David was indeed a trained architect, he told me over lunch he'd ended up in a dead-end junior job in some government department after graduation, re-drawing official plans for minor construction projects that never became real. "Busy work. Everyone knew better than to imagine someone would actually build them." One day several years ago, he noticed a tour bus pull up beside a square in Old Havana and several dozen tourists spill out. The tour's operator had apparently designated the morning as free time. But the tourists seemed uncertain where to spend their free time so, on a whim, David approached them.

"Would you like me to show you around?" He'd made twenty CUCs that first morning. Eventually, a friend of a friend introduced him to Lío, who matched him with tourists keen to discover more about the architecture of Old Havana.

"How long have you known Mariela?" I asked.

"Ah, Mariela," he said, "the love of my life." He looked at what must have been my ashen expression, laughed, punched me playfully on the shoulder. "The love of yours, too, if I'm not mistaken. No need to worry, my friend. We can share our love for Mariela." He paused. "How did we meet? She was working for Lío. I was working for Lío. After my father kicked me out of our family's apartment, she found me a place to live."

"With Mariela?"

"Mariela lives there as well. But it is not like that. The building has been condemned. No one is supposed to live there. So we are— ¿como se dice?—squatters, illegal occupants."

"Why did your father kick you out?" Why hadn't I asked that first? It felt like one of those seven-second radio tape delays playing in my head.

"Because I liked Michael Jackson too much," he parried. "But that was my dad's fault too. When I was a kid, one of my father's relatives in Miami sent us bootleg cassettes of American pop songs. I became obsessed with Michael Jackson. Billie Jean...beauty queen...." David had an excellent voice. "I played them over and over. That's how I learned to speak English. So I could understand the words. Not that they ever made all that much sense to me. Later, I would play DVDs of movies over and over, British movies especially. *From Russia With Love, A Hard Day's Night, Life of Brian....* That's where I get my accent.

"Anyway, my father wasn't too happy when I started to dress like Michael Jackson. Called me all sorts of names, some of them true. I mean, I knew I was gay since the day I understood such things."

Gay! He didn't look—what the hell did I know? Gay...was good.

"So you and Mariela?" I was still trying to be sure.

"Best friends," he said. "I tell her everything. She tells me some things. Right now, she's helping me through my latest drama. My boyfriend is leaving next week, going back to Italy. He's one of the managers at the Club Arena, a little Italian resort just past the beach where we were yesterday. I met him about six months ago at Mi Cayito, the gay beach." I looked at him. "Mariela and I went for a walk there yesterday. She was giving me courage to say goodbye to him. He's going back to his wife and family. He never told me he was married. Bastard!"

"What does she tell you? Mariela, I mean. You said she tells you some things...."

"Not so much about you, not exactly," David replied after a moment's hesitation. "Oh, she likes you, I'm sure she does. But we talk about other things. She has many sadnesses."

She did. I was sure of it. But what were they? I waited in vain for him to elaborate. He didn't. He sat in silence guarding Mariela's secrets, like a true friend.

MARIELA AND I HAD AGREED TO MEET AT BRUNO'S AT SIX. HER DAY HAD already been spoken for. She had to guide a delegation of Australian trade unionists around Havana. "Their accents are even odder than yours, mate," she'd said by way of hello.

By the time she arrived, I was well into my second cup of Bruno's deadly concoction. He had recognized me, greeted me effusively in Spanish, and I had responded with my best, badly accented attempt at his language, opening my arms in pretend embrace. *"¡Un abrazo fuerte, mi amigo!"* When I returned to Halifax, I wanted to tell him, I intended to sign up for Spanish lessons. But I didn't yet have the words to explain, so we quickly settled into companionable, nothing-more-to-say silence while he waited tables and I waited for Mariela.

I was happy for the quiet time, happy for the drink, happier for the second one—liquid courage, which, if it didn't kill me, would make me strong. I was leaving Havana late the next afternoon. Lío had agreed to drive me to the Varadero airport, back to the late-night charter flight to Canada filled with its by-now exhausted collection of sun-sated holiday makers, people who had probably never ventured beyond the boundaries of their beach resorts and didn't know what they'd missed, back to Halifax, back to my lost job and my dead father and my non-life.

If I didn't say something now—in other words, if I did what I always did, which was to say nothing, do nothing, be no one—I would never know. I needed to know. At least that.

"David tells me you're sad," I began after Bruno greeted Mariela with an actual hug and handed her a drink before retreating back to the bar. "Are you? Sad, I mean?"

"Aren't you?" she replied. "Isn't everyone? I believe we all have our sadnesses."

That had not begun well. But it turned out to be just an inauspicious prelude to what transformed itself into a grown-up version of "I'll-show-you-mine-if-you-show-me-yours."

I showed her most of mine. I told her about my job, about my father, even about the circumstances of his death and the guilt that clung to me from time to time.

Mariela told me about her father, who'd died of a heart attack when she was eleven. "It is strange to say but what I remember most is not some specific memory of my father but of how our living circumstances changed after he died." Before he died, Mariela, her parents, and two older brothers all lived together with her father's parents and her uncle and his family. "Don't look so surprised, my friend. That is just the Cuban way. There were no houses or apartments available, even if my parents could have afforded one." She was lucky, she said. "I was the only girl, so I got to have my own bedroom at my dad's mother's place. But after my father died, we moved in with my mother's mother. It was a much smaller apartment and I had to share a room with my mother." She laughed. "I blamed my father for that. And for the Special Period too."

Mariela was barely a teenager when the Soviet Union collapsed.

"I don't know if it's true, but my mother says life was different here before. We were poor. Everyone in Cuba was. But we were all poor equally. Doctors, fishermen, teachers, everyone the same." She sounded like Silvia. "The state provided education, health care, jobs, rations. No one got rich, but no one starved. And everyone was happy. Or that is what they say."

Mariela's own memories of the Special Period were vivid and concrete. She remembered the empty refrigerator that had been disconnected because there was no electricity to run it and no food to keep cold. "At school, we often ate radish, water, and rice for lunch and called that a meal. I was always hungry. And I got sick. I remember one time I had the 'flu or a fever, and our neighbour agreed to kill her chicken so my mother could make me chicken soup—for the protein. But I was so dehydrated I fainted into the soup." She laughed at her own tumbling memories.

"When you were growing up," I said, trying to steer the conversation into the on-ramp of the highway I wanted her to travel down, "did you have many boyfriends?"

She laughed. My purpose was more transparent than I intended. "Not many. Just one, actually. His name was Alejandro. I called him Alex." It sounded to my ears like Alix or perhaps Alice. "We grew up on the same street, attended school together. At first, Alex was our class imp, then our class troublemaker, and, finally, at around the time of my *quinceañera*, the time I became very interested in boys, he became our class 'bad boy.' He gelled his black hair into a spiky crown like that American actor, Leonardo DiCaprio. He kept his shirts open to the navel to show off his brown skin and the muscles of his teenaged belly." I sucked in my gut involuntarily. "But most important, for me at that time, he knew how to play the guitar and all the words to all the American pop songs. That was when I fell in love with Alex, or at least with the idea of him."

"And what happened? With Alejandro…Alex?"

"We got married." She looked at me then. What did my face tell her?

"And you? Are you married, Mr. Eli Cooper?" When Mariela spoke to me now, she seemed to prefer pronouncing my full name rather than just Eli, which did not trip off her tongue, or Cooper, which she now understood was incorrect. I was fine with whatever she wanted to call me.

"No," I said. "Never."

"If you were a Cuban, my friend, I'm sure you would have been married many times by now."

"Why do you say that?"

"Cubans don't take marriage as seriously as people in other countries, that's all. Uncle Lío? He's been married four times, and he'll probably marry at least once more before he's done. Maybe it's because religion isn't as important here in Cuba, or because there is nothing to fight over at the end. In Cuba you fall in love, try it on for a few years and, if it doesn't work, you get divorced. In Cuba, all it takes is one hundred pesos—that's five American dollars—and you're divorced."

"Did that happen with you?" I asked hopefully. "Are you divorced?"

"We are not together," she answered, not exactly answering my question. I recalled her turn of phrase when she'd recounted her conversation with the US foreign service officer. What did "no living husband" mean?

"What is he like?" I asked. I considered "was," fishing for additional explanation, but decided to let her lead.

"He's not like me," she said, speaking in the present. "We're very different."

Mariela had been the youngest in her family by many years, a shy "little mother" whose favourite schoolyard game consisted of teaching younger schoolmates their sums and letters. She always knew she would end up a teacher, she said, always understood she would marry and have children and grandchildren and never stray far from the place where she was born. "That was me...then."

Alex, on the other hand, was born restless, impatient with the classroom. He had grander dreams. He quit school after Grade 10, landed a job on the grounds crew at a Varadero resort. But he didn't rake lawns or pull weeds for long, Mariela said. Alex chatted up the tourists, charmed the bosses, eventually sang-and-danced his way into an audition to be a backup performer in the entertainment department, filling in whenever one of the travelling regulars was sick or couldn't make it.

"He's a very good musician, a wonderful singer." After the shows, Alex would bring out his guitar and play by the pool for those tourists who weren't ready to call it a night. He made friends, and more. "He was very good at making friends," Mariela said, without apparent judgment.

The tourists had called him Alex, or Al, and marvelled that his last name was Jones. When he recorded a CD to sell to the tourists, Mariela told me, Alex billed himself as "the Cuban Tom Jones." He was going be a singing sensation, he told everyone, and not just in Havana, but in Hollywood. "He believed that."

"What happened?" I asked. "With you and him?"

"We got married. In 1998. He was twenty-two, I was twenty-one."

I did the math. She had been born in 1977. Which meant she was now thirty-one. And I was fifty-four. Twenty-three years in the difference. *Jesus!*

After their wedding, Alex had moved into her grandmother's apartment with Mariela, her grandmother, her mother, her older brother Frankie, and her even older brother Fidelito. Mariela's mother had volunteered to move into her own mother's bedroom so the newlyweds could have privacy. "But, of course, there is no privacy in Cuba. Just frictions. Always. Alex would play Willy Chirino's music on his boom box, even quietly in our bedroom, and my *abuela* would order him to turn it off or leave the apartment. 'Willy Chirino!' she would scream, and then make as to spit on the floor. *'¡Gusano!'* She called him a worm."

"Who's Willy Chirino?"

"You have much to learn, Mr. Eli Cooper."

"Teach me," I said.

"My abuela divides her life into two unequal parts," Mariela explained around my actual question. "Before Fidel and After Fidel. Before Fidel was bad, awful, 'worse than you can ever imagine, little girl.' After Fidel, my grandmother learned to read and write, became a proud revolutionary. She convinced my parents to name their first-born son Fidel in honour of her El Jefe." Mariela laughed. "But Fidelito was the first to leave." One night soon after Alex had joined the household, Fidelito left for a three-day business trip to Havana. He never returned. "My mother only learned he'd left the country when a policeman friend of hers showed up a week later to ask questions and to commiserate with her on her loss."

"Where did he go?"

"He disappeared. We never heard from him again."

"You're kidding me," I said.

"The good news is that, after Fidelito and Frankie left, my mother got her own room."

"Frankie left too?"

"Everybody leaves."

A few years later, Frankie—a doctor—received a visa to attend a medical conference in Montreal. Once he got there, he slipped away from the Cuban delegation and snuck across the border into the United States. Mariela shook her head, the bile bitter in her throat. "The Americans let him stay. Just because he had set foot on American soil. He had arrived illegally, but he had arrived, so that made it OK."

"Is he still there?"

"We think so. At first, he moved to Los Angeles where he became a taxi driver because he wasn't allowed to practise medicine. He lived with an American woman, a hairdresser, and her two teenaged daughters. He would call my mother sometimes, telling her how much he missed her, and Cuba. He would send pictures too, but my mother refused to look at them. At some point, he told her he was thinking of starting over in New Mexico. And then he stopped calling, stopped writing. So...we don't know."

"Jesus," I said. "That must have been awful for your mother."

"Worse for me, I think. It is hardest on the last child left, especially if that child is a girl. How do you leave your mother? I could never do that."

What was she saying? "But you just applied for a visa to go to the United States."

"To visit. Not to stay."

"Why bother then? Why does it matter that they said no?"

"It's a...personal matter." That hiccup again. "Not worth talking about."

I tried to think of some response that would elicit a response, that would keep this thread unspooling. I couldn't. The silence stretched into a chasm, lying heavy between us. How had we gotten here? I needed to trace back the thread. Oh, right....

"Willy...Chorizo?"

She let out a hearty, full-throated laugh, leaned her head back, blew away that dark shadow. "*Chirino*! Willy Chirino."

"So who's he?"

"You really don't know?" I shook my head. "Willy Chirino is one of the most famous Latin American pop singers in the world. He's from Cuba. Or at least he was born here. He grew up in Miami and became famous. He hates Cubans—or at least those of us who stayed. Have you ever heard of '*Nuestro Día Ya Viene Llegando*'?" I shook my head yet again. "I will have to educate you, Mr. Eli Cooper. In English, the song is called 'Our Day will Come' and it is like an anthem for the exiles in Miami. They really think they're coming here and taking back Cuba again, just like in the old days."

"And your grandmother—"

"She hates Willy Chirino. Couldn't stand to hear him sing. But Alex, he loved the sound of his music. He played that song over and over. When my abuela would complain, he would just shrug and say, '*Sólo música*.' It's only music. And she would yell back at him, '*¡No música! ¡Vete!*' Get out. And he would leave. He would take his CDs and his boom box and disappear—for an hour, for a night, for a few days." She paused, emptied her cup. "I should have confronted my grandmother then, said, 'He is my husband. He lives here too.' But I never did. And you want to know something?"

"What?"

"I never asked Alex where he went either. I thought if I said nothing, maybe everything would work out. But, of course, nothing ever does."

Doesn't it? I had begun to believe the loss of my job and the death of my father were really just nature's ways of working shit out, of leading me here to Havana, to Mariela, to my destiny. I hadn't sorted through all the details yet—that would have to wait until I returned to Canada and had access to the internet—but I was certain living in Cuba would be cheaper than living in Halifax, and the weather would be better too! Perhaps I would write that novel I'd never written but must have planned to once. And now I had something to write about.... Was I letting my fantasies leapfrog our reality? *Our* reality?

"Is that what happened? With you and Alex?" I asked.

"I knew there were foreign women among the friends Alex made at the resort," she said more quietly. "And I knew he was unfaithful. Of course, I know there are Cubans who take up with foreigners at the resorts and use them as their ticket out of the country. I knew Alex had these crazy Hollywood dreams. So I told him, 'I'm not leaving Cuba.' 'Neither am I,' he told me. But he lied."

"So that's what happened? He just left?"

She stopped, slammed on the brakes of her testimonial. We had just started down the off-ramp and she turned to me with a stony stare.

"You know, Mr. Eli Cooper, you ask many questions. Time for me to ask questions and for you to give answers. Tell me more about you."

I thought for a moment, told her some. But not all. "There isn't much to tell. I have a sister. One. Older. She left too. She's a lawyer in Calgary, the other side of the country from where I live. I know what you mean about being the child left behind. I didn't feel like I could 'abandon' my parents either. So I stayed. But here I am. And, that's thanks to my sister too. This was all her idea." I wasn't certain Sarah would have agreed to "all."

"I would like to meet her someday," Mariela said. "To thank her." I wasn't sure my sister would have agreed to that either.

Bruno had been picking up the drained cups and depositing full ones in their place while we talked. I had no idea how many I'd drunk. But I knew I was ready. Finally. I lifted the plastic cup to my face, closed my eyes, and swallowed the liquid whole. I didn't even cough. "I'm not very good at this," I began, looking her in the eye now, trying to focus. "I'm out of practice. Actually, I've never had much practice at all." No detours, Eli, no sideroads. Forward. "But these last few days, this place, these people...." I swept my hand around as if I meant these people in this bar. I didn't. Don't try to explain, I told myself. "I feel like a different person since I arrived in Havana. And the best part of being here in Cuba has been meeting you." Was I drunk? I was drunk. *En el ron, la verdad*...my version of *in vino veritas*. I tried to lock on her eyes. But she was looking down now, at her cup, at the table, at nothing. Was I embarrassing her? Was this a mistake? "I've never said this before..." I had. Of course I had. But that was then, and this was now. "God, this is hard." It was. "But I think I'm falling in love with you. I do."

I'd said the words, and the words hung there, out to dry, for what seemed like forever. My face flashed hot, then cold, then clammy. Was it the alcohol? Or the saying it out loud?

Mariela looked up finally. Her eyes—those eyes—were wet with tears. She blinked, wiped away her tears with her left hand. With her right hand, she reached out, took my hand in hers, squeezed. The silence again, but this time not so heavy and dark.

"We should walk," she said finally.

* * * *

At some point, sometime long after darkness settled over the city, Mariela and I found ourselves at the far end of the seawall, at the far end of my imagination. She didn't want to go back to my casa. "Silvia will tell Lío, who will tell everyone." And she refused to take me back to her place. "No, not there...let's walk."

So we strolled along the Malecón, which was pulsing with Habaneros, mostly young, clustered in nesting, nuzzling couples or raucous groups of half a dozen, dotted here and there with lone musicians playing for tourist change, or jineteros waiting to pounce on the unsuspecting. I held her hand. We walked past the Hotel Nacional, past the US Interests Section, past the Avenue of the Presidents, which she told me the locals called "G."

When the wind rose off the water, I put my arm around her shoulder. She did not resist. Instead she melted into me. Melded. Not that she stopped performing her tourist-guide shtick. "Did you know the Malecón is an eight-kilometre stretch of coastal street and seawall? Construction began in 1901 and wasn't completed for fifty years, so you can see we were inefficient, even before the Revolution—" I stopped, turned, kissed her on the mouth, stilled her talk.

The kiss seemed feels-so-right natural but also, in the same moment, life-altering consequential. I do not come from a family of touchers, let alone kissers. When Sarah came to Halifax after our father died, our hugs had been—for both of us—tense, perfunctory, moments to endure and get past. There had been no kissing, certainly not on the mouth. I hadn't kissed anyone on the mouth since...well, since Wendy Wagner. But that shouldn't count. The time before that? I remembered. How could I forget?

Mariela and I were tentative at first, my lips on hers—soft, warm, wet—her mouth slowly opening up, prising mine open, my tongue finding hers, hers mine. We did not embrace. Instead, we held each other's hands by our sides, leaned our faces toward one another, the rest of our bodies not touching. I could have stayed in that moment forever. Finally, Mariela pulled back, let go of my hands, reached up with her right hand, and pressed a finger to my lips. "So, Mr. Eli Cooper," she said.

* * * *

I would like to tell you the earth moved, as in Hemingway's *For Whom the Bell Tolls* or Carole King's song, but that would be a lie. I was drunk. She was drunk. We balanced precariously on a narrow concrete wall with the Malecón roadway on one side and the rock-studded shore on the other, kissing, grabbing, fondling, fumbling aside clothing, assembling our body parts so they fit together at the correct angles so we didn't suddenly, inadvertently disconnect our connected connectors, all the while ignoring the horns and shouts from passing cars and the studied indifference of the occasional passing Habanero, who'd apparently seen it all many times before. At some point, sometime just before it would have been too late, Mariela produced a condom from somewhere—Where? And why hadn't I thought to do that?—and expertly applied it before allowing me entry.

This was not the way I'd envisioned the universe unfolding the first time we made love. But that was the point. It was the first time. There would be other times in better places where we could conduct, at leisure, all our lovers' explorations of all our bodily hills and valleys, desires and fantasies.

We.

Our.

How long had it been since I had imagined in first-person plural?

"Do you know what I'm thinking?" I asked. We had readjusted our clothing, rearranged our bodies, and were now sitting facing the lapping waves, the water, our legs dangling over the side of the wall. "Besides the fact I really am in love with you, I mean." The words did not yet roll off my tongue, but they had begun to feel more natural to speak. There was time for them to feel more lived-in.

"What are you thinking, Mr. Eli Cooper?"

"I'm just thinking about what it would be like to live here. In Havana. If I sell my house in Halifax—maybe fix it up first like my sister says—we could live here on what I earn from that until my pension kicks in. I can start collecting my Canada pension—that's the government one—when I'm sixty. It won't be much, but when my company pension kicks in at sixty-five, there'll be plenty of—"

"I'm sure that will be very nice for you," she cut me off, the chill in her voice suddenly colder than a nor'easter. We were still seated physically side by side, thigh to thigh, heat to heat, but there was a now psychic iceberg between us.

"Us," I said quickly. "I meant us."

"I know what you meant," she replied without any change in tone.

We walked back to my casa. She did not hold my hand, her body did not meld into mine. She offered a terse no when I offered to walk her home. "Good night, Mr. Cooper," she said. And was gone. Without even a kiss goodbye.

THE IDEA—LÍO'S IDEA—WAS THAT I WOULD BUY THE CELLPHONE FOR Mariela but register it in my name, and then leave enough cash behind to cover the costs of the cell service and any calls she'd make to me.

"Mariela like," he said, though I realized later he'd never asked her if she would. And David agreed. "More practical than an engagement ring," he told me. "It's a gift that keeps on giving."

So David, Lío, and I had spent my last morning in Havana standing in an endless line outside the Old Havana offices of ETECSA, the Cuban telephone company. When we finally reached the desk, Lío and David did the talking. I did the signing and paying. No one questioned what we were doing, even though ordinary Cubans, I had learned, were not supposed to own cellphones. "Only government, big people," Lío explained. But every second person I'd seen on the streets of Havana seemed to have a cellphone glued to their ears.

"Everybody do," Lío conceded. "Nobody care. Unless they do."

It was his go-to explanation for why everything that wasn't supposed to happen in Cuba actually happened.

"Cubans aren't allowed to own cellphones, but foreigners are" was David's more fulsome explanation. "So Cubans get foreign friends to buy cellphones in their names, then give them back to the Cubans to use. Sometimes, the foreigner pays, sometimes the Cuban. It depends."

In my case, I would pay. "So she call you," Lío explained.

After I finished paying, Lío suggested we walk over to Mariela's apartment so I could present the phone to her in person. After last night, I wasn't sure that was a good idea. I had shuffled the deck of our conversation, tried to make sense of the words, sound out the silences between the words. "Good night, Mr. Cooper." Sobering-up second thoughts? Lover's remorse? Something I did? Or didn't do? There had been a time—perhaps before last night—when rejection, if that's what it was, would not have bothered me. I would have moved on with barely a backward glance. It didn't matter. Now it did. Which may have been why I didn't tell Lío or David about what had transpired the night before, allowed them to believe—tried to believe myself—that there was something to this self-created myth of Mariela and me.

"*Mi casa, tu casa,*" David had bowed as he opened the gate for us. "And Mariela's casa, of course." He led us up a wide circular concrete staircase. "Watch the railings," he said. There were no railings. "And careful of those hanging wires. We 'borrow' our electricity from the building next door." The second-floor landing was a rubble of broken chunks of concrete. "Now you see where the staircase to the third floor ended up," David continued sardonically. "Luckily, we have this ladder." It was not so much a ladder as a collection of mismatched boards cobbled together in an approximation of a ladder. "After you." He held the ladder while Lío and I climbed to the top and then he scrambled up after us. The rear of the third floor was open to the sky. "The roof collapsed a few years ago," David said. "That's when they condemned the building. And people—me, Mariela, others too—moved in. Because we needed a place to stay."

While he led us down a hallway past closed doors and curtained-off rooms, I tried to square what I was seeing with my visit to Lío's house in Cerro, to Silvia and Esteban's third-floor casa. Was this what Mariela had meant when she talked about how life had become more unequal after the Special Period? Halfway down the corridor, David pulled back a curtain and invited me to look inside. There were perhaps a half a dozen older men in their undershirts sitting around a table, smoking, drinking, playing dominoes. They looked up at us, nodded. "This is our condo's games room," David said grandly. "And totally free for the use of the residents." He continued, stopping at a door where cardboard boxes were stacked one on top of the other, each one filled to bulging with empty rum bottles. "*Mi tía* Eva lives behind this door. She drinks to forget. But she never forgets to save her empties so she can take them back to the bootlegger and get more rum.... And this is my room," he said as he reached into his pocket, pulled out a key, unlocked a padlock, invited us inside. It was nothing like Esteban and Silvia's casa, but still night-and-day different from the rest of this building. There was paint on the walls, for starters, hot pink but paint nonetheless. And a tacked-up poster of Michael Jackson, a fully stocked bookshelf, a living room chair, a coffee table weighted down with architectural and art books, some open and scattered across the surface, and a double mattress in one corner. "Home sweet—"

He stopped. Mariela had heard the noise and come to investigate. She was not amused. I did not understand her words in Spanish, but I immediately understand the daggers-in-all-directions look she gave us. *Why did you bring him here?* Him, meaning me.

"Uh..." David seemed clearly taken aback. He sputtered something about ETECSA and mobile, and he waved his hand around the room, perhaps to implicate all us in whatever she was accusing him of doing, or not doing. Lío looked down at his feet, knowing better than to interject.

"I...we..."—should I invoke the deflective "we" here to spread the blame?—"We got you this." I held up the box. "It's a phone." The box showed the phone. "For you."

"I don't need a phone," she replied.

"Everybody need phone," Lío jumped in finally, trying to be helpful. "I text where you meet client...."

I wondered if that was really what the phone was for. Lío's convenience. Was this all some sort elaborate set-up for a scam I didn't yet understand?

Mariela ignored Lío, waved away my offer of the phone. "So now you know where we live," she said, turning to—on—me. "Still think you want to live like a Cuban?"

And with that, she turned and went back down the hall, entered her room, closed the door behind her. At least she didn't slam it.

We stood for a few minutes in awkward silence. Finally, Lío held out his hand. "Phone. I take. Give her. Later." So the phone was for Lío.

"You know," David said finally, "on days like this I'm glad I'm gay." We all laughed at that. Because we couldn't think of anything else to do.

* * * *

I hadn't known Mariela had already asked to hitch a ride to Cárdenas with Lío when he drove me to the airport, or that David would decide to accompany us, or that he would decide to sit up front with Lío, perhaps to avoid being caught again in Mariela's crosshairs, or maybe to allow Mariela and me to talk.

Not that that happened. Despite my best efforts at small talk—Will you be staying with your mother? What will you do in Cárdenas? When will you go back to Havana?—her cryptic, mono-syllabic responses did not encourage follow up.

Luckily, David had brought along a bootleg CD (*50 Best Songs— The Motown Years: Michael Jackson & The Jackson 5*), which he played through Lío's stereo system at high volume, negating the need to fill the silences. After a while, I gave up my futile attempts to engage Mariela in conversation and breathed in the lush beauty of the Cuban countryside one last time.

When we arrived at the airport after a quick stop in Jibacoa to pick up my duffel, I tried again. "I'm so happy I got to meet you," I said, sliding—as unobtrusively as a man dressed in shorts with sweaty bare legs could slide across a plastic-covered seat—toward her half of the seat. I put my arms out, hoping for a melt/meld. She shook her head like a wet puppy, continued to look straight ahead.

"Can I at least, maybe, call you sometime...on *our* phone?" I asked. The faintest flicker of a smile. And then it was gone.

Lío and David got out of the car to hug me on my way. "Don't worry," David said. "I'll talk to her. My turn to be the one giving advice." Lío shrugged in Mariela's direction, whispered in my ear. "Be OK. Will see."

I wanted to believe that, wanted it to be true. Sitting alone in the airport departures lounge surrounded by troops of exhausted, desultory tourists, all waiting for flights back to their own real worlds, I knew exactly what I needed to do. I needed to run back out of the airport, forget my luggage, find a cab, and instruct the driver to take me to Cárdenas—wherever that was—and be quick about it. Once I found Mariela—I would find her—I would beg, plead, cajole, convince her she was as in love with me as I was with her, and that we could live happily ever after. I would—I didn't need that. I hadn't disappeared down a bottomless hole like this since...well, since then. And where did that get me? I got up, walked over to the nearest duty free, bought one bottle of Havana Club and one bottle of Ron Santiago for new times' sake. I found a seat as far from the crowd as possible, and wondered if there really was, as Esteban had said, sweetness in a lime.

BAY OF CÁRDENAS

*T*he dream always begins the same way. Mariela standing beside the blackboard, teaching her class. She doesn't know what she is teaching. It doesn't matter. Suddenly, there's a commotion in the hallway. Maruchi, Uncle Lío's eldest daughter, bursts into her classroom, shouting at her. "They're leaving! Alex! Tonito! All of them! On the raft! Hurry! Quick!" On the raft? Roberto's and Delfin's raft? Alex and Tonito? It couldn't be. He wouldn't. Not with her Tonito.

This is the part where Mariela wishes she could change what happens next in her dream, as if that could change the ending in real life. Because she didn't believe what she couldn't comprehend, she takes time she doesn't know she doesn't have. In molasses motion, she goes to see the principal. "Can you ask someone to watch my class?" she asks. "I have a family...situation." While the Mariela in the dream explains to the principal all the lessons she's planned for the children for the afternoon, the Mariela dreaming the dream wills the other Mariela to hurry up. She sees Maruchi hopping around like she is about to pee her pants. "We have to go," she says again and again. "Before it's too late."

But it is already too late. The dream speeds up. Too fast now. By the time the two of them finally arrive at the docks at the Bay of Cárdenas, the raft is a speck on the sparkling green-blue horizon. She cannot identify anyone aboard, or even if there is anyone aboard.

So, in the beginning, Mariela in the dream—and in life—refuses to believe, even as reality chips away at her dreaming disbelief. The raft does not return. The days go by, then the weeks. No one phones from Florida to say they have arrived safely. No one calls at all. After a while, *everyone in Cárdenas, even in Mariela's own family, accepts that what happens has happened, that this is Cuba and that there is nothing to do but to move on with the life of the living.*

Mariela can't. She reshapes her own dream, sculpting threads of reality into at least the beginning of a more hopeful ending. In this dream, it is still the night Tonito disappeared. What happened has happened. Mariela lies alone on Tonito's bed in the corner of the bedroom she will no longer share with anyone. She smells the smell of her son on the sheets, on the pillow. She feels around under the pillow, searching for something she does not find. She smiles to herself. Tonito is safe. Mi Toni is with him.

Mi Toni, a stuffed doll, has been Tonito's protector against monsters and bad dreams since he was a baby. If Tonito has taken Mi Toni on the raft with him, they will both be safe. She knows it.

The dream skips ahead like a scratchy recording. Now they are somewhere—there are pinks and blues and yellows and greens—but they are nowhere Mariela recognizes. Suddenly, out of the swirl, Tonito emerges. He is clutching Mi Toni, holding his doll out toward her. She runs to greet them, reaches out to swallow both of them in her arms and...she is holding air. Again.

COOPER'S CASA

HAVANA, 2017

I EXAMINE THE EGGSHELL BLUE PAINT ON THE SITTING- ROOM WALL. HERE AND there, air bubbles bubble up beneath the surface. Near the ceiling, I note peeling paint. Havana's humidity? Lío's black market supplier? Our contractor's slapdash workmanship? Whatever, I will need to have the room repainted again soon. One more expense at a time when room revenue is falling.

It is early evening now. Charles and Sandra—the only guests we have scheduled this entire week—have left for dinner. Tony is watching cartoons in the family quarters. Mariela is still out somewhere with the American businessman who hired her to act as his guide and translator during his business trip to Havana. I do my best to reign in my jealousy. I fail. I tell myself my jealousy is a sign I care. I tell myself not to tell that to Mariela.

The paint....

I have become the King of the Casa. Casa Havanada...Havana... Canada...Havanada. Get it? The year I moved here semi-permanently, the government issued decrees legalizing the buying and selling of automobiles and houses. While there had long been a black market in both—witness Lío's acquisition of his Cerro house from that departing Cuban family—it suddenly became legal to engage in such transactions.

Lío had helped Mariela and me find a large-but-down-at-the-heels second-floor apartment in a structurally sound building in

Havana Centro that proved ideal for my ambitions. Mariela bought it with my money, since foreigners are still not permitted to own real estate in Cuba. That, of course, made Sarah nervous. "I love Mariela, I really do, and I trust her," she told me, "but you need to have a written contract. Just in case." She emailed me a draft agreement, which I did not ask Mariela to sign, did not show her.

Truth? Mariela had seemed as nervous as Sarah, if not more so, about our domestic arrangement. Our decision to "go home" may have been Mariela's, but it came smeared thick with dollops of regret and remorse. Mariela was still mourning, still trying to sort out her own conflicted feelings about me, about us, about all that had happened and was about to happen. I have come to understand nothing that happens now or in the future will change her past, replace her loss, fully heal her wound. So we keep on keeping on, not talking about what she will not—cannot—say.

As for the casa, Mariela had insisted from the beginning, "It's yours." In fact, that became her unacknowledged declaration of independence from me. She would continue to work as a tour guide, she informed me, while I became responsible for renovating the old apartment and then running the new casa.

And so we would live together—and separately—happily ever after.

My renovator responsibilities had consisted mostly of accompanying Lío to nondescript buildings in shabby neighbourhoods on the outskirts of Havana. While Lío bartered with sketchy-looking Cubans I would not want to encounter in an alley in the middle of the afternoon, shouting in a rapid-fire, often angry-sounding Spanish I couldn't begin to decipher, I waited, mute, by his side. When they finished, the men would laugh and embrace, and Lío would tell me how much to pay. Since Lío never asked me for money for his services, I assumed he got his cut from the vendors. I never knew—never asked—how much of what I paid ended up in Lío's pocket. Probably a lot.

A few days or weeks later, the construction materials we'd ordered, which I'd never actually seen during any of our negotiations, would magically "fall off a truck"—often an official-looking truck—near the entrance to our building. Tiles, paint, nails, pipes, appliances, everything we needed.

Still, it took another year after that for our "contractor," a moonlighting, jack-of-all-trades soldier Lío had hired and I paid Lío to pay (yet another cut for Lío!), to arrange all the tiles, paint, nails, pipes, appliances, and so on in their proper places.

Which had been followed by a seemingly inevitable six more months of work by me, this time with help from Silvia, to hopscotch my way through all the many and various bureaucratic hoops in order to be licensed as a legal *casa particular.*

And to give my own life its current shape and purpose.

We modelled our casa on Esteban and Silvia's Casa Centro. Let me give you the quick tour. There are three guest bedrooms, each with its own ensuite toilet and shower, a personal-sized fridge, and an air conditioner. There is a common sitting room at one end of the apartment—the room where the paint is now peeling—where guests can gather and where we serve not-included-with-the-price breakfast each morning. The sitting room spills out onto the balcony overlooking the streets. At the other end of the apartment, past the guest rooms, there is a small kitchen where Alma, one of the neighbourhood women who works for us, prepares the breakfasts, and beyond that, our own still unfinished living quarters, which consists of a combination galley kitchen, sitting room, and TV room, and two bedrooms off to one side. No air conditioning. That is for the paying customers. And, sometimes, for Mariela's mother. Big Maria, as I call her (though not to her face), is an endlessly cheerful lady who dotes on Tony. Whenever she visits us and it's available, we put her up in the biggest guest room. She loves the air conditioner, and often invites Tony to sleep with her "in the cool."

The larger bedroom in the family quarters, which is not nearly as large as the smallest guest bedroom, contains a double bed and dresser where Mariela and Tony sleep.

The smaller bedroom, the one I now call mine, features a single bed and desk. That was not the plan, but let me come back to that.

DELUSIONS OF
ELEANOR

"So what do you think?" Sarah asked, sipping her stress-free peppermint tea, fondling one set of drawings and then another, and another.

"I think they'd all be too expensive," I replied. Sarah had asked Arthur, an architect friend of George, who was a lawyer friend of Sarah's, to stop by our father's house and suggest some renovation options for us to consider and commit to.

"George and I worked together in Calgary," she'd told me. "Then he got posted to Halifax for two years to handle a big offshore project for one of our major international clients." After he and his wife purchased a house in the city's expensive—naturally—south end, "they hired Arthur to do a major makeover for them," she explained. "Major. I mean he gutted the place. But now it looks fabulous."

No doubt. Arthur appeared to be big on fabulous. He had come up with three different options—"depending on the price range"—for renovating my father's house. They were: fabulous, even more fabulous, and beyond fabulous. Even the least fabulous of these, I was sure, would set me back more than my father's house could ever command. He and Sarah had spent several hours going room to room, measuring, and tut-tutting, and oh-dearing, while I trailed behind.

"Do you really think I could get my investment back?" I asked Arthur after he sketched out the options on his drawing pad.

"Well," Arthur allowed after making a few more notes, "this is Halifax and not Calgary." He seemed to be directing his answer to Sarah more than to me, even though I was the one asking. "And we're talking the north end, so there's a limit to what this market will bear. But Halifax isn't close to its peak yet and you're on the peninsula, which is where people want to be.... So yes, I do think you could make your investment back. And more."

After that, Arthur had taken his leave, "So you two can discuss what you might want to do."

Sarah repeated Arthur's economic justification and upped the pro-reno ante. "There's no mortgage, so it's all equity. You could borrow what you need against the value, then pay it back when you sell."

"If I sell."

Sarah breezed past my caveat. "You don't really have a choice, you know, especially if you don't find another job soon. Have you even looked?"

I hadn't, not really. How could I when I still hadn't decided where I wanted to be, or with whom, or even what I wanted to be when I grew up? If I grew up? Now that I couldn't help but grow up.

"I'm looking," I said.

"I'm not sure you should consider another newspaper job," Sarah said. "Saul and I gave up our subscription to the Calgary *Herald* last year. And he wants to drop the *Globe* too. Everybody is reading online now, and it's free."

I wanted to tell her it was only "free" because morons like my sister and her husband imagined real news didn't cost money to produce. But I didn't want to turn down that low road, in part because some piece of me didn't want to acknowledge she was more right than wrong, and, in part, because I didn't want her visit to end badly.

We'd had a falling out nearly six months ago, soon after I'd returned from Cuba—over Mariela, of course.

"She was just a fantasy," Sarah had pronounced after she called to find out how my trip had gone. "I understand you needed that. After...everything. But a woman like that is bad business. I was talking to a guy in our office who specializes in immigration." There was always a "guy" in her office. "He says women like her prey on vulnerable men like you. Looking for money, looking for a way out of whatever third-world shithole they're stuck in. You were her ticket—"

I hung up on her. She called back a week later, didn't even mention how our last conversation ended. Instead, she told me spring wouldn't be a good time for me to visit Calgary. "Things are really busy at the office, and Saul and I are trying to start this renovation business on the side. Oh, and Amy's coming home from college at the end of the month—she had a great semester, loves law—and, well, I just think it would be the wrong time for you, for us. Is that OK?"

"Sure." I'd forgotten she'd invited me.

"But I'll still come down at the end of the summer. Help you go through mum's and dad's stuff, get all that organized. OK?"

"OK." She had arrived. And organized. And conquered. And now she was all packed for her return flight. We had not mentioned Mariela since I'd hung up on her that night nearly six months ago. Until today. She couldn't help herself.

"I really hope you're still not pining after that Cuban woman. What was her name?" Sarah had already called the limousine service.

"Mariela. Her name is Mariela."

"Well, really, it would have been a terrible mistake for you to get involved with someone like that. I know what you're like. You remember the last time you did that. Mooning over that girl back in high school...I'll bet you don't even remember her name now."

Sarah may not remember, but I do. Her name was Eleanor. She had been my first love. Until Mariela, I thought Eleanor had also been my last. Who knew? Perhaps I'd been right.

I tried not to think about that. I only knew that, after all my years of needing no one, I now found myself desperately wanting someone. Whether that was Mariela or just someone, anyone, I still wasn't sure.

* * * *

After Sarah left, I sat in the kitchen, poured myself a glass of Havana Club—my small, insignificant show of solidarity with Esteban, with Cuba, with the Revolution—and contemplated my Sarah-set tasks ahead. She had mounded a mountain of stuffed green plastic garbage bags in one corner of the room, the last remnants of the contents of my parents' closets, drawers, attic storage, and basement boxes, all of which she had carefully sorted and organized for disposal or pickup. There were written instructions on the kitchen table to call Big Brothers Big Sisters. Sarah had scheduled a truck from the consignment furniture shop to pick up our parents' furnishings. "It'll be easier to renovate if the house is emptier," Sarah explained. I didn't tell her I still wasn't sure I would. "Besides, it's all worn and out of fashion." As if I cared.

Sarah had taken only a few small pieces of my mother's jewelry for herself. She gave me our father's war medal and left the urn of ashes on the mantel in the living room.

"I can't deal with that now," she explained. "Later?" Worked for me.

She also left the family photo albums, all except her own baby album, on the bed in my parents' bedroom for me to sort. I would do that...later.

I wished I'd had a photo album of my trip to Cuba. But I didn't have a single photo of Mariela, nothing to compare, no proof she had even existed. Truth? The longer we were apart, the less I found myself able to fit even the picture pieces of Mariela's face back together in my head. I couldn't forget her eyes, of course, but the rest? Dimples? Did she have them? I believed she did. How big was her nose? Did her mouth turn up, or down?

In the first months after I returned to Canada, I frequently dialled the number of the cellphone I'd bought for Mariela. Lío was the only person who ever answered. So, the phone really was for him. He promised to pass my message on to Mariela. "She call." I left my number. "Tell her to call collect." She never did. After a while, no one answered the cellphone at all. I tried the casa email address I had for Esteban and Silvia. Silvia wrote back cryptically, "Not a good time." I also emailed David, who for some reason had a Spain-based email address, but he didn't reply at all.

I had starred in this life movie once before, too many years ago, and it had ended badly. For me. I won't pretend to you that I didn't know how I'd screwed up that first time, or what I should do this time to avoid ending up in the same wrong place again. I needed to go back to Havana, talk to Mariela. But in truth, I was more afraid Mariela would reject me than I was hopeful she would not, and that fear paralyzed me. Twice, I'd gone online to book a flight to Havana. Twice, I'd snapped my browser window shut after I'd filled out my credit card information but before I'd hit Confirm Booking. Déjà vu, this time on the internet.

Mariela had become my fantastic, phantasmagoric fantasy woman. Not my first fantasy, of course. But I now understood, better than before, that my fantasy of Eleanor had led me to more than thirty years of an anesthetized, feelings-free, nothing-nowhere existence, which is what I'd somehow assumed must be my personal happy place. This had lasted until Mariela's presence jolted me into an understanding I really did have feelings—strong ones.

How long had I known Mariela? Two weeks? No, not even that. I took the calendar off the wall, placed it on the kitchen table. Every Christmas, Sarah would send my father the same Friends of Canadian Broadcasting monthly calendar filled with photos of nostalgic Canadian TV shows I'd never watched, and my father did not remember. Every year, I would replace last year's edition with this year's and then forget to change the months until the next calendar arrived. The latest one had not been turned since January 2008, which made it easy to find the month I was looking for. I counted the days. Mariela and I hadn't actually met until three days after I'd arrived in Cuba. Did the car ride to Havana count? She was in the front seat. I was in the back. We barely exchanged five words. That morning at the Bodeguita? Yes, that would be a more logical starting point, but I was already six days into my two weeks in Cuba by then, which left only a dozen hours—probably not that many—in the physical company of Mariela? How could I have imagined I'd been in love, that we'd been in love?

The problem, I eventually decided, was not so much that my relationship with Mariela had not worked out as I'd fantasized, but that the prospect of that relationship had changed my relationship to relationships. Now I wanted one. Perhaps my wanting one had nothing to do with Mariela at all. Perhaps my newly discovered lovelorn angst simply reflected the reality I no longer had my job or my father to anchor my waking hours, to give them a sense of purpose, or at least routine. I had gone from—how did that line go?—alone but never lonely, to pathetically lonely and parenthetically alone.

But if not Mariela, Wendy? Please god, no. Not that she would have had me. I still shuddered to imagine her day-after remorse. Liv? We were never lovers like that, never would be. Besides, she'd already decamped for Toronto and a maternity-leave editing gig at the *Post*, which she hoped might lead to something more permanent. The revolution would have to go on without her. Or not.

With that, I had exhausted all the semi-available single women of my quasi-acquaintance. I test-drank my way through a series of local bars, which *The Coast,* our alternative weekly, had advertised as the city's best pickup bars—the Dome, the New Palace, even, by accident, Reflections, which I'd neglected to note was a gay pickup bar—neither picking up nor being picked up. I was too old for pickup bars. And too young for Irish singalong pubs.

Which is how I eventually found myself at an online dating site called Plenty of Fish. A week before I lost my job, I'd edited a wire-service feature—a cutesy Valentine's Day business feature—about the startling international success of a Canadian internet mating service whose founder had managed to net $10 million a year from his apartment in Vancouver, working no more than ten hours a week. I remembered those details, and also that I'd wasted more time than should have been necessary drowning the reporter's tortured fishy word play—"casting their nets," "virtual online sea," "hooked," "best thrown back in the pond," and blub, blub, blub—but I could not now recall suddenly salient-to-me details like how the service worked, or whether it actually did. As I Googled its website, it was no longer lost on me that I had not so much lived a real life as created a facsimile of one out of all the stories I'd edited.

I filled out the forms. *Longest relationship?* "Prefer not to say." *Body type?* "Prefer not to say." *Looking for?* This time there was no prefer not to say choice, so I chose "I don't care," which seemed a little too blasé, but there it was. I also took the "world famous" Plenty of Fish personality test: *I am comfortable interacting with strangers.* "No," I answered, but then I changed it to "Yes." Who wants to interact with a stranger who doesn't want to interact back? *My own thoughts and feelings sometimes scare me.* They do, but that might make me seem like a serial killer, so..."No."

Plenty of Fish claimed more than a half-a-million users. Surely one among them would want to love me as much as I wanted them to love me. It did not seem so. I did have online "interactions" with a number of women who'd read my profile and were interested enough to respond. Once. A few agreed to meet for coffee, but then didn't show up. I understood that. I had done the same to others in my turn. Second thoughts? Fear? Avoidance? All of the above, probably.

I did meet one woman face to face. Her name was Catherine. She was a pleasant enough former Ontario public school teacher a few years younger than me. After her twenty-year marriage—"no kids, thank goodness"—fell apart, she decided to start life over again on the east coast. "Is that crazy?" We had coffee. We talked. We laughed. All good. At the end, I asked if I could call her again. She said yes. I never did. And she never called me either. I don't know why she didn't. I know why I didn't. Whenever I tried to think about life with her, all I could think of was Mariela. What was Mariela doing while I wasn't?

"**T**RIB–30–SIX" HAD BEEN THE CRYPTIC SUBJECT LINE IN PEGGY Aylward's email invitation to an end-of-summer barbecue and reunion she and her husband organized for the *Trib*'s former newsroom staff members. "The '-30-,'" as Peggy explained, unnecessarily and unnecessarily loudly sometime after her third beer, "represents the original telegrapher's symbol for 'end of transmission,' signifying the end of the *Tribune*. The 'Six'—you'll note I spelled it out rather than use numbers, in deference to the Canadian Press Style Guide (cheers, laughter)—that's to indicate it has now been six long months since the *Tribune* published its last." She held up her empty mug. "Long may it reign over us, God save the *Trib*!"

To the *Trib*.

Liv, no longer among us, no longer offering her revolutionary fuck-the-Man toasts, sent an email greeting from Toronto, which Peggy read aloud. In it, Liv offered her heartfelt thanks to everyone for the friendships and the memories. Peggy teared up. As she did again when she asked us to raise our glasses in memory of John Gibson, "our editor and leader forever." Gibson—I'd never called him John—died of a heart attack two months after the paper shut down. "He died of a broken heart," Peggy said, though I guessed his many decades of three-beer lunches to wash down his cheeseburger and fries had been at least a contributing factor.

Most of the rest of us who hadn't leaped from the *Trib*'s sinking ship to various floundering-but-still-publishing newspapers elsewhere had come to Peggy's gathering to see what everyone else was doing—and if they were doing better than we were. Some, including Peggy, had landed well paid and pensionable provincial government jobs as "communications specialists" or "policy advisors" to the same cabinet ministers they'd once written about. Others found short-term gigs working at the CBC or PR firms.

"What are you up to these days?" people kept asking me, phrasing it that way to avoid asking if I was still unemployed.

"Living the dream," I would say. "Staying loose." I did not mention my Cuban holiday, nor the fact I still didn't have a clue where, or if, I would ever work again, or what I would do if I did.

"You should think about marketing," my sister had suggested before she took her leave. "We just hired two former journalists at the firm to develop our website and market our services to clients." I didn't tell her I couldn't imagine a worse fate, or one for which I was less well suited. I had spent my career becoming more and more skilled at less and less, and none of the skills I had developed involved creating HTML-PSP-CMS-HTTP-BLAH-BLAH-BLAH web pages for ambulance-chasing lawyers or schmoozing with "clients" about developing "marketing messages."

What I'd liked most about newspapers, in fact, was that they were repositories for those without discernible social skills. I'd discovered my own career path near the end of my first year of university. Fresh out of my disastrous high school graduating year and all that followed—I'll come back to that—I'd stumbled blindly into university and one day accidentally wandered into a campus newspaper recruitment meeting for want of anything better to occupy my time before my next class. I saw immediately they were all misfits and, immediately, that I fit. I stayed. Toward the end of my third year, a former *Gazette* editor who'd landed a job at a start-up tabloid called the *Tribune* told me the paper was looking for weekend night-shift editors. I applied, landed the gig, never graduated, and never left the *Trib*. Until it left me.

"Hey, Eli!" It was Wendy Wagner. "You're looking good," she said.

"You too," I replied, meaning it. In six months, her teen-goth-moth look had butterflied into sophisticated young urban professional. She'd deep-sixed the nose ring and the heavy makeup, allowed the natural colour back into her hair, lost some puppy fat. Though she was dressed casually for today's occasion in jeans and a top, it was also clear she'd put time and thought into what she wore, and how she wore it.

"How goes the job?" I asked.

"Great! I'm learning a ton, which means I'm, like, still learning how much I don't know," she said. "I wish you were still there to answer my questions." She laughed. "Now I'm the one the other reporters come to and ask questions."

"I'm sure you do fine," I replied, and meant that, too.

Since I'd returned from Cuba, I'd occasionally picked up *Morning Hi* and discovered, to my surprise and despite its execrable name, it wasn't awful. It wasn't the *New York Times*, of course, or even the *Tribune*. But with an editorial staff that seemed to consist of Wendy and two or three reporters—all even more fresh out of J-School—the paper managed to fill its local news columns, sometimes with more and better local stories than the *Herald* did with twenty times its editorial resources. The stories were invariably bare-bones brief and without detail, let alone analysis, but the paper appeared to be finding a readership. Whenever I happened to spend time in coffee shops—an occupational hazard of the otherwise unoccupied—I'd notice well-thumbed copies of *Morning Hi* decorating the tables.

"Are you...?" she asked.

"No, not yet," I answered the question she hadn't found the words to ask. "But I'm living the dream, staying loose, you know." I needed a better line.

"If you're not too busy, I'd love to get together sometime, maybe like for lunch or coffee," she said. "There's some stuff I need to talk to you about."

Stuff? Like that time in the bathroom at the Shoe? "Uh, sure," I said. "That would be nice."

"How about Wednesday? There's a great new sushi place near our office, which I think is actually in your neighbourhood. We could meet there at, like, one o'clock if that works for you."

"Sure...OK."
"My treat," she said.

* * * *

Even as a child, I rarely spent time in my parents' bedroom. We were a family that valued our privacy, if that's what you'd call it. Now I sat on my parents' lumpy double bed, my father's side worn into a rut by his extra twenty years of living and sleeping, and I contemplated the collection of photo albums Sarah had left for me to sort. I leafed through random ones, surprised by their number and by the number of eras they reflected. A few must have been passed down from my grandparents, all of whom had died before I was born. There were no captions, though each photo was neatly arranged and inserted into photo corners. I recognized a photo of my father as a teenager, at the beach with his sister, Abigail, and a boy and girl I didn't know. Were they friends of theirs, or perhaps Abigail's boyfriend, Arthur's girlfriend? Could she have been the "fucking cunt" of my father's dementia delirium? I really should visit Aunt Abigail, bring along the albums and ask her to identify who was who and what was going on. I would probably not do that. I already understood as much.

Luckily, there were no albums from my father's final years. I had only just begun to let go of the vivid mental images of those— Dad's sallow face, wax-paper skin, haunted eyes, shock of unkempt white hair, his incomprehension about who I was, or who he was, or why he was. I'd attempted to replace them in my head with other, better flash memories—Dad teaching me to throw a baseball when I was five, presiding benignly over Sunday dinners while my mother served and my sister and I talked excitedly about our days. There were no actual photos of any of those moments. I began to doubt those memories were real. Did my father teach me how to throw a baseball, or did I just wish he had? I'm almost certain I borrowed my memory about idyllic family dinners from a television sitcom.

The final album was an oversized school-project-style scrapbook with a homemade brown paper cover featuring a stencilled title, "ELIJAH," which my mother must have compiled. There were no candid snaps but a seemingly complete collection of "official" photos glued in chronological order in its pages. These were class photos and head shots from Grade Primary to high school graduation, various hockey and baseball team photos, even an official graduation prom picture of a dorky-looking me and—yes, of course, I remembered her name—standing on a fake bridge with fake flowers in a corner of the gym with its hopeful "Good Luck to the Graduates" banner as a backdrop. And then there was the cast photo from the high school musical in Grade 11. Eleanor stood in the front row of the chorus, with me on one side and Donnie Brandon on the other.

Are high school relationships explicable? Friendships? Donnie was my best friend. I was from the city's working-class north end, the son of a low-level provincial civil servant. Donnie lived in the richest corner of the deepest, upper-crustiest south end, the son of a corporate lawyer who served as the minister of something or other in the government. Donnie was the star quarterback on the football team. I cheered from the sidelines. Donnie had a new girlfriend every month. I had my first—and only—girlfriend during my last year, which would have been too late for me to tell Donnie about her.

Donnie died on the May long weekend of our Grade 11 year. A car accident. He and two friends from the football team were on their way to his parents' summer house—it wasn't just a cottage—in Chester when they careened off the road, hit a power pole, flipped over, and tumbled down an embankment. Donnie was driving. Too fast. He was drunk. They all were. And then they were gone. Forever. This was in an era before school grief counsellors, so those of us left behind were left mostly on our own, trying to cope with the adult world of loss before our time.

I handled it by telling everyone I was supposed to have been with Donnie and the others that weekend—the fourth in his father's car—but had had to cancel for some reason at the last moment. I can't remember now why I said I couldn't go. But I do remember I told that story so often and for so long I believed it was true. It wasn't. I wasn't friends with the others. Donnie had never invited me to spend a weekend at his parents' summer place. Donnie and I were never as close as I claimed. Why did I lie? I had many reasons, not the least of which was to insinuate my way into Eleanor's heart. I wondered now if I had really been that calculating.

I leafed through the album again. There was only that one photo, at the graduation prom, of just Eleanor and me. Photographs show the laughs.

MARIELA NEVER DID RETURN MY CALLS. BUT ONE DAY, APROPOS OF nothing I could discern, an email arrived. It had been sent from David's Spanish account. There was no explanation for that either.

> Dear Mr. Elijah Cooper,
> Dear Mr. Eli Cooper,
> Dear Elijah,
> Dear Eli,
> Dearest Cooper,
> I know it is not really your first name, but I would like to call you Cooper, the name I first heard you called. Do you mind?
> The reason I am writing to you today is to say I am sorry for the way I behaved the day you left. I had my reasons.
> I am often frustrated by the ways in which foreigners romanticize my country. And I detected some of that when you talked about moving here. I may love my country—and I do, with my whole heart—but I also know how hard it can be. I do not romanticize life here. I want you to love Cuba too, but the real place with all its faults and not some idealized paradise.
> I realize therefore I should have welcomed it when David brought you to our building so you could see how we really live. But that is part of my contradiction. As much as I want you to know the real place that is Cuba, I do not want you to know my real place, if you understand what I mean.

I was grateful when you bought me a mobile, but resentful too. Another contradiction. Why should I need you to provide me with charity? Why should I need anyone?

At the same time, I did not want to take advantage of you, did not want to become one of those awful women hanging off the arm of their sugar daddies, exchanging sex for CUCs, or for a ticket to some life of riches unattainable in Cuba.

That is why I rejected your generous gift of the phone. Later, when I had a chance to think about what I had done and how foolish I had been, I decided I would go to Uncle Lío and get it back. But then I discovered I had waited too long.

I confess I am not unhappy about that. I can express myself in English more clearly on the page than with my voice.

I will try.

I must be honest. I did not, in the beginning, think of you in any way other than as a client. But then I came out of the Interests Section reeling, and I heard you call my name. Your eyes exuded warmth and sympathy, and—even though you had no idea what had happened to me—a kind of empathy. You wanted to help me. I was grateful.

Perhaps that is why what happened between us happened. It shouldn't have. I know that now. I did not mean to lead you on. I was vulnerable, and you were kind. But kindness is not enough to serve as the basis for a relationship between us. We come from different worlds. We have lived different experiences. It would be foolish for either of us to think or act otherwise.

I am writing today to apologize if I led you to believe we could be anything other than friends. But I do hope we can be friends.

If you ever return to Cuba, dear Cooper, it would be my privilege to be your guide.

Your friend,
Mariela

I knew Mariela didn't intend it that way, but I read her email as encouragement. She had written to me!

* * * *

"I'm sorry. I really am." She was the still-late, still-apologizing Wendy Wagner. Dressed today in a neat, business-like black pant-suit with a gold top, she looked her new role. And sounded it too.

"We just got a whole bunch of FOI/POP responses this morning and I needed to make sure someone was following up on a couple of them."

The Wendy Wagner I remembered wouldn't have known a free-dom of information protection of privacy act request from her dis-carded nose ring. The new Wendy was assigning reporters to do what she herself wouldn't have been able to accomplish six months ago.

"Most of what we got back is blacked out or total crap," she confided, "but there's some stuff about a contract for a new school in the minister's riding that looks, like, really juicy."

The waitress had returned. She seemed to know Wendy. "The sashimi sampler and Perrier, right?" she said.

"Right," Wendy replied. Now I knew where the puppy fat had gone.

"And for the gentleman?" Was our waitress thinking *the father?*

"I'll have the Bento 2," I said, ordering a lunch special that would do nothing to dissipate my own old-dog fat. "Oh, and another Sapporo." I'd already finished most of a first waiting for Wendy to arrive. What the fuck? Wendy—aka *Morning Hi*—was paying and I had nothing to do this afternoon that required sobriety.

Wendy prattled on about her job, and the paper, and the surveys that showed how well its new format was working. "Our readers like it short and sweet," she allowed, "with lots of pictures.... But that doesn't mean we can't do real journalism too. We do." I still had doubts, though I kept them to myself. "What I really miss is having all you guys—you, Liv, Peggy—to show me the ropes. I learned so much from all of you in such a short time. I really loved you guys, especially you."

If I remembered correctly, this sounded like the beginning of the conversation that had ended with sex in the bathroom. Wendy seemed oblivious. Did she even remember that? Part of me hoped she did, most of me prayed she didn't.

"And, now," she continued, "I'm like the most experienced person in the whole newsroom. Crazy? Right?"

Right.

"That's one reason I wanted to talk to you. The publisher says we're doing so well he's authorized me to hire a columnist. Our first. Freelance, of course. I talked to Liv and Peggy, and they both suggested you." Had she offered them the gig first and only thought of me after they'd turned her down?

"I don't know," I said. "I've never written a column."

"Liv says you have all sorts of great opinions, like, just waiting to write." She did? Did I? "What do you think? Do you want to give it a try? I can't pay much, just a hundred a column to start." One hundred dollars a column! "I can see that look on your face. I know, I know. It isn't much, but we don't have all that much room for copy either. You'd only have to write, like, three hundred words." Three hundred words! "But—"

"What about copy-editing?" I offered. As much as I'd admired the new paper's energy and feistiness, its pages were rife with Wendy-like typos, grammatical errors, missing facts, missed connections. That I could help with. "I could maybe come in and do some copy-editing for you."

"Oh, we don't do any editing in Halifax," she replied breezily. "We send everything to Toronto and they, like, do all that stuff there." Using real people or algorithms, I wanted to ask her, but didn't. "I wish we did. I'd love to have you in the office."

"Listen, Wendy, you know, I just wanted to say I'm really sorry about...." What was I sorry about, and how could I say that now?

"Never be sorry," she said. "Life happens. And life goes on. We're OK." She paused, looked straight into my eyes for just an instant, and then breezily returned to the subject at hand. "So will you think about it? The column, I mean."

"I will." I wouldn't.

The food arrived. We ate. Wendy finished. I had ordered too much.

"Can you pack this?" I asked the waitress, thinking it might save me the trouble of cooking dinner, wondering if Wendy would see it as a sign of my penny-pinching or poverty, or both.

"You went to Cuba last winter, right?" Wendy said, making conversation while we waited for the bill.

"I did."

"I thought somebody told me that at Peggy's party. Anyway, my boyfriend and I are thinking of going this winter." Boyfriend? Wendy had a boyfriend? "Did you have a good time?"

Did I have a good time? What did "good" even mean in that context? But that wasn't what Wendy was asking. "I had a great time," I answered. "I highly recommend it, especially Havana."

"Good to know. But did you hear the news this morning?"

"What news?"

"About the big hurricane. Bigger than Katrina. I just read it on the wire. They say it's going to kick the shit out of Havana."

* * * *

It began very badly, and then it got much worse. The shit-kicker hurricane Wendy had referred to was Gustav, already the third named storm in what those who were paid to know about such things were gleefully predicting would be an especially destructive 2008 hurricane season.

Gustav—birthed as a nondescript tropical depression in the warm waters southeast of Haiti—had suddenly, inexplicably morphed into a full-blown, raging hurricane, and set off on a swirling, whirling rampage targeting Haiti, the Dominican Republic, Jamaica, the Cayman Islands, and Cuba. Since Gustav's final destination appeared to be New Orleans and since it might make landfall exactly three years to the day after Hurricane Katrina decimated the city, its trajectory became worthy of breathless American cable news coverage. As an editor, I understood the journalistic joy of anniversaries combined with serendipitous coincidences, and I appreciated CNN providing round-the-clock coverage for its American viewers. But I was now an ex-editor and all I really wanted and needed to know was what the fuck was actually happening in Havana.

I had been trying for three days to get through to Mariela. No one answered her cellphone. I called the landline number I had for Esteban and Silvia's casa, but all the phones seemed to be dead. Emails disappeared into the void.

"Meanwhile…"—it was the CNN announcer again with his "aside" voice after reporting on the latest news from New Orleans—"people in the Caribbean are cleaning up from the mess Gustav left. The State Department estimates half-a-million people have been affected by the storm in communist Cuba, including in the capital of Havana where waves crashed over the Malecón and flooded already crumbling seaside neighbourhoods."

The screen showed images from mid-storm as huge waves washed over the seawall. Images from the aftermath followed as rescuers in rubber dinghies navigated Central Havana's narrow streets. I was certain I saw a shot of the street where Mariela and David lived. Or did I just imagine that? The streets all looked the same.

"We'll be right back," the announcer said, "with more on the latest from New Orleans."

Within days of Gustav's dissipation and before anyone could recover, Hurricane Hanna stormed by, delivering Cuba another glancing blow in its wake. Its mere existence left me paralyzed, transfixed in front of my television awaiting the Next Big One. Which turned out to be Ike. As Hurricane Ike barrelled toward Cuba, news reports said 2.6 million Cubans had already abandoned their homes to seek shelter from the storm. That represented almost one-quarter of the country's population! Where could they have gone? Was Mariela among them? She must have been.

By the time this storm passed over, thirty thousand Cuban homes had been destroyed across the island, another two hundred thousand damaged. In Havana, sixty-seven buildings—four in a single block in the old city—had collapsed. While CNN showed close-up images of rubble it said came from collapsed Havana infrastructure, the announcer gloated. "The Castro regime likes to brag no one in Cuba dies in hurricanes. That may technically be true, but the communists are far less willing to talk about what happens afterward. Like much of Havana, this apartment building in downtown

Havana"—on the screen, a fleeting image from mid-storm of what could have been Mariela's and David's home—"was in sad shape structurally even before Ike. After the storm passed, some residents tried to return to their home here. But the building collapsed with them inside. A man and a woman are believed dead."

Fuck!

"SO IF WE'RE ALL HERE, COMPAÑEROS, I THINK WE SHOULD GET STARTED," Jack began, scanning the earnest faces of the dozen or so folks squeezed tonight into his small dingy living room, sitting on his saggy couch and mismatched living-room chairs, or perched on the hard-backed, garage-sale wooden chairs he'd imported from the kitchen for the occasion. One young man—one of the few among us who might be described that way— sat cross-legged on the floor.

"We've got a long agenda and lots of urgent items tonight, especially about hurricane relief," Jack said. "But before we get to that, I want to welcome our newest member. I know some of you met Eli Cooper at the fundraiser on Wednesday." Nods and greetings. "Eli and I go way back. The old *Dal Gazette* days, right Eli?" Right, I nodded. "Back when revolution was still cool, back before Eli sold out to the Media Man." He laughed his familiar room-filler laugh. I smiled weakly. No one else paid attention. "Just kidding, Eli," Jack jumped into the silence he'd created. "Anyway, the good news is that Eli has finally discovered the power and beauty of that wonderful little island we've all known about forever, and he has decided to join our little cell. Welcome *compañero*."

I am not usually—you may have assumed this already—a joiner, even of groups that might welcome me. But here I was, joined, welcomed. I dimly remembered Jack from university. He was one of a small group of political hangers-on who attended *Gazette* staff meetings but never seemed to write a word. Even so, he championed others who proposed stories interpreting Chairman Mao's *Little Red Book* for the peasant masses among our readership of party-hearty college students, and loudly criticized what he called "rightist tendencies" in stories lesser revolutionaries had written about issues that actually had something to do with what was happening on campus. I lost touch with him after I joined the *Tribune*, though I recalled hearing from someone he'd become a welder because he refused to put his university education "to the service of the Man." He also occasionally published pamphlets attacking multinational corporations and local business owners about topics which the *Trib*'s lawyers inevitably deemed too libellous for us.

Jack's interest in Cuba was longstanding. During the seventies, he told me, he'd travelled by tramp steamer to Cuba to be part of a brigade harvesting sugar cane, and he still flew back to the island at least once or twice a year for conferences and to support the Revolution. He was now the president of NovaCubaCan, a small pro-Cuba group, mostly, it seemed to me, because no one else wanted the job. NovaCubaCan had sponsored last week's "Cuba Hurricanes Relief Fundraiser," which Jack had organized, and I had attended.

He had begun those proceedings by reading a letter from a national Cuba solidarity organization of which NovaCubaCan was obviously a branch plant.

"Cuba has been assaulted in quick succession by three powerful hurricanes," he began as if the storms themselves had been part of a planned attack against the island. "That Cuba should be a victim of the increased frequency of such 'natural disasters' is both unnatural and a striking injustice," the letter continued. "Under the inspired leadership of Raúl and of their workers' and farmers' government, Cuba is the country least to be blamed for the deteriorating climatic conditions that fuel hurricanes."

Ah, yes, climate change as an imperialist weapon of mass destruction. I wished I hadn't sat so far from the exit.

"As usual," the letter continued, slowly circling its point, "Canada's government is providing no aid to Cuba in this time of crisis. And the Canadian media, which has reported extensively on hurricane damage in Louisiana, has been all but silent on the devastation in Cuba. In the face of this inaction and silence, it is imperative for those of us who are supporters of the Cuban Revolution to show our solidarity."

Jack paused, looked around the room. "*Viva!*" he shouted. "*Viva Fidel! Viva Cuba!*"

"*Viva!*" a few voices shouted back, while the rest of us mumbled something incoherent, approximating *viva.*

Was I a supporter of the Cuban Revolution? Mostly, I was desperate to find out if Mariela was all right. I'd attended the fundraiser after seeing a notice about it in *The Coast*. I contributed two twenties when they passed around the baseball cap. "For Mariela," I said to myself as I tossed the bills into the collection of mostly fives and tens.

During the milling and socializing after the official fundraiser, I'd met a Cuban Canadian couple named Lily and Umberto. Umberto, dark, young, and virile, was dressed for the seasonably cool fall night in sweatpants and a T-shirt. Lily, a doughy, middle-aged university librarian, was wearing a full, almost floor-length peasant skirt over fire-engine red sneakers. Her husband, Lily told me, had lots of relatives in central Havana. "If they don't know your friend," she assured me, "they will know people who will."

Umberto looked doubtful.

"I try," he said.

He was calling his cousin later in the week. He would ask him to check on Mariela.

Which was the real reason I'd decided to attend NovaCubaCan's regular monthly meeting tonight. To find out what Umberto had found out. Unfortunately, Lily and Umberto arrived late, so I'd had to wait while Jack waded his way—democratically, slowly, painfully—through all the interminable urgent items on his agenda. It began with a report on the "tremendous success" of an ongoing letter-writing campaign in support of the Cuban Five, Cuban intelligence agents in prison in the United States. There was a lengthy discussion about arranging a visit to the city by the Cuban ambassador to raise public consciousness about the need for donations to rebuild after the devastation and a decision, reached after what seemed an endless debate, not to send the pitifully small one-hundred-and-forty-three dollars raised during the fundraiser to the national organization immediately, but to wait instead until we could assemble a "more respectable sum reflecting our commitment to the cause."

"So, thank you again, *compañeros*, for your continuing support for the Cuban Revolution, for the Cuban people," Jack summarized. Finally, we were coming to the end. Somehow—mostly because Lily had agreed to chair it—I'd volunteered to serve on a committee organizing the collection of supplies to send to Cuba.

"*Hasta la Victoria…. Viva!*" Jack called out like a high school cheerleader. "*Viva Fidel! Viva Cuba!*"

"*Viva,*" people replied in distinctly lower-case voices as they scrambled for the door.

Lily found me. "Great news," she said. "Umberto's cousin knows someone who knows your Mariela. She is OK, she is fine. She told him to tell you she has your number and she will call you tomorrow night."

5

THERE WAS STILL ONLY ONE PHONE IN THE HOUSE, THE BLACK ROTARY DIAL number on the little table outside my parents' bedroom. The next evening, sometime before seven o'clock, I pulled out the small, uncomfortable bench seat from under the table and sat down in front of the phone. I stared at it, willing it to ring, dreading what I might hear when it did. I fretted, rehearsed, discarded, revised, and then rehearsed anew what I would say to Mariela when it rang. If it rang....

Three hours later, the phone did ring. I waited, took a deep breath, picked up the receiver.

"Hello," I said, trying to calm the quaver in my voice, the quiver in my soul.

"Hello." A woman's voice. But not Mariela's.

"Hello?"

"Mr. Elijah Cooper?"

"Yes?"

"Mr. Cooper, my name is Kimberly Sanderson...." She paused, hopeful, as if that might mean something to me. It didn't.

"Yes?"

"My mother's maiden name was Pattison...Eleanor Pattison."
Silence. More silence.

"Do you know who I mean, Mr. Cooper?"

I tried to find my breath, which had seemed to have been sucked from my lungs.

"I do," I gasped.

"I'm her daughter," she said, "and I believe you're my father."

I tried to think of the right words to say. I couldn't. A long pause.

"How's Eleanor?" I asked.

I know that was not the right—certainly not the appropriate—first question to ask the daughter I didn't know I had, but it was the question that had been bubbling at the tip-top of my simple, single-tracked mind for thirty-six years. There was a time when I knew not only the number of years I'd been waiting to ask it, but also the months, days, hours, minutes. Time does not heal. A love wound may eventually scab over and the scab fall off, but the wound memory remains—and it remains real.

Eleanor Pattison was my girlfriend. My first. My only. When we met in Grade 11, she was my best friend Donnie Brandon's girlfriend. I was not jealous. Eleanor was so far out of my league as to be beyond my galaxy. She was a high school cheerleader—beautiful in that blonde way that was popular back then, probably still is—petite, perfectly proportioned with tousled, down-to-her-breasts hair—and therefore the perfect arm-candy complement to Donnie's football star quarterback

I never understood what Eleanor's father did for a living, but it seemed, at least according to what Eleanor eventually told me, he did most of it on his yacht. I was never invited on his yacht. I never even saw it. I did see their house, which resembled—and may have even been modelled on—a castle.

After the car accident in which Donnie died, Eleanor seemed to gravitate toward me. She asked me to sit with her at his funeral, to go with her to his interment, to "be there for me" when we all went to his parents' home after the service for tea and tears. In the days that followed, we met each day after school, walked together down to the coffee shop below the Lord Nelson Hotel, drank coffee and ate rice pudding ("Donnie's favourite") while she talked about Donnie, and I listened.

I only realized years later, and in a very different context, there was nothing unusual—or necessarily "about me"—in how Eleanor reacted. In 1998, I served as the main editor on the *Tribune* newsroom team that covered the crash of Swissair Flight 111, a New York-to-Geneva passenger jet that flew into the sea near Halifax, killing all 239 people aboard. Part of our ongoing coverage included stories about unexpected post-crash relationships between family members of the victims, mostly high-powered New Yorkers, and locals who lived near the crash site, many salt-of-the-sea fishermen.

Peggy Aylward interviewed a psychologist who explained what he suggested was a common phenomenon. "When someone loses a loved one in such sudden, unexpected circumstances, they naturally gravitate to people who might have been closest to their loved one, physically, emotionally, at the time of their death. It's just their way of closing the distance, of connecting with the one who is gone."

Of course, my story—my made-up story—that I was supposed to be in the car with Donnie played neatly into that psychological narrative. I kept the clipping because it seemed to me as good an explanation as I would find to explain why Eleanor Pattison fell in love with me.

By the end of the summer after Donnie died, Eleanor was referring to me as her boyfriend. At first, I had trouble wrapping my head around the concept Eleanor could ever be "my girlfriend." But the more time we spent together—and we spent more and more time together alone—my mind and body seemed to relax into the idea. I almost believed it.

Not that we had sex. Not then. I didn't drive. Neither did Eleanor. She never suggested we go to her parents' house, and I certainly never considered bringing her to mine. We spent a lot of days walking in Point Pleasant Park. Occasionally, we'd wander away from the well-travelled pathways and into the deep woods, find a quiet space, sit down, talk, lay down, cuddle, make out...never quite going all the way. Eleanor didn't stop me. I stopped myself. Was I saving myself for something I didn't understand? Was I afraid of defiling Donnie's memory? Or just afraid I'd screw up screwing.

Summer turned into fall, and fall became unseasonably cold for making out in the woods. Then it was winter and there never seemed a right sometime or right somewhere to take the next step. We held hands in the school's hallways as we moved from class to class. "No touching, Mr. Cooper, no touching," the hall monitor inevitably admonished, an admonition I just as inevitably ignored as soon as we passed out of her sightline.

I walked Eleanor home every day after school, my arm wrapped protectively around her shoulders, her body tucking comfortably into mine. We always parted a block from her house—for reasons unspoken but understood—after a few too-brief minutes of deep kisses and roaming hands beneath heavy coats.

In May of our last year of high school, Eleanor and I attended a memorial service to mark the one-year anniversary of Donnie's death, and then I walked her home. Our deep kisses that evening were deeper, our roaming hands more urgent. "I want to," she said as we reluctantly, finally separated our bodies. "Soon."

"Soon" came a month later, sometime after three o'clock in the morning during an all-night after-grad party in a cottage near Chester. The cottage was really a mansion, with both a pool and ocean frontage and a sailboat at the dock. It was owned by friends of Eleanor's parents whose son was one of our fellow grads. His parents hired a bus to bring a dozen of us to the party and back to the city the next morning. This was in the days before alcohol-free grads. His parents just wanted to give us a space where we could all get blotto together one last time, parent-free, but without any of us ending up like Donnie. Donnie's undying legacy to the rest of us was understood. Do not die drunk in a car accident.

I was drunk and stoned. So was Eleanor. I had to pee. So did Eleanor. We ended up, accidentally or not, far from the rest of the party, alone together in the parents' upstairs master bathroom. The bathroom was bigger than my bedroom at home, with a huge walk-in tub in one corner and an incongruously, oversized wicker chair beside the tub. We started in the chair, moved up against a wall and ended, gloriously naked, shudderingly sated, in the empty tub.

I'd like to believe I recall every delicious moment, every delectable touch and tingle that passed between us that night, but I don't. Over the years, I know I've honed and layered, massaged and manipulated my memories to the point where I no longer know which among them is truth and which is simply part of my made-up Myth of Eleanor and Eli. At some level, it doesn't really matter. In the end, it was that myth—and my desperate need to see my myth as reality—that determined the rest of my life.

Until the new Myth of Me and Mariela replaced it.

The day after grad, Eleanor departed for eight weeks as a counsellor at an expensive summer camp in Quebec, which her father and Eleanor had both attended as campers, and which he now underwrote as his do-good gift to the sons and daughters of his done-well friends. I had a summer job bagging groceries at a Dominion store. Eleanor and I agreed to write each other every day. And we did. In the beginning the letters consisted largely of day-to-day tidbits from our mundane existences—"One of my campers broke out in a poison ivy rash and the whole camp is on lockdown." "There was a big staff meeting today because the cash didn't balance at the end of the day yesterday, and the manager is threatening to fire whoever is to blame."—coupled with pledges of eternal love and modestly racy descriptions of what we would do to, and with, each other when were finally together again. In early August, however, Eleanor's letters suddenly took on a more ominous if elliptical colouration. "We have to talk...there's something important we need to discuss...I need to see you now."

I feared what I thought would be the worst—that she had fallen in love with a fellow counsellor—which made the eventual reality seem less worse. To me at least. At first.

Eleanor flew home the week before camp officially ended and called immediately to arrange to meet that night. We kissed when we met, but she quickly cut off my embrace. "Let's walk," she said. Our small talk was small as she led me off the park's main trail and into a clearing in the woods where we'd spent many happy hours the previous summer. She sat on a fallen tree trunk. I sat beside her, expectant, dreading.

"I'm pregnant," she said simply, unemotionally.

It is strange to comprehend—even for me today—but, at the time, the possibility Eleanor might have become pregnant as a result of our one sexual encounter had never occurred to me. Perhaps I was so self-absorbed in my own sweet-shocky surprise she might actually love me in this unexpected way I never bothered to ask who was responsible for what. I know we had not used a condom. Perhaps I had assumed Eleanor was "taking care" of that. I knew other girls in our class were on the pill—or at least that's what some of the boys claimed—but I never asked Eleanor if she was too. Or maybe I just didn't want to break the spell by asking the question that might have cooled our ardour and ended my first time before it could become such.

"Shit," I said finally. "Really?"

"Really." She'd gone to see a doctor in Quebec the week before. He told Eleanor about a doctor he knew in Montreal—I'm guessing now he probably meant Henry Morgentaler—who could perform a safe abortion in his clinic.

"But I could never do that," she said. I didn't ask why.

"So?"

"I don't know. I just know I have to tell my parents tomorrow tonight after my dad gets home."

"I could come with you," I said. "We could tell them together."

"No," she replied firmly. "That would only make everything worse." I didn't ask her why that would be. I figured that out later.

We agreed she would call me after she talked to her parents. I sat by the phone—the same one I would sit in front of many years later waiting for Mariela to call—but Eleanor never called. I tried to call her the next day from the pay phone near work. But the voice on the other end of the line—her mother, I'm sure, her voice stiff and icy—simply said "Eleanor isn't available." I was afraid to leave a message. That night I stood for an hour at the corner where we usually parted, hoping she would telepathically receive the message I was sending and come find me. She didn't. The next night I ventured closer to the entrance to her house, but there was no light outside the door, no lights from inside I could see at all. The night after that, I screwed up my courage and knocked on the door. No response at all.

Finally, on the fifth night, I saw a light on in an upstairs room. I knocked. And waited. Knocked again. And again. Finally, her father—dishevelled from sleep or drink, I couldn't tell—opened the door, stared me down.

"Uh...hello, Mr. Pattison. My name is—"

"I know who you are." Flat, hard, with more than a hint of danger.

"I was just...I mean, I was hoping to talk to Eleanor—"

"Not here."

"Oh." I hadn't considered that possibility. "Well, then, can I—"

"She's not here. I already told you that. And she won't be here. Not for you. Not now. Not ever."

I hadn't realized how tall he was. Maybe because he was standing in the doorway while I was on the step below, or maybe it was because he'd puffed himself up, father-protector-like, to appear even more intimidating than I already understood him to be.

"But—"

"You should leave if you know what's good for you, young man. You're not welcome at this house. Don't come back—and don't ever try to contact my daughter again."

"But—"

"My daughter has gone away. And she won't be back. She doesn't want to see you again. If you persist in trying to contact her, there will be consequences, serious consequences. Do you understand?"

"But—"

"Do you understand?"

"Yes, but—"

"You will leave now, young man, or I will call the police."

With that, he stepped back into the house and closed the door so hard I could feel the air from its slamming slap me on my face.

It was only after my encounter with her father that I realized how isolated from the rest of our world Eleanor and I had become. I had no one to call, no one to ask, What now? In the months after Donnie's death, Eleanor had quit the cheerleading squad ("What's there to cheer about now?"), gave up hanging out with her former girlfriends, and spent all her time with me, talking about Donnie, about life with Donnie, about whether there was life after Donnie. As for me, I had always been a loner. If not for my friendship with

Donnie, which had briefly brought me out of my own one-man-shell of a happy place, I'd never have met Eleanor.

But the result was I had no one I could ask where she'd gone. I called a few of her cheerleader friends, but they appeared to blame me for the fact Eleanor had grown distant from them. They claimed not to know where she'd gone. They might even have been telling the truth. I would have talked to Sarah, but my sister—who'd been big-sister fascinated with little brother's love life that summer—had already left for Calgary to prepare for her first year of law school.

So, in September of 1972, I went off to my first year of university without Eleanor, without Donnie, without anyone I cared about from high school. Every morning, I boarded the bus near my parents' house in the north end for the crosstown ride to the Dalhousie University campus in the south end, attended my classes, and then returned home at the end of the day to spend my nights alone in my room. I did not join any campus group, did not attend any campus event until the very last day of first term. After I finished my last exam, I noticed a sign advertising an end-of-exam blowout dance. Everyone welcome. Why the fuck not?

I went alone. I drank alone. I drank a lot. At some point, I decided the time had finally come to confront Mr. Pattison. Why the fuck not? So I walked from the campus toward the Pattison castle, rehearsing the speech I'd been practising since that night in August when he'd told me to get lost. I'd show him. Except....

Except when I got to the house, there was a sign on the lawn. SOLD. I knocked on the door. Loudly. Repeatedly. No one answered. I walked around the house. There were no curtains on any of the windows. I managed to hoist myself up a wall, look in one of the windows. No furniture. I walked around the house one more time, pissed on the front door, left.

And that was that. There should have been more to it, a greater sense of occasion, but that was that. And that was all.

When Sarah returned home at Christmas, I broached the subject with her, explaining that Eleanor and her family had moved away after high school without leaving a forwarding address so I didn't know where or how to find her, not explaining Eleanor had been pregnant or that her father told me never to darken their door again. Sarah's reasonable big-sister advice was to forget about Eleanor.

"Everybody has a first love they think is the one," she explained sagely, "but she never is. You'll meet all sorts of other more interesting girls at college."

I didn't.

"You'll forget all about her."

I didn't.

I know now there were resources—even then, even before the internet—I might have marshalled to track down Eleanor. I could have started at the library, looked up her house address in the *City Directory,* found her parents' first names (George and Alice, as I later learned), discovered where her father worked, contacted his business, learned where they'd moved, tracked him down through Directory Assistance, called him, insisted he tell me where Eleanor was, boarded a bus or plane or train or boat or whatever I had to in order to go to where she was, tell her I loved her, and wanted to marry her so we could love happily ever after.

But I was eighteen and hopelessly naive. I didn't have the journalistic smarts then to know how to begin such a search. By the time I'd learned how to do it, the trail had long since grown cold. Whatever her father had done for a living, I learned when I did look him up, he'd listed no employer, no office I could contact. Perhaps that's why he conducted all his business on his yacht. But he wasn't listed as having been a member of any yacht club in the city. There was no record of his existence in the library's extensive newspaper clippings files, or in the *Tribune*'s less extensive local biographical indexes either.

Eventually, I gave up. Almost. Occasionally, after the web cleaved open the world's secrets, I would amuse myself to sleep on nights after my shift ended and I'd had too much to drink. I plugged search terms into the newest of the ever-evolving numbers of ever more comprehensive search engines. I did find an obituary for a George Pattison, investor and philanthropist, who died in Detroit in 1998 and had lived "briefly" in Halifax with his former wife, Alice, but there were no references to a child by that marriage. Perhaps Eleanor was dead, but that didn't explain why she wouldn't be listed. Perhaps the second wife, the current widow, had written Eleanor out of obituary existence for some reason? For what reason? And why just her and not her mother? Perhaps I had the wrong George Pattison. I fell asleep.

I'm sure, in retrospect, I could have done more—or better. I could have hired a private detective who specialized in missing persons searches, for example. I did consider that at one point, but ultimately rejected it. I'm not sure why, but I think, when I am being honest with myself, which is not often, I didn't want to find her. I came to prefer the Delusion of Eleanor to the possibility, the likelihood, I would find her and she would reject me.

I couldn't help but acknowledge (though I never really did, not really) that, in all the years since I'd last seen her—thirty-six—Eleanor had never once tried to contact me. That must have meant something.

Still, I remained faithful to Eleanor. Or to my fantasy of her. When I did finally, half-heartedly, begin to date again—I was already working at the *Tribune* by then—I compared every fellow journalist, every secretary, every Friday-night bar pickup, to Eleanor. I compared sex with them to graduation night with Eleanor in the wicker chair, up against the wall, in the tub—and found everyone and everything else wanting. Over time, I became less and less interested in looking. Sex became an occasional meaningless release with someone like Liv, someone I understood was also looking for her own meaningless release. And then, of course, there was the occasional unfortunate accident with someone like Wendy, who was too drunk to know I was not what she wanted.

"How's Eleanor," I asked again into the phone. "Your mother, I mean."

Kimberly paused, seemed to consider. "I think we should meet. I can tell you everything, and you can tell me everything."

MARIELA NEVER DID CALL ME, BUT SHE DID SEND ANOTHER EMAIL FROM David's account.

I am sorry I didn't telephone you when I told your friend I would. Things here are very unsettled, partly because of the hurricane, but also because of some other reasons. I will explain all that when I see you again, if you are still willing to see me.

As I said, there were reasons for how I behaved, but those reasons were not good reasons. I would like to see you again, my dear Cooper, to rewind back to that moment on the Malecón when you said you loved me and start again from there.

Muchos abrazos fuertes, mi amor,

Mariela

Mi amor? Mi amor! I printed Mariela's email so I could read, and re-read, and then re-read it some more. "I would like to see you again...."

I decided to concoct myself a celebratory Esteban mojito, but discovered there was no lime in the fridge to cut the sweetness of the sugar. Who needed lime when life was so sweet? I drank my Havana Club neat. Mi amor.

* * * *

"I won't kid you," he said after I'd finished laying out some of the facts. "What you're talking about is eighty per cent of my business these days. A guy—women too, lots of women, maybe even more women—they travel on their own to some exotic spot for a vacation, adventure, whatever. Usually the Caribbean, but hey, also Asia, eastern Europe, the former Soviet Union, all these such-and-so-stans, countries I've never heard of, with names I can't pronounce. So they go to these places, maybe they get too much sun, maybe they drink too much, maybe they're lonely, whatever. And then they meet some local Casanova, or whatever a lady Casanova is called, and they get romanced and loved like they were never loved or romanced at home, so, naturally, they fall in love and, naturally too, they want to bring their new joy-toy back home with them, get married, have beautiful brown or yellow babies and live happily ever after. Whatever. Nine times out of ten? It ends badly. Bad, fucking-ly bad. Is that the kind of situation you're talking about, compadre?"

No...well, yes. Maybe. Was it?

I'd ended up in the office of Vincent—"call me Vince"—Peterson, Attorney and Immigration Consultant, under what might be described as a slightly misleading artifice. I'd explained to his secretary I was a freelance magazine writer working on a story about a trend I'd noted on the internet. This was partly true. I might one day become a freelance magazine writer, and I had indeed discovered on the internet what seemed to me to be a disturbing trend. North Americans seemed to be falling in love with Cubans to no good end. I even found one web forum called "Cuba, No Amor" filled with shared horror stories about...well, about the impossibility of getting a Cuban government exit visa for your Cuban lover, about the improbability of getting a Canadian government visa for your Cuban lover to come to Canada, about the disillusionments, the betrayals, the recriminations, and inevitably, about the inevitability your relationship will go south after your lover comes north. I didn't want to believe.

"There must be some happy endings," I said to Vince.

"Sure, there are," he replied, "But few and fucking far between in my experience. I said nine out of ten ends badly? Make that ninety-nine out of a hundred."

"But if I...if *someone*, say, wanted to marry a Cuban and bring them back to Canada, what would be the process?"

I had now decided my mistake with Mariela had been in suggesting I'd move to Cuba to be with her when the right answer was the one behind door number three. I would apply to bring her to Canada to live with me. The real reason I had asked to meet with Vince was to figure out how to go about it.

"How many years do you have, pal? I'm not trying to discourage you...or someone," he said, arching his eyebrows in my direction as if to indicate he was on to me, "but it's a very complicated, time-consuming process. And expensive, especially if you want to involve me. She has to convince the Cubans they really don't want, or need, her around anymore, and then you—someone—has to convince the Canadian government this is a legit fucking relationship, in the best sense of that term, and not just a way for her to get the hell out of Cuba. You have to guarantee the government she isn't going to end up on the public tit when she gets here. Given what I told you—nine times out of ten, ninety-nine times out of a hundred—you can understand why the government might be a little skeptical your situation is going to end up any different.

"My advice? What I tell my clients all the time. You're in love. Fine. Go down there. Be in love. Love. Have sex. Bring a few presents for her family. Play the big man. Three, four months. And then get the fuck out before Big Mamma and all her family and friends get their claws too deep in you. That's my advice, compadre."

Thanks.

"By the way, what magazine did you say this was for?"

7

"PLEASE CALL ME KIM," KIMBERLY SAID AS SHE SAT DOWN ACROSS FROM me at the table in the restaurant.

When she first entered, looked around, I'd called out, "Kimberly!" Although she had no social media profile and no online photos I could find—of course I checked!—I would have recognized her anywhere. Tiny, perfect—in that same blonde Eleanor way. Except that she was pregnant. Six months, she told me after we hugged hello. Is this what Eleanor looked like when she was six months pregnant? I hadn't seen Eleanor then...or ever after. I stared at Kim as she eased herself into the seat, searching for something of me in her face, her hair, her manner? If there was, I couldn't see it.

Should I have said "Call me dad"? I shouldn't. I didn't.

We'd agreed to meet at Jane's on the Common. "It's my favourite restaurant," I said. It was, though I hadn't been back since that night with Sarah, the night of the "you-deserve-a-break" Cuba ticket, the night my life began to change.

"You can't go wrong with their daily special," I said, trying not to let my mind wander off the track.

We both ordered the special. Kim asked for a club soda.

"My doctor says I'm not supposed to drink any alcohol until after the baby is born."

I asked for rum. "What kind of rum do you stock?" I wanted to know.

"Appleton. It's from Jamaica," the waitress answered.

"You should get Havana Club," I suggested. "From Cuba. It's very good too." I was stalling, not sure if I should start, or how to start if I did, or where this might go. "But yes, Appleton will be fine. Thank you."

"My mother died three months ago," Kim said finally. "I didn't want to tell you that on the phone.

I didn't want to hear that, not on the phone, not in person.

"I'm sorry," I said.

"I'm sorry too," she replied. "I'd really hoped she'd live to see her grandson. It's a boy, by the way."

How could Eleanor be dead when she was still eighteen? I realized, even as I thought such thoughts, these were wrong thoughts for me to be thinking. How could I still obsess about this person I had known only flickeringly briefly in the context of my whole life, and hadn't seen in the flesh since 1972, when my actual daughter, flesh of my flesh, sat in front of me now, carrying inside her my grandson, a next generation me! Part of me wanted, needed to know everything that had happened in the thirty-six years since my sperm had commingled with Eleanor's seed in the bathroom of that cottage/mansion in Chester to create this Kim person now sitting, full-grown, pregnant herself, across from me. But another part of me didn't want to know, couldn't wrap my mind around the reality I had an actual daughter. Before, the idea of having fathered a child—I had not known Kim had a gender or a name until very recently—had been an abstraction. I did not carry her inside me for nine months, was not there for her birth, or her growing up, or her all grown up. We never had the chance to father-daughter bond, to share experiences, to care about one another. But perhaps that was just another excuse for my lifelong failure to connect, to care, about anyone beyond myself. And yet, here I was, sitting across from my daughter, caring suddenly, deeply about who Kim was, and where she'd come from, and who she'd become. Maybe I didn't need the ghost of Eleanor past. Or the (im)plausibility of Mariela future.

"Tell me about you," I said. She didn't, not exactly, not at first. Instead, she told me about everyone around her. It turned out they were all dead—Eleanor from cancer ("three months from diagnosis to death"), Charles, the man Kim had called "dad," from a heart attack two years before that, both sets of grandparents, including George and his wife, from various age-related causes many years before.

The father of her own child, she said, a tax advisor at the same Toronto firm where she worked in human resources (she'd moved there for university and trained as a psychologist), was "not in the picture." Like I had not been in her picture? "And I'm an only child," she added. So there hadn't been another. "Which means I have no one." She paused. "Except you."

She had only accidentally discovered my existence and my fleeting but significant (seminal) role in her life while helping her mother organize Charles's papers after he died, and discovered her adoption folder among them.

"They never told me," Kim explained. "Mom said they always planned to, but then they kept putting it off and it got harder and harder to bring it up. So they just let me think Dad— Charles—was my father."

It wasn't until after her mother was diagnosed with cancer and Kim's pregnancy had been confirmed that Kim finally began to press her mother for details. "I wanted to know for me, but I really needed to know for the baby. And that's when she told me about you."

What did she tell you, I wondered?

As Kim recounted the story, Eleanor's parents had shipped her off to the west coast, to Portland, Oregon, in August 1972, where she lived with her mother's sister until after Kim was born.

"My great-aunt took care of me while my mother went back to school, to community college for a year and then to Portland State. That's where my mother met my dad. They got married right away. I'm not sure she ever really loved him, but he was a good husband, a great father. He adopted me. I wasn't even two, so I never knew him as anyone but my dad, and no one told me any different."

Never really loved him.... "When you were talking with your mother when she was, you know, in her last months, did she talk at all about me, about what happened?"

"A little. She told me you were really sweet to her, that you became her best friend in high school, that I was an accident but a lucky one." She stopped, tried to decide where to go from that. "What can you tell me about Donnie Brandon?"

"Donnie?" Me trying to decide too. "The three of us," I said. "We were best friends. Why do you ask?"

"Well, just before she died, my mother was talking to me about those times, just rambling on, maybe medicated, and she said this Donnie person had been the love of her life, but that he had died." She stopped. The silence hung between us until I couldn't bear it.

"Yes," I said finally. "He did. A car accident."

Eli loves Eleanor. Eleanor loves Donnie.... I need to go to Havana before it's too late.

"All right," she said finally. "Now you know all about me. Tell me about you."

THE
MONEY DANCE

1

THE MAN IN THE TAN UNIFORM WITH THE *MINISTERIO DEL INTERIOR* BADGE ON
his breast pocket was polite but insistent. "This way, sir. *Por
favor.* Bring your luggage. All of it." He led the way—as I pushed two
suitcases, balancing a cardboard box on the larger one—into a small
windowless room away from the luggage carousel.

Two other men, also in uniform, waited inside the room with
a tail-wagging dog that had the colouration of an Irish Springer
Spaniel but probably wasn't.

The older man nodded toward the dog. "Only routine."

"Of course," I said. What was I supposed to say?

I had flown into Havana's José Martí International Airport
from Toronto late that night. Because it was no longer tourist season,
there had been no direct flights from Halifax to Varadero or one of
the other Cuban tourist destinations. It was after midnight when
we landed, and the airport was mostly deserted as we stumbled,
bleary-eyed, toward Customs. My fellow passengers were different from those I remembered from my first charter-flight holiday.
There were a few all-weather tourists, of course, and some others,
dressed conspicuously in suits, probably deal-seeking businessmen,
but many, perhaps a majority, appeared to be lone older men. Like

me. A few women too. Most were well-dressed, tropical-casual. I'd noticed them when we boarded the plane in Toronto, but I became more conscious of what brought them to Havana as we waited in line for our luggage. They were already on their cellphones, connecting with people beyond the airport exits, making arrangements. Too late for me, the Cuban government had made it legal for Cubans to own their own cellphones soon after I bought Mariela's. Were these men calling their Cuban wives or girlfriends? As their luggage spit out onto the carousel, I noticed the men scooping up oversized hockey bag after antique steamer trunk after awkwardly stuffed cardboard box...booty for their Cuban families? Was I the same cliché?

I had arrived better prepared than on my first visit. Instead of a duffel, I'd brought my newly acquired, matching, big and not-quite-so-big red soft-sided suitcases, each with four-wheel rollers. The smaller one contained my clothing, much of it the same as on my last trip, but with a newly acquired bathing suit and fresher socks and T-shirts, which left plenty of room for the spillover from the larger suitcase's collection of gifts for Mariela. There were towels, sheets, toilet paper, soap, vitamins, shampoo and conditioner, toothpaste, makeup, moisturizer, deodorant, even feminine hygiene products, all chosen by Lily, my new NovaCubaCan friend.

"I know Cuban women," she said. "Your friend will appreciate these." Cuban women, maybe, but Mariela? Charity? I would soon find out. Lily had also packed a separate cardboard box of gifts for her husband's cousin in Central Havana, the one who'd helped find Mariela. "Don't worry," she said, "he'll come to your casa to get it."

As the dog sniffed the box's exterior, I realized with a start I had no idea what Lily had packed inside. The younger officer held up a box cutter and waved it in the direction of the cardboard box.

"Uh, OK," I replied. Did I have a choice? He carefully sliced open the box along the tape lines, reached his arms in—he was wearing latex gloves—felt around, removed a few items of clothing, held them up, put them back. He pulled out a couple of vitamin bottles, opened the screw tops, checked carefully to see that the seal had not been broken, replaced them too. After he'd completed his silent search and gave the mutt his doggie reward, the older officer began questioning me. His younger partner now opened my large suitcase and began picking up each item individually. He seemed especially interested in the half dozen bottles of shampoo, handling each one carefully, opening the top, sniffing, closing.

"So Señor...Cooper...." The older man was holding my passport, my tourist visa. "Your airline ticket says, 'open return.' Why is that?"

"Well, I don't have a job," I began, smiling. Neither man seemed to see the humour. "I mean I'm sort of retired, so I don't have to be back for work on a particular day or anything, so I thought I'd...." *Shut up, Eli.*

"This is not your first time in Cuba?"

"No." I decided to answer only the questions I was asked, to volunteer nothing until I understood what this was about.

"When were you last in our country?"

"February."

"Yes. I see that." He was looking at a piece of paper. "For two weeks. Correct?"

"Yes."

"You flew into Varadero. You had a reservation at a resort hotel in Jibacoa, but you did not stay there the whole time. Correct?"

"Correct." Perhaps I should answer more fulsomely, I thought, get this over with, or at least figure out where all these questions were leading. "I was bored at the resort and decided I wanted to see Havana."

"And yet you chose not to go to our capital on an official excursion. Correct?"

"Yes. But there weren't any excursions to Havana during that week." Stop volunteering.

"So, tell me, Señor Cooper, how did you get to Havana?"

Shit. Was this really all about Lío driving me into Havana? *No one care...unless they do. And then I in trouble. Big trouble.* "A friend drove me."

"This friend of yours? Would his name be Virgilio Montes?"

Silence.

"Perhaps you knew him as Lío."

"Yes, that's him," I said reluctantly, feeling like I was being sucked deeper down into a rabbit hole with no exit.

"You say this Lío is a friend of yours. How long have you two been friends?"

"Not long then. Actually, we'd just met."

"Just met?" the older officer arched his brows. "And yet you say you were friends?"

"We became friends. After. I asked the bell captain—" Christ! Throw everyone under the bus. "I asked someone at the resort to find me a drive and they—"

"Do you remember the name of this 'someone'?"

"No."

"Could that someone have been—" he consulted another piece of paper—"Reynaldo Sánchez?"

"Yes. Maybe. I don't know." I really still didn't remember. Just that his name started with an R.

The younger officer finally closed the lid on the small suitcase. He nodded a "no" to the older one.

"Did you buy a mobile telephone for your friend Lío?"

"No...I mean, yes, but it wasn't...." Shit. I couldn't implicate Mariela in this, whatever *this* was. "Yes, I did," I said finally, "but as a gift. I hadn't realized I couldn't use my credit card in Cuba." I stopped. *"Bloqueo!"* I declared with what I hoped was the proper vehemence. "Lío helped arrange for my sister in Canada to send me money. Legally." I only hoped now that what Lío did had been legal. "So I bought him a phone. It seemed the least I could do. For...his... help."

"Are you sure you didn't buy the phone as a gift for...." I had begun to realize the man only paused to look down at his papers for effect. He knew exactly what was written there. "Ah, yes, here it is... Mariela Pérez. Is she also your *friend?"*

"Uh, yes, she is. A friend." What did he mean? What did he know? "It was for both of them really."

"For both of—"

"Virgilio Montes?" It was the younger officer, impatient now. Was he the one actually in charge? "Did Señor Montes ask you to bring anything into Cuba in your luggage for him on this trip?"

"No."

"Did anyone ask you to bring anything into Cuba for them?"

"No. I mean...." Did he mean all the supplies I was carrying? "No one asked me. These are just gifts. After the hurricanes, I thought—"

"That is all, Señor Cooper." The younger officer looked dismissively at the older one, as if to say we have learned everything of importance we need to know. It is time to put an end to this. "You are free to go," he said. "Please," he added, "enjoy your visit to our wonderful country."

And then they disappeared back out the door, leaving me alone with my luggage and Lily's no-longer-sealed cardboard carton, as well as the uncomfortable feeling that for some unknown reason my life had become an open book in Cuba.

* * * *

Lío had been arrested. He was in Villa Marista, a Havana jail run by the Ministry of the Interior.

"Bad, very bad," Esteban whispered to me as he hauled my luggage from the taxi up the three flights to the casa. "Not his fault."

Since there were other guests—two British couples—already enjoying Esteban's mojitos in the kitchen, he escorted me back into his and Silvia's private quarters. I'd never been there before. It was clear the renovations had stopped with the guest area.

Over rum and cold cuts, Silvia unfolded the story. One of Lío's occasional customers, a Mexican businessman who travelled to Havana frequently, had asked Lío to deliver a package to an address in Miramar. It wasn't an unusual request, and Lío thought nothing of it. He dropped off the package that same day. The man at the door thanked him and handed him a ten CUC tip on top of the twenty the Mexican had already paid him.

"Lío leaves, go back to his car," Esteban said, returning from another round of guest drink–making, and picking up the story.

"And...." He threw his hands up in the air. "Arrested. Like that. Other man too."

"Why?" I asked.

"*Policía* say package contain...boom...*bomba!*"

"Not a bomb," Silvia clarified, "but pieces to make bomb. Lío says the officers told him there was C3—plastic explosive?—in the shampoo bottles."

So that was why.

"Lío no know," Esteban insisted. "Just package is all. No know."

"Who? Why?" I asked. None of this made any sense to me. Except I now understood the sudden interest in me and my luggage at the airport.

"Miami," Silvia said simply, as if that explained everything. "They want to destroy the Revolution."

"What about Lío?" I asked, wanting to get back to the issue at hand. "What will happen to him?"

"I think they will let him go," Silvia replied. "I hope. Lío is a good man, a good communist."

We sat in silence for a few minutes. I wanted desperately to change the subject to the one that had really brought me back to Havana. "Mariela?" I said finally.

Silvia smiled, happy too to move on. "She's waiting for you. At Lío's. She and David live there now. Until Lío gets out."

2

THE TAXI DRIVER WAITED OUTSIDE LÍO'S DARKENED HOUSE WHILE I KNOCKED on the door. It was the middle of the night in Havana. There were no streetlights, no lights in any of the homes along the street, no illumination, in fact, in any of the neighbourhoods we'd driven through to get here.

"I wait," the driver said. "Make sure someone answer."

Ah, yes, I thought. I was back in Cuba, back where people looked out for one another. And then I thought of Lío.

Mariela answered on the first knock. She'd been sitting, waiting in the dark for me. She wore a short shift dress that might have been a nightgown, and bare feet, but she also sported lipstick. For me?

"My darling Cooper," she greeted me, wrapping her arms around my neck. "It is so good to see you again." I inhaled her perfume, kissed her neck, then my lips worked their way up to her cheeks, her lips. In the distance, I could hear the taxi slowly drive away, its engine labouring from too many years of service to the Revolution.

"No electricity...again...always..." she said to explain the lack of lights anywhere. She shrugged, pulled away from my embrace. "Come." She took my hand, led me through the living room, past the kitchen with its gleam-in-the-dark stainless-steel appliances, and out into the small backyard where candles burned in Lío's barbecue pit. We sat on lawn chairs, she pulled hers closer to mine.

"I missed you," she said.

"Me too," I said. I meant it. Did she? "Are you OK? I mean the hurricane, Lío, everything that's happened."

"I'm good. Better now that you're here."

We were not even touching, and I could already feel myself grow hard, my mind grow soft. Was love sex, and sex love, or was that just men, or perhaps just me? Mariela told me about the hurricanes. Like everyone else in her Havana neighbourhood, she and David had been evacuated to a shelter away from danger. Not once, but twice. "The first time was not so bad but when we came home the second time, even the staircase to the second floor was gone, washed away. There was still water everywhere. We slept for a few nights outside in the park, Coppelia, where we had that ice cream"—I remembered—"and then, because of the hurricane, there were some cancellations at Silvia's casa, so she let us stay there for a few nights," Mariela continued. "Uncle Lío had already been arrested by then, but no one knew what was going on until Esteban was allowed to see him, and Uncle Lío told him to tell us we could live in his house until he gets released."

"When will that be?"

"No one knows, but soon, we think, we hope. Radio Bemba says."

"Radio Bemba?"

"Gossip. That's what we call it. It's how we find out what's really going on. They say the investigators already know Uncle Lío didn't know what was in the package, but they need him to testify against the Mexican and the other one—the Cuban in the pay of the Americans, the one he brought the package to—so they'll keep him in jail until after the trial."

"Is he OK?"

"Uncle Lío?" She smiled. "He's always OK. He's probably selling the guards cheap construction materials to fix up their apartments." She yawned then. With meaning. "I have some clients early tomorrow morning. Some Spaniards I met at the hotel." I looked at her. She smiled again. "If Lío can do it, why not me?... So, we should go to bed."

There was no discussion, no negotiating dance. She led me upstairs and into what must have been Lío's bedroom. Even in the dark, I could make out the fussy, over-decorated Mediterranean dressers, the oval king-sized bed, the mirrored tiles looking down from the ceiling. Lío's style, I thought.

"David?" I asked. Were we alone?

"With his Italian," she replied. "He came back to Cuba for a visit last week and I haven't seen David since."

She pulled the dress up over her head, dropped it to the floor. My eyes adjusted to the lack of light very well.

"Better than on the Malecón?" she asked. She wasn't wearing a bra. She stepped out of her panties. I had never seen her naked before.

"Much better," I said. "Much better."

Mariela undressed me. This was so much different, so much better than that first night—I suddenly remembered the condom. I was not eighteen this time. No excuses. I'd bought a box, plain, no colours, no ridges, no ostentation, at a drug store in Halifax before I left and stuffed it into my shaving kit. For whatever reason, the inspectors had not inspected that. Before leaving Silvia's tonight, I removed one packet from the box and placed it in my wallet. Just in hope. And hope seemed about to be rewarded. But as I fumbled for the wallet in my back pocket, I felt my pants fall to my ankles.

"Condom," I said, pointing down vaguely.

Mariela giggled. "On the night table. I am prepared."

I laughed. "Me too. In my pants pocket. Ready also!"

She turned serious. "We will use yours. Mine are Cuban condoms. Made in China. The government gives them out, but they are not very good. They irritate, and sometimes they break."

"Canadian it will be then," I said. "Just like me."

The sex was, unsurprisingly, much better this time. Gentle at first, probing, exploring, circling, hands darting here and there, speeding up, backing off, then speeding up again, becoming more intense with each pass, more urgent, sweat mingling skin on skin, lips pressed against lips, against teeth, tongues inside mouths, the mind wanting the moment never to end, the body with a mind of its own. When it ended—finally, and too soon at the same moment—I was spent, physically, emotionally, mentally.

We laid on our backs for a while, let our breaths settle back to their normal rhythms, our sweat cool the heat inside our bodies. We stared up at ourselves in Lío's mirror, laughed at the incongruity of it all, me—for a change—not even cataloguing my own many imperfections.

"I've been thinking," I said finally. I had. About Vince, the immigration specialist. About nine out of ten, ninety-nine out a hundred. About being that one in a million who finds true love in this unlikely place, in this unexpected way. Why not me? I thought about Eleanor too. Eleanor, loving the Donnie she could never have at the same time I was loving the Eleanor I had never found. And now she was dead. I thought about all those missed opportunities, all those wasted years. And for what?

I hired Vince—"Five hundred bucks, friends and family price, for your 'friend'"— to help me navigate the process before the process, which entailed gathering my birth certificate, preparing my legal proof of un-marital status, my Canadian certification of non-impediment to marriage abroad, getting all those official documents translated into official Spanish, then having them notarized by the Cuban consulate in Montreal. Just in case. Just in case I worked up the courage to actually ask Mariela to marry me. Just in case she said yes.

Vince had thrown down warning flags. "If she says yes—and why would anyone say no to you?—the real fun begins. Getting her out of the country. But let's fall off that particular crazy, swaying suspension bridge when we get to it, OK?"

OK.

I had not told anyone of my plan. Who was there to tell? Certainly not Sarah. If Mariela said yes, of course, I would have to tell my sister about her new sister-in-law. But until then, I had no desire to venture out on to that bridge only to have it come tumbling down.

"I'm not someone who falls in love easily, or often," I began now, circling, still looking up at the mirror instead of over at Mariela, trying, and failing, to read the expression on her face at this distance. "So this is very hard for me."

It was. I had been rehearsing this conversation, at home in Halifax, in my head, for weeks, ever since Mariela's email, probably since long before that. Since when? When did I fall in love with Mariela? Not that first day in the car with Lío on the drive from Jibacoa to Havana. I couldn't even have imagined falling in love then. Perhaps it happened that night on the roof bar at the Ambos Mundos? Mariela had seemed smart, funny, beautiful, too young, beyond my hopes or expectations, and therefore someone I could love because she wouldn't have to love me back, and nothing would happen, and life could go on without interruption. My kind of love. Or maybe I realized I was in love that day outside the US Interests Section when I'd first sensed that other Mariela, the one who was pained, vulnerable, needing someone. Me? No, not me. Not then. I only wished. Or could my I-have-officially-fallen-in-love moment have occurred the morning before our day at the beach when I mistakenly connected the romance dots between Mariela and David, and realized I was jealous. How could I be jealous if I didn't care?

Forget the when for the moment. Why? Why did I fall in love? Why now? Why here? Why with Mariela? What the fuck is love, and what's love got to do with anything anyway? I only knew enough now to know I knew nothing—and I didn't care. Perhaps that was love.

"That night when we were at Bruno's, before the Malecón, before...." Before we did what we did, I didn't say. "I probably shouldn't have told you I was falling in love with you. I didn't mean to scare you. But it wasn't just the rum talking. I was. I am. I can't explain where it comes from or why, and I know it's crazy, and I know you'll think I'm crazy—" Stop babbling, I told myself, this wasn't the way the speech had unfolded in your head—"but I do know I want to marry you." There. I'd said it.

Mariela edged closer to me, wrapped her left leg over my body, turned her face in my direction. I kept staring up at the ceiling.

"It doesn't matter to me where we live," I told the mirror. "Havana? Halifax? Maybe we can go back and forth. Winters here, summers in Canada. I've already got the forms we need to start the process. We can—"

She reached out, wrapped her fingers around my jaw, turned my face to hers. "Yes," she said simply. "Yes." And kissed me. I could feel the wet of her tears.

We made love again, a second act I would not have believed myself still physically capable of performing until I did. We used her Cuban condom this time since I'd only brought one with me. This time, when it was over, we stayed wrapped in each other, me still inside her for as long as possible, not wanting to break that bond.

"Let's call this our 'Special Period,'" she whispered finally, drowsy, her hot breath in my ear.

"I thought that was a bad time here, the Special Period," I said.

"It was," she answered, "Fidel's Special Period. But I still like the sound of those words inside my head. The phrase seems magical. The 'Special Period,'" she said again, almost whimsically. "That time when you're first in love, and there is nothing but love. Do you know what I mean?"

I did. She meant that Special Period before....

Before what?

T**HE NEXT MORNING, M**ARIELA MADE US CAFÉ CON LECHE. "I'M SORRY
there's no food in the house," she apologized, opening and closing Lío's massive stainless-steel fridge to confirm the fact. "I usually
just buy bread on my way downtown."

What had really happened last night? Mariela, who'd basically
refused to even look at me when I tried to get close to her the day I
left Havana in February, and who had not responded to almost any of
my six months' worth of phone calls and emails and messages since,
had greeted me last night as "my darling Cooper." As her long lost.
We'd had sex, the best sex I could remember. Was it? What about
Eleanor? How soon you forget. I thought about Vince.

"Don't ever let them get too close, my friend, or they'll take
you for more than you're worth."

I thought about Sarah, who would say "I told you so" when it
all went to shit.

"You're very quiet this morning," Mariela said, sliding up
beside me, offering a cheek to kiss. "Are you OK?"

"Oh, yes. I am...OK." I kissed her cheek. "Just thinking. About
how wonderful last night was."

She smiled. "Me too," she said. Did she mean that? Or were we
in When-Harry-Met-Sally territory? Fake orgasms? Fake love? Why
was I allowing myself to wander into that messy morass?

She gave my arm a squeeze. "I've been thinking too. About the
wedding. Silvia's sister's daughter got married last year. She had a

wonderful dress. We're about the same size, so I'll talk to Silvia, see if I can borrow it.... We could have the reception at Bruno's. Just a small group. I can ask Silvia to supervise the making of the wedding cake. And—"

This was fast. Too fast? What was the rush? But, of course, I was the one who'd asked Mariela to marry me. And why would I want to wait? I didn't. But...now that we were engaged—were we?—I sensed the webs of our relationships must inevitably spider outward to include Sarah, Mariela's family....

"What about your mother and grandmother?" I asked Mariela. "Should we go to Cárdenas and tell them our good news?"

"No," Mariela snapped, too quickly, it seemed to me. "I will tell my mother and she can tell my grandmother. It will be better that way. My mother will be afraid I will leave forever. Like my brothers."

"Will they come to the wedding— your mother and grandmother?"

"No...maybe...." Her verbal hiccup had returned. "My mother doesn't like Havana," she explained. "And my grandmother's health isn't the best. We will see." She stopped, retreated inside herself.

What did I really know about Mariela? About her family? About her life before me? About her current relationship with her first husband—what was his name?... Alex? Not that Mariela knew anything about me either. I'd never mentioned Eleanor, but that was different. It was. Really.

"I have to go now, and find my clients, or they will wander off on their own," she said as if she hadn't said what she'd just said. "Let's meet for drinks after. At Bruno's. You will be OK here by yourself?"

"Yes," I said. "I'll be fine." I would need all the hours left in the day to rearrange the dangerous thoughts in my head, to swim back from edge of that abyss I was creating in my mind and back to the beautiful still pool of love from the night before, to my special place and my own Special Period.

* * * *

"There is something I have not told you," Mariela declared as Bruno deposited a second round on the table. "About Alex and me." I waited for the other boot to kick me in the head.

I had put in the hours before I met Mariela strolling the Malecón, noting how few permanent scars all those hurricanes, one after another, each one worse than the last, which had dominated my every waking hour and sleeping thought for more than a month, had actually left on this city. The water-roiled streets of my television-screen memory had long since been sucked back into the Bay of Havana, leaving no obvious trace, save for a few missing chunks of concrete, which may or may not have been missing before the storm. Though it had been just a few months since the last of the storms swept through, no one I encountered among my admittedly so-far small sampling of the city's population—Mariela, Esteban, Silvia, Bruno—even brought up the subject unless I raised it first.

"Hurricanes are just part of life for us," Mariela had insisted when I asked her what it felt like to live through one. "Like...snow for you in Canada."

Not quite. I had tried out my Rosetta Stone *"¿Huracán?"*—pronouncing my best who-ra-CAN—on Bruno, who seemed to understand. He also appeared unperturbed by the storms, even though, as he admitted to me, he lost a week's worth of business while he waited for the knee-deep water inside his courtyard bar to dissipate and for his customers to return from their temporary shelters. *"Pero es bueno,"* he told me with a shrug, adding as he raised his cupped hand to his mouth. *"Todos beben más."*

Mariela did drink more. And it felt like I was about to, too.

"I told you Alex and I were not together, but not how that happened," Mariela continued. "You remember that day, after we met outside the Interests Section, I was complaining how unfair it was for them to turn me down for a visa after I had gone through all the proper channels?"

I did.

"But that if I had jumped on a raft and sailed to Florida, they would have let me stay, no questions asked?"

Yes.

"Well, that is what Alex did. He left on a raft."

No! So, while Alex and Mariela were "no longer together," that was only because Alex was in Florida! Which was why Mariela needed a visa— Stop! Don't allow yourself to leap ahead of yourself. Let her tell it—and then leap off that bridge.

"I had no idea he was even planning to do such a thing," Mariela continued. "I mean, everyone knew about Delfín and Roberto." *Delfín? Roberto?* "Delfín was Alex's cousin, Roberto his best friend. They were our age. We all went to school together. Roberto's family lived in a little house on the edge of Cárdenas. It had a shed on the property near the seashore where the three of them used to go to talk and drink rum. But Alex never told me he was part of their plan."

"Sorry? Part of what plan?"

"I apologize, Cooper, I'm not explaining myself. Like I told you, I explain myself much better in English when I can take the time to think and then write everything down. Anyway, I knew Delfín and Roberto were building a raft inside that shed. They'd been building it forever. They tied a bunch of old planks and pieces of driftwood together on top of some metal barrels. Roberto claimed they were fixing up an old engine to power it, but he told me it would have a sail too so they could save on gasoline. Nobody said anything to the authorities. Perhaps no one told because no one believed them. I did not. They were *no muy brillantes*. Alex and I even joked about what a crazy idea it was and how stupid the two of them were to think they could sail it to Florida. Alex never told me he was helping him, or that he planned to go with them."

"To Florida." I had to be sure.

"Yes. And that was the last I saw of...Alex."

"He didn't call."

"None of them did."

I tried to process that. So that meant....

"They died," Mariela answered the latest question I didn't have the language to ask. "At least that is what everyone in Cuba believes. It happens very often. People set off for Florida in their homemade rafts and they are never heard from again."

"So, is that what happened to Alex? He died?"

"Yes. I am...certain." She did not seem certain. Her hiccup had returned.

"I'm sorry for your loss." I chose to believe her. It was easier for me to feel genuine sympathy for Mariela if Alex wasn't alive and well and waiting for her in Florida.

"It is OK," she said. "As I told you, things were not good between us even before. I think we both understood by then our marriage had been a mistake. Maybe that made it easier for him to leave but, if he hadn't gone off on that raft, I am sure we would have been divorced by now anyway."

"So, you're not actually divorced?" My spidey sense sensed danger. Why was nothing ever simple?

She smiled. "Don't worry, my darling Cooper. I will fix that before we get married. In Cuba, a few things are not so difficult. Like divorce."

My spidey sense relaxed. That, I would only discover much later, was a mistake.

I held up my cup to get Bruno's attention. I needed another drink.

T HE EMBASSY WAS ALSO A MISTAKE, BUT I'D KNOWN THAT BEFORE IT
happened, even before I'd invited Mariela to join me.

"It'll be fun," I said. "An introduction to Canada and Canadian culture."

"You're sure it's OK?" she replied. "I mean, I'm a Cuban and—"

"Soon to be the *wife* of a Canadian," I said, brushing past her reticence, "which must make you at least half Canadian already. It'll be fun," I said again. What had I been thinking?

I'd discovered the existence of the Polar Bar, a biweekly party for expats at the Canadian embassy in Havana, when I met with officials there to go over what I would need to do to bring Mariela to Canada. I knew most of it already, from Vince and from the immigration website, but I thought it wouldn't hurt to introduce myself face to face.

"You say you're planning to marry the young woman here, even before you apply to sponsor her to come to Canada," the man at the embassy said when I explained my plans. He introduced himself as William, and he looked to be in his late twenties. "You do understand there are no guarantees she will be accepted."

"I do," I said. I did, of course, but it seemed only logical to me that applying to sponsor a woman who was already your wife would show commitment, give the application gravitas.

Vince had tried without success to point out the error of my ways. "You're talking logic, I'm talking immigration," he said.

William had said much the same thing, but in a kinder, gentler, more bureaucratic way. He'd been non-committal about how long it would take to get an official response to an application—"It depends on many factors"—and even less committal about what that response would be. "I really can't say, Mr. Cooper."

That said, he was friendly enough when he stopped talking official-ese after I stopped asking the questions that required him to speak that foreign language. We talked about the state of the newspaper business.

"I was going to be a journalist once," he confided, "but my parents talked me out of it. A good thing too, I guess, from everything I hear. What are you doing now?" I tried to explain I was still considering my options.

"I'm sure you know this already," he continued, "but they'll look more favourably on your application if you can say you have a job."

I did know that, which was why "Find Job" was at the top of my to-do list for after I returned to Canada.

"Is there anything you miss about Canada?" I asked. I was curious. What if they turned down my application to sponsor Mariela? Could I really live here?

"Everything," William replied. "Winter. You won't believe it, but I miss the seasons. Luckily, my four years here are coming to an end, so we'll be heading back to Ottawa before next winter. Ha! Be careful what you wish for, my wife tells me. And the internet, of course. I miss that. We have it here in the office, but it can be painfully slow. And the Canadian government frowns on it if you illegally download movies. But there's no internet in our apartment, so...what else? Beef! I do really miss Canadian beef. I was born in Alberta. Real beef is hard to get here.... Speaking of which, the Polar Bar is tomorrow night. A party here at the embassy. By the pool. There'll be burgers—Alberta beef—and Canadian beer. 'Where the burgers are grilled and the beer is chilled,' as we like to advertise. You should come."

"That sounds great," I said. "Is it OK if I bring my fiancée?"

"Mmmm," he said. "It's usually just Canadians, I mean for people with Canadian passports. But, well, let me think...." He thought. "There probably won't be a lot of people, since it's not high tourist season...so...why not? I'll leave a note for the guy at the gate."

I took that as unbridled enthusiasm and translated it into a personal request when I told Mariela.

"William—that's the guy's name at the embassy—says he'd really like to meet you."

"Why me?"

"Because you're my fiancée. Because we're going to be married. Because you might become a Canadian. If you want."

"But I won't know anyone."

"You'll know me."

I should have known. William had been right. It was a small crowd, perhaps a dozen people, some of them certainly embassy staffers who had to be here, a few scruffy backpackers returning from travelling around the country, one of the guys from my Toronto flight, whom I'd rightly assumed must be here to do business, doing business by the pool with other random business-looking types. There was a Cuban DJ playing music, Canadian songs whose titles he could not pronounce and Cuban songs whose lyrics I could not understand. The music was too loud for real conversation, not loud enough to discourage people from trying.

"I'm Jack," declared the tall, tanned, silver-haired man who'd materialized in front of me, sticking out his hand for a shake that could have broken a few bones in mine. He ignored Mariela. He worked for a big multinational accounting firm based in Toronto. The firm had opened its Havana office a year ago to provide services to the increasing numbers of its clients trying to do business in Cuba. "Why they want to try, I have no idea. Fucking Cuban bureaucracy," he said, taking a swig from his beer. It was clearly not his first. "Anyway, I got the short straw, so I'm stuck in this shithole." He looked at his watch. "For two more months, three days, and four hours."

I glanced at Mariela. She was staring at nothing across the pool.

"So I come here every two weeks for a little beef and some real Canadian beer." He raised his can.

I should have said something, defended Cuba, protected Mariela. I didn't. I saw William standing alone. "Hey, honey." I'd never called Mariela honey before. "There's William over there. He's the one from the embassy, the one I told you about. I should introduce you to him." I turned back to Jack. "Look, it was great to meet you," I said. "Enjoy your burger." I should have said *Fucking asshole*. For Mariela, as well as for me. But I didn't.

William was diplomatically proper, unfailingly polite. He welcomed Mariela, congratulated her on our engagement, pointed out the ambassador who was standing with a group by the pool. "See the guy to his right," William said to me. "Gregory. A lawyer. Smart guy. Married to a Cuban. He's lived here forever, even during the Special Period, I think. You should talk to him." Talk to him? Was William sending me a subtle, or not-so-subtle message, like forget getting permission to bring Mariela to Canada and start planning the rest of your life in Cuba.

"Thanks so much for inviting us," I said to William. "It's been great. But we should go. We have some stuff we need to do for the wedding."

Mariela smiled for the first time all evening.

I thought, that went well.

I **I** T'S A TRADITION," DAVID EXPLAINED OVER THE NOISE OF THE BAND AND the raucous sounds of drunken celebration. He was pointing uncertainly at a rainbow of coloured ribbons spraying out from the bottom of the wedding cake. "A Bruno tradition," he explained. "He bakes ribbons into the bottom layer of the cake and then, during the reception, all the unmarried women—men too, maybe, who knows?—get to pull on a ribbon. At the end of one ribbon, there is a ring. If you are the lucky one and get the ring when you pull on the ribbon, then you'll be the next one to be married."

"Like a garter," I replied. He looked puzzled. Perhaps traditions do not travel well. When Sarah and Saul married, she'd tossed her ceremonial garter over her shoulder for a similar purpose. "Never mind," I said to David. "It's a Canadian thing." Or maybe it was Jewish? I hadn't been to that many weddings.

"There is another part of Bruno's tradition," David continued, "but I doubt Silvia would have allowed such a terrible thing." He took another swig from Bruno's bootleg rum. He was drunk. I was drunk. I could feel my eyes slitting. "Sometimes he will attach a thimble to one of the ribbons," he said. "And the one who pulls that one is doomed to be an old maid forever."

We stood for a moment in silent contemplation of the cake.

"Silvia wouldn't," I said.

"Not Silvia," David agreed.

I looked around the room, filled with perhaps two dozen people, most of whom I didn't know. I knew David, of course, and now his Italian lover, Ale, whom David had introduced to me. And Silvia and Esteban. But that was it. Was everyone else here to celebrate my wedding? Or Mariela's? How many of them did Mariela even know? How many had showed up just to drink the free bootleg rum I'd paid Bruno to serve? I didn't know but I couldn't complain. Bruno really did know how to throw a party. The walls behind his bar had been decorated with yellow streamers and a handmade Bristol board sign that read *"¡Felicidades, Cooper y Mariela!"* in bold red-and-green block lettering. The platters on the plastic-covered tables on either side of the bar groaned with tiny, church-supper-style sandwiches and all manner of sweet treats, which Bruno had to keep refilling as the party proceeded. Bruno had rearranged the rest of the tables and chairs around the edges of the space to create a dance floor. The band, which had set up in another corner of the room, was playing danceable (for Cubans, if not for me) popular music. There was no stage, which made the mood somehow cozier, more intimate.

I watched Mariela dance past with someone else I didn't know. She was beautiful, smiling, her green eyes still mesmerizing, her hair—freed now from whatever upswept hairdo she and Silvia had concocted for the ceremony—hung loose the way it should. I was less enamoured of her dress. David had tried to describe the features of the wedding dress to me—the puff sleeves, the scalloped neckline, the basque waist, the tulle skirt...I had no clue what he was talking about. I only knew her neckline didn't scallop quite far enough to do justice to Mariela's fine stand-up-and-salute breasts. Her midsection—was that the basque?—seemed sausage-wrapped. To me, the dress looked like what it was. Someone else's. Nipped and tucked. I didn't say that, of course. I told Mariela she looked beautiful, which she did. She told me I was *hermoso* in the white guayabera and matching pants she'd chosen for me.

Now I smiled across the dance floor at her, blew her a kiss. She air-kissed me back. Even across the room, I could see the sweat beading on her forehead and above her lip. I wanted to kiss it away.

My bride! My wife! I was finally, officially, a married man. The ceremony itself had been muted, almost anticlimactic. Silvia was Mariela's bridesmaid, Esteban my best man. We'd arrived early in the afternoon at the *Palacio de los Matrimonios*, the white "palace on the hill" where Cubans officially marry in civil ceremonies in a converted pre-Revolution mansion. There were couples ahead of us, couples behind, a veritable wedding assembly line of soon-to-be-coupling couples. *Good day. Do you? I do. And you? I do. I now pronounce you...goodbye.* All in Spanish, of course. Perhaps it was the language barrier, or more likely, my lifelong aversion to cant and ceremony. Whatever, the actual wedding—the monotonal reading from something called the *Código del Matrimonio*, the repetitions of all the foreign words and phrases, the finger-ringing, the document-witnessing, the awkward public kissing at the end—left me unshaken, unstirred.

It was only after the official stuff was all over, seated regally with Mariela on the parade boot of a red 1959 Ford Fairlane convertible Esteban had borrowed and spit-polished for the occasion, laughing, kissing, waving, driving through the streets of Havana on our way to Bruno's, Esteban hard-honking the horn while drivers from the other cars honked back and people on the street shouted out their good wishes—*¡Suerte! ¡Lindísimo! ¡Felicidades!*—that I began to understand the enormity of what I'd just done.

At fifty-five, I had gotten married for the first time in my life—married to a woman who was younger than my daughter. Sometimes, I will confess, that difference in our ages gave me pause. I'd read all the stories, edited a few, all about the creepy older guy who weds a girl-woman. No good can come of that. But that wasn't me. Or Mariela. There were other times too, I'll admit since I'm admitting, when I simply marvelled at my good fortune, at the very idea someone as young and beautiful as Mariela could really love someone like me.

The song finally came to an end. Mariela's dance partner, a slim young man about her own age, bowed ostentatiously, removing a bill from his shirt pocket, and carefully pinned it among the others on her dress.

The money dance, I'd already learned from Bruno, was yet another wedding tradition, although I eventually came to realize most of Bruno's traditions were ones he'd created himself. When guests danced with the bride, they would present her with gifts of cash, which they would pin to her dress. For her new life with her husband. I told Mariela I was uncomfortable with the idea—we clearly didn't need the money nearly as much as its givers did—but she had brushed past my objections. "If we tell them not to, people will be offended."

It was only later I realized she was building up her own cache of cash. This was not, if I am to be truthful, the first, or only thing Mariela and I disagreed about when it came to the wedding preparations. But I'd expected that. Over the years, I'd also edited more than my share of spring wedding-plan pieces—"Wedding planning can be the most stressful time in a young couple's relationship"—so I understood it all came with the territory.

"Pastel de boda! Pastel de boda!" Bruno shouted to quiet the crowd as a beaming Silvia pushed a small cart topped with the wedding cake into the centre of the room. "Made me," Bruno tried out his English on me, pointing at himself. "Tres cake...blanco...." He gave up then, pointed proudly instead to the plastic bride and groom atop the cake. With Mariela's left arm wrapped around my waist, we held on to the knife and cut through the top layer in unison. Everyone cheered, and whooped, and toasted. We passed around the cake and doled out our own gifts for the guests—each woman received a delicate purse Mariela had chosen specially (and into each of which I had secretly inserted, at the last moment, a new twenty CUC note). Each man got a dazzling knockoff wristwatch, sans cash.

Finally, a couple of eager young women insisted it was time to pull out the ribbons.

"You too," I said to David, pushing him into their circle. "You're single too."

David pulled the ring. There was a surprised silence, then cheers as David presented the ring to Ale. And the band resumed playing.

* * * *

Sometime later—the band was still playing, the drinks still flowing—there was a commotion near the door. It was Lío, freshly sprung from Villa Marista! He was accompanied by two embarrassed-looking men in uniform, each hefting a case of Ron Santiago rum.

"For party," Lío yelled, seeing me. "Best rum! Best party!"

After everyone finally stopped hugging him, crying, cheering, slapping him on the back, Lío climbed on a table, supported by his two guards—who were smiling reluctantly, unsuccessfully attempting to appear intimidating—and began to speak.

David, who was standing beside me, translated. "He says he wouldn't have missed this party...this wedding...for the world." David slipped the English seamlessly in between Lío's Spanish. "He says he wants everyone to toast the bride and groom with the best Cuban rum.... He's telling Bruno to put out some cups and instructing the guards to pour.

"Unbelievable," David said to me. "Un-fucking-believable." After the drinks had been poured and passed, Lío raised his glass. "*Salud, Mariela y Cooper. Salud siempre!*" He emptied his cup, smiled, poured another. "*Viva Raúl! Viva Fidel! Viva Cuba!*"

Before the crowd's own shouted *viva* responses—much more effusive than any I'd heard at NovaCubaCan meetings—could fade, Lío spoke again, back to sentences longer than I could understand. David thankfully stepped in again. "He says he has a special gift for the newlyweds. He's sorry it's not gift wrapped, he says, but he has been a little preoccupied." The laughter erupted only a moment ahead of David's translation. "What he is giving the happy couple is the gift of privacy, something much valued here in Cuba, my friend Cooper." More laughter. "Tonight, he says, he will stay with his friends, Esteban and Silvia, so the newly wedded couple can do what newlyweds should do." I saw Lío wink to more cheers. "*Y David?*" Lío began again. David nodded in recognition. "And now he's speaking to me. He says, 'David, you had better stay away too.'" Laughter. "Don't worry, my friend," David spoke directly to me now. "Ale and I will be staying at his hotel. The place is yours." And he held out his cup to mine. We clinked cups.

* * * *

It was not quite morning when I woke up, more thirsty than hungover. Mariela and I had not made love, despite Lío's gift of privacy, despite even Mariela's new racy lingerie that was also, I had discovered, yet another popular wedding custom.

"I am so tired," she had said, yawning, perhaps for effect, as she entered the bedroom wearing a new sheer white peignoir with matching lacy panties and bra she had acquired for the occasion. She sat down on the bed beside me, placed her hand, affectionately rather than lasciviously, on my thigh. "Could we?... Would you mind? I would like the moment to be special, romantic but I am too tired right now. I should not have had so much to drink, but Lío kept insisting, '¡Otro! ¡Otro!' And I kept having one more."

"Me too," I admitted. The truth was I was not disappointed. I was tired too, and woozy from the drinks, and already wondering if I would be able to perform my husbandly responsibilities. It all seemed silly when I analyzed it. We were not teenagers, we were not virgins, we were not even unfamiliar to each other. Why this pressure to consummate a relationship that had already been well and truly consummated, simply because it was our wedding night?

"Hey," I said, putting my own hand on hers, also more affectionately than lasciviously, and squeezed. "Not to worry. We have the rest of our lives to have sex."

She laughed. We kissed, still more affectionately than lasciviously, and slid into Lío's bed, side by side on our backs, bodies touching, hands entwined, staring up at the mirror on the ceiling. "But if anyone asks," I said finally, "we did. Many times. In many different positions. And it was good. Very good."

She laughed out loud then, rolled over and kissed me. "I love you very much, my darling Cooper," she said.

And that was the last I remembered. Until now. The room was still dark (the electricity must be off again, I thought) and the lack of noise on the street outside sent its silent signal of just how late, or early, it must be. I needed a drink of water. I remembered I'd left a bottle (I still drank my water from a bottle like a tourist) on Lío's dresser, so I got up to get it, navigated my way past my white pants, white guayabera, white boxers, which had all fallen where

I'd shed them, found the bottle, opened it, took a swig, replaced it on the dresser, and returned by the same path to the bed. Only then did I realize the bed was empty. *Fuck!* I panicked. Was this my *Dallas,* Bobby Ewing, it-was-all-a-dream moment? Had I woken up to discover that none of this—not Mariela, not Cuba, maybe not my father's death nor my lost job—had actually happened? No, that couldn't be true. I looked around. Even in the dark, there was no mistaking that this was Lío's bedroom, Lío's mirrored ceiling.... So where was Mariela?

I treaded down the staircase carefully—it was even darker on the stairs, no windows, and I was mindful of Lío's warning the marble tiles could be slippery. Once in the kitchen, I could see the faintest, flickering light emanating from Lío's backyard. When I reached the door, I could see Mariela, wearing a housecoat now, sitting silent, cross-legged, on the ground in front of Lío's barbecue pit. She was holding something in her hand.

"Hey," I said as softly as I could. She started, hastily put whatever she was holding into the pocket of her housecoat. "I didn't mean to disturb you. Are you OK?"

"Yes, yes," she said, raising her face to face mine. "I'm OK. I had a nightmare is all. I sometimes have them. No reason. I just do." I was about to ask her about her nightmares, but she had already moved on. "And now...I was just thinking about how...happy I am."

I could see tears on her cheeks.

BEHIND GLASS

She emerges from the void, enveloped in a jumble of colour confusion-profusion—vibrant, fully saturated pinks and blues and yellows and greens, all mixing together in a mélange of wild swirls and crazy swoops. Eventually, the colours settle into shapes, the shapes into focus.

She is standing in the centre of a manicured neon-green lawn-carpet, dotted here and there by tall, shady, forest-green magnolia trees, each in full white bloom. Off in the distance, she can see what looks like a palace of a house—its coral-coloured stucco walls and wet-earth-brown roof tiles set off by pulsing white-in-the-sun trim. Somewhere in the distance, there is a black wooden fence that seems to extend to the sky and to the end of east and west. To keep people in? To keep them out?

Mariela has never been to Florida, but she has seen photos. She must be in Florida.

She sees children run around her and through, chasing each other as if she doesn't exist. Does she? She reaches out. Her fingers smack into a wall of glass she hadn't realized was there. Is it? She is trapped like a moth inside a glass jar. She can see the children, but she hears nothing. Are they laughing, shouting? Playing tag, you're it? Is it someone's birthday party? Is it?—

She sees Tonito then, running among them, oblivious. He is older than when she last saw him. Six or seven now. Perhaps it is his birthday....

At the edge of her vision, a woman appears. Old, kind-faced, perhaps a grandmother or a faithful retainer. She carries a tray with a pitcher of some fruity pink liquid and a number of glasses. The children stop what they are doing and run to her.

All except Tonito.

Tonito stops, turns toward Mariela, stares at her with those eyes— those eyes that are hers—for what seems like forever. Finally, he opens his mouth, shapes a single word, "Mami?" Though she cannot hear him speak, she understands, with a kind of ineffable anguish, that the delighted "Mami" of that first dream has been reimagined and is now a doubtful, questioning voice. "Mami?"

Does he know who she is? She tries to run toward him, but the glass stops her. She rushes back and forth, around, but there seems no end to the glass, no way past it. Finally, Tonito himself walks tentatively up to the glass, put his small palms on its surface, peers in. She places her palms opposite his.

"Tonito!" she shouts. "It's me, Mami!"

She can see the tiniest spark of "I know you" in his eyes before the entire image begins to dissolve back into its confusion of colour and there is no longer anything or anyone beyond the glass.

And then she wakes up, her fists balled so tight her fingernails draw blood from her palms and tears stream down her face, her silent scream trapped in her throat.

WANTS AND NEEDS

HAVANA, 2017

THE IMAGE ON MY COMPUTER SCREEN BOBS AND WEAVES. TONY MUST BE talking and walking. Again.

"Tony, Tony! Tony! You have to stop doing that. You're making me nauseous."

"What's nauseous?"

"Feeling sick to my stomach."

"Are you sick, Papi?"

The idea of these weekly IMO video chats had seemed like a good one. We'd even tested the app together before I left Havana. But we are now 3,000 kilometres apart. I'm in my basement apartment in Halifax staring at a jumping-bean image of Tony on my computer screen while Tony is with his grandmother at an outdoor Wi-Fi hotspot in the middle of Havana, wandering back and forth on the sidewalk, waving the mobile as he talks at me.

"No, Tony. I'm OK," I tell him. "It's just that I need you to hold the phone steady. Remember. Like we talked about last time."

I shouldn't complain. Who would have even imagined this would ever be possible? In the eight years since my first visit to Havana, mobile phones have become ubiquitous. Internet access, which used to be the preserve of privileged foreigners and important public officials, is increasingly seen as a public necessity, at least in theory. Which means I can stay in regular video contact with Tony even when I'm up north. I can see and hear him, and he can do the same. I don't want him to forget me while I am back in Halifax for my annual Canada-imposed 183-day exile. I travel back to Halifax each spring, then wait until the end of the fall hurricane season to return to Havana. I do this because Canadian government rules dictate I must reside physically in Canada for six months plus one day each year in order to maintain my health care eligibility. So far, I haven't needed to avail myself of that. Despite my age, I am in excellent health, give or take the odd, mild touch of arthritis in my knees, which I only notice when I first get out of bed. The few times I've needed to see a doctor in Havana, the kind fellow at the local clinic where Mariela goes sees me without asking to be paid or wanting proof of my Canadian insurance. Instead, I do what's required. I bring him "black-bag" gifts, such as some chocolate for his wife, a bottle of rum for him, a shopping bag filled with juices, sodas, eggs, meat, or other groceries for his family. My good health notwithstanding, I spend my requisite six months plus a day back in Canada. Just in case.

That's also why Tony was born in Canada. Just in case. So he would have Canadian citizenship as his birthright. On his birth certificate, he is Anthony Elijah. I call him Tony. Mariela calls him Antonio.

Mariela and I don't talk much about how we reached this time and place in our lives. Or whether it—whatever "it" is—is what we really want. But...how does that song go? You may not always get what you want, but you get what you need. Mariela needed this, needed me, needed Tony most of all. That's not to say she doesn't have regrets. How could she not? "One cannot replace the other," she tells me. And she still has nightmares. They occur less often now but, on some nights, I still hear her moaning from the next room. Tony—now our little log!—sleeps through it all. If I ask Mariela about her nightmare the next day, she will answer simply, "The same." So I have learned not to ask.

Me? Is this really what I want? When this journey began eight years ago, I believed I wanted nothing. Then I discovered I wanted everything. Now? Perhaps I too have ended up with what I need.

After Tony was born, we stayed in Halifax for a few months while I arranged my affairs. I semi-renovated my parents' house, removing the padlocks from the doors, ripping up the shag rugs from the main floor, and painting every surface a boring neutral colour. Sarah, who was now teaching at the local law school, took it upon herself to de-clutter what little was left of the clutter of my human existence, then artfully staged the house as an inviting, lived-in yet un-lived-in home, complete with the homey smells of cinnamon wafting from a pot simmering on the stove whenever potential buyers came for a showing. I put the house on the market for the outrageous price Arthur the Architect believed reasonable—and got every penny of it. I handed half to Sarah's investment guy, Peter Someone-or-other, who has since invested it in some sort of magical money beans he insists will allow me to live out all my legally permissible days in Havana in relative comfort.

While I'm in Halifax, I live in the basement apartment of a house Wendy Wagner and her husband bought with my help. They'd wanted to buy the house but couldn't afford it, so I agreed to rent the apartment, then paid my first years' rent in advance out of the proceeds from the sale of my house. They added that to their down-payment, thus convincing their bankers they had the wherewithal to carry the mortgage. They were grateful. I am grateful.

Tony has never lived in Canada except for his first few months, but Mariela and I agree he will spend at least part of each summer here with me when he's older. Sarah has promised to help take care of him. While I'm in Halifax, Big Maria, Mariela's mother, lives in my bedroom in Havana and looks after Tony so Mariela can continue working.

While I'm in Canada, I miss Cuba, miss my family, miss Tony most of all. I still refuse to think of myself as one of those foreign sugar daddies who breeze in and out of Cuba for a few months at a time, lavish gifts on all and sundry, live like a Cuban king on a Canadian pauper's salary, and feel themselves fulfilled. But I am. And I do.

Does it make a difference I now consider Cuba my real home? I find things to occupy my time in Halifax, of course. Last summer I made weekly visits to Aunt Abigail in a seniors' residence, staying for dinner, befriending her friends. The home's "life coordinator" eventually recruited me to be part of what she called the Memory Project, interviewing the residents about their lives for a book she plans to get printed. My hope—that I would encounter someone who had known or served with my father and could tell me the story behind the story I still didn't fully understand—proved vain, but listening to all the stories I didn't know about lives I hadn't lived inspired me to begin researching and writing my own family history. For balance, I'm learning more about Mariela's family story too. Big Maria has a head full of family stories from before and after the Revolution, all of which need to be recorded and preserved. I'm trying. For Tony.

"Is your abuela there?" I ask finally, interrupting yet another Tony monologue about his imaginary adventures in the snow with Olaf.

"She's talking to *una mujer*. Should I get her?"

"No, no. It's OK. Just give her a kiss for me, will you."

"OK."

"And here's one for your mother." I blew him a kiss. "Did you catch it?"

"Yes."

"And one for you."

"I caught it!" he yelled as the image on my screen flipped and flopped. "Papi?"

"Yes." He fumbled with the phone, held it in one hand, held his Mi Toni in the other, pushing the doll's face at the screen.

"Mi Toni is kissing you too. Did you catch it?"

I did.

WELCOME
TO
CANADA

Y ET ANOTHER PLANELOAD OF WEARY, WARY, BORED, BOUNCY PASSENGERS disgorging from escalators, spilling out, expectant, into the arrivals area at the Halifax airport. But not Mariela. Not this flight.... The black beans! Lily's recipe. Cuban, from Umberto's grandmother. *Muy rica!* Lily assured me. Those beans now simmering on the stove at home. Burned dry? Burned down the house? Would Mariela really want her first Canadian dinner to be Cuban beans and rice, overly familiar food territory, or would she perhaps crave the Big Mac and fries she'd heard about but never experienced? What would she think about Jane's on the Common? Gloves! Goddamn! I'd remembered to buy her a duffel coat, boots of indeterminate size and style, even a scarf to protect her neck against Halifax's late winter winds, all now hanging neatly over my arm, waiting only for her to step into them. But I'd forgotten to remember winter gloves. How could I have?...

No matter. We were only going to get into the limo anyway. When she arrived (not *if* anymore, but *when*!) I would need to remember to call the number on the business card so the limo driver would be waiting for us outside after we picked up her luggage. Would she think a limo too ostentatious? Airport limos are no big deal in Canada, I'd tell her, just glorified taxis. But would she then assume that was the way I always travelled? Why hadn't I learned to drive? What if she'd changed her mind? Maybe she'd never boarded.

More de-planing passengers descending escalators, exiting, meeting, greeting...I already knew she wouldn't be among this group either. The arrivals board said her much-delayed flight wasn't scheduled to land for another twenty minutes. But you could never be sure. Maybe the arrivals board hadn't been updated. Maybe...not her...not yet.

My mind skittered, careened, crashed into itself. I needed to slow down, breathe. Everything had happened more quickly than I'd expected.

"These things take for-fucking-ever, compadre," Vince had warned when he helped me fill out the formal application to sponsor Mariela to become a permanent Canadian resident the day after I'd returned from Havana a married man. "Months...years...if you're lucky. Be prepared." Which is why Vince had suggested coupling that application with a temporary visitor's visa application so Mariela might, possibly, at least, get to spend some time with me in Canada while we waited. "Let her experience a Canadian winter," he joked. "Then we'll see how much she loves you. Seriously though," he added seriously, sensing the sugar plums already dancing in my head, "the Canadian government will probably say no to a visitor's visa until they consider the permanent application. Even if the Cubans say yes, which they won't...don't get your hopes up, my man."

I hadn't. I'd filled out the official visitor's visa letter-of-invitation application form—"Kind of relationship (Please specify)"—which Vince had then notarized and couriered, along with my $224 Canadian processing fee, to the Cuban embassy in Ottawa. According to Vince, the embassy would eventually send the invitation, "probably by courier pigeon," to Cuba's Ministry of Foreign Affairs in Havana "where some non-functioning functionary will sit on it for a few months before, maybe, blessing it with some legal-bullshit stamp and then sending it on to some other cash-grabbing money-suck who will want even more of your money and take more of our time, and finally, they may—or may not—say yes. Or nothing at all. In my experience anyway. They claim the whole thing should take three months. I think the truth is more like Celsius-to-Fahrenheit. Double that and add thirty-two. Like I said, compadre, I'm happy to take your money. Just don't expect results in return."

But the Cubans had said yes! In half of the time Vince had predicted. And then the Canadian government conferred its blessing on Mariela's temporary visitor's visa.

"That's fantastic," Vince said, not sounding fantastic, "but you're not there yet, not even close. First you gotta read all the fine print, the print where it says even a valid visa is not a guarantee of entry into Canada. Some fucking border guard can still say no at the port of entry for some reason or no reason, and your *chica* is on the next plane back to Havana."

Mariela's plane had landed! The screen now officially declared her flight "Arrived"...if, in fact, she was on the plane. Was she? She'd lent the cellphone I bought for her—the one I bought to replace the one Lío now seemed to think was his—to David.

"I won't need it when I'm with you," she'd explained sort-of logically the day before she was supposed to fly. But her initial flight from Havana to Toronto had been delayed, her connecting flight to Halifax cancelled and then rescheduled for today because of a blizzard here, and I couldn't get in touch with her. That's when I began to panic that she'd decided not to come at all.

Some days I liked my life better when I didn't care.

Which reminded me. I would need to call the office to let them know I wouldn't be back today. I had an office. I had a job I needed to keep. I was now a Vice President and Senior Content Strategist at Coastal Communications Consultancy. My embossed business card boasted C3 was staffed with "Canada's finest full-service public relations and crisis communications management team." Including me.

I'd only applied for the job because Vince said having one would bolster my application to sponsor Mariela, and because Peggy Aylward heard I was looking and promised to put in a good word for me with her friend who owned C3, and because Wendy Wagner—Wendy!—had offered to write me a letter of reference. "You'll be great," she said. I only wished I believed she knew what she was talking about.

Luckily, Steve LaChance, the owner of C3, had the PR professional's misplaced reverence for journalists. "I hate fucking PR types," he'd declared, even though he was clearly a public relations lifer. Steve hired me immediately, offering an excellent—much-better-than-the-*Trib*—salary, but on a month-to-month contract with no benefits and no guarantees any of it would last beyond the next paycheque. "We're in a volatile business environment," he told me. "Everything is contract to contract."

"Fine with me," I said. But the job had turned out much better than I could have hoped. Back in the newsroom, I'd been expected to do my job without getting praised for doing it. At C3, Steve and his account executives seemed to want to heap praise on my every breath. "I can't believe how fast you came up with that", "You have such a way with words", "I wish I could write like that."

It was bullshit, of course—they were PR types, after all—but I was happy to let it go to my head. Just as I was happy to let go of my newspaper editor's fixation on facts.

"But that's not accurate," I remembered telling Steve the first week about some fluff he'd asked me to write for a client.

"Don't worry," he'd replied. "In our business, facts are aspirational." It was a liberating moment.

That said, Steve was smart enough to recognize I should not be allowed anywhere near C3's corporate clients. I think the rumpled mismatched sports jacket and pants, golf shirt, and sneakers I wore for my interview were his first clues. So, despite my lofty title, I served mainly as support for Steve's stable of inevitably attractive, inevitably young but also inevitably whip-smart female account executives who faced-to-face with the clients. They promised. I delivered. They thanked me. It worked well, so long as I did not let myself think too deeply about what I was really doing. *Think Mariela. Think sponsorship application.*

Steve didn't know about Mariela—I'd kept that on a need-to-tell basis, which so far had been limited to my surprised, and surprising, sister, Sarah—but he'd been quick to acquiesce when I asked last week for a few days off for "personal stuff."

"No problem, Writer Man," he'd replied, using one of his many something-Man names for me. *Word Man, Speed Man*...occasionally *Solitary Man, à la* Neil Diamond, whenever he saw me eating alone in the lunchroom. "Whatever you need," he added. "We don't do time-cards here. Just check in on Thursday. We're expecting word on that Emera contract, and we may need some of your speedy words. OK?"

"OK." But of course I'd forgotten. It was now Thursday. I'd need to—

There she was! On the escalator. Still as beautiful as I remembered, reconstructed in my mind. Wearing, despite the winter-like weather outside, a flowered summer dress with only a thin white cotton cardigan. Thank god I'd brought a winter coat. No gloves—forget the gloves! Mariela had landed. She saw me, smiled her radiant recognition smile. Or perhaps it was just relief. Had she also worried whether I would be waiting for her?

"I am so happy to see you," she said, wrapping her arms around my shoulders, kissing my neck.

"Me too," I said, pulling her closer, feeling her heartbeat. "Me too."

The rest was a blur. Waiting at the carousel for her luggage (the big red suitcase I'd left behind during my last trip to Havana, now stuffed to bursting with her life), listening while Mariela recounted her hassle-free journey through customs—"The nice woman agent," she marvelled, "said, 'Welcome to Canada,' and told me I could stay for six months"—remembering to call the limo, forgetting to call the office.... The limo ride was uneventful. We sat, thigh to thigh, on one side of the back seat, my left hand smothering her much smaller right, her face pressed against the window, transfixed by the snowbanks whizzing by. I tried to imagine what that must be like, seeing snow for the first time, realizing this had to be the new rest of your life.

"Over there." I pointed past the driver as he crested the suspension bridge from Dartmouth to Halifax. "There's your new home." She turned to look, just as a moving van passed in the other lane. "Too late," I said, and kissed her on the lips.

I gave the limo driver five twenties and told him to keep the change. I couldn't remember if the fare was $65 or $75. No matter. He was unseemly grateful. I practically had to wrest the suitcase from his hands to prevent him from accompanying it—and us—up the stairs and into the house.

"My house," I announced to Mariela, looking at what was, in reality, a nondescript two-storey wooden house on a street of nondescript two-storey wooden houses. Her eyes—those eyes—went wide anyway. "Your house now," I added.

Part of me wanted to lift her in my arms, carry her up the dozen concrete stairs and over the threshold, just like newlyweds in the movies. But I didn't want to make a fool of myself slipping and falling on the icy steps, and besides, there was her luggage to carry. Not to mention a long, narrow box leaning against the front door, blocking the entrance. Where had that come from?

Inside, while Mariela stared at the opulence I knew was merely dowdy, I unwrapped the brown paper covering the box, opened it, glanced at the card. I handed the bouquet to Mariela. "For you," I said, adding, not quite believing, "from my sister."

Mariela took the flowers, read the words on the card.

"Welcome to Canada, Mariela!

Welcome to the family!

Your sister-in-law, Sarah."

* * * *

My far too long delayed conversation with Sarah—"I'm married to that Cuban woman and, oh, by the way, I'm also the father to a long lost love-child daughter who is about to make me a grandfather and you a great aunt"—had taken place more than a year earlier, a month or so after I'd returned from Havana. It had not unfolded in any of the ways I'd hoped, expected, and feared it might.

"Hey," I said when she picked up the phone. "I have some news." Get the worst out of the way fast, I thought to myself, and then deal with the fallout.

"Eli!" Sarah almost shouted in response. "You must be psychic." There was a strange edge in her tone. Hysteria? "I was just about to call you. I have news too. So much!"

"You go first," I said quickly. Anything to put off the inevitable.

"How to begin?" she began. Unlike me, she knew how to begin. "Amy's a lesbian!"

I hadn't seen *that* coming. Amy, the good daughter dutifully following her mother and father into the family business of law, was a lesbian? How should I respond? *I'm sorry*. No. Commiserating at this point might be presumptuous. What then?

"She is?" I said, neutral, let Sarah lead.

"I'm OK with it, I am, really I am," Sarah continued, responding to the question I didn't ask. "It's her father who's not." OK. More information. Keep quiet. Let it happen. "She told us this spring when she came home from Yale. That's the part I really can't believe. She was doing so well in law school. Straight A's in every course, and she gives it all up. Just like that. She quit law school."

"She did?" And being a lesbian had what exactly to do with law school?

"I was going to call, tell you then. But I knew you were dealing with your own stuff. Dad. Your job. That Cuban woman. I didn't want to add to your burden." Thanks. "Besides, I thought it might be temporary, you know, a passing fancy." Amy being a lesbian? Or that Cuban woman? "But now Amy's moved to Vancouver, moved in with her undergraduate thesis advisor. The woman's almost my age, for heaven's sake."

"Oh."

"They actually became lovers—that's what they call it—when Amy was still an undergrad. That woman could be fired. She *should* get fired. But...I mean, it's fine. I raised my kids to believe they could be anything they wanted to be. I never even guessed," she continued. "I mean, there were no signs. Amy was so popular. Boys lined up to invite her to her high school prom. And she had boyfriends. She even lived with a boy during her second year at UBC. I told you about that, right?" No. "It doesn't matter. But, I mean, how are you supposed to know these things? As a parent, I mean? If they don't say? Thank god for Jacob. He's been a mensch. He keeps me sane. Unlike his father."

His father? Her voice faltered. Was she crying? "Saul's left me," she said finally. "Thirty-three years of marriage. And then gone. Just like that. He says he couldn't deal with Amy, couldn't deal with *me* dealing with Amy. Like I'm to blame." She was sniffling now. "So he moved out. But he didn't just move out. He moved in too. With a junior associate in the firm. He was supposed to be mentoring her. Instead, he was fucking her." I couldn't remember my sister ever using the word fuck in my presence. "I complained to the firm's professional ethics committee," she said, "not because I expect those fucks to actually do anything about it but because I wanted to watch the worms squirm." She laughed. It wasn't a funny laugh. "So now I have a daughter who's living with a woman my age, and a husband— former husband—who's shacked up with a woman young enough to be my daughter."

"I'm sorry," I said. "I really am." I was. "Is there anything I can do?"

"Tell me something that will make me happy," she said.

So I did. And it did. I hadn't expected that. I told her about Kim, and about Kim's son, who then was due any day.

"I never thought I'd be an aunty," Sarah said. "And now a great-aunty in the bargain. How wonderful!"

I told her about Mariela, about our wedding in Havana, about the status of my application to sponsor her to be a permanent Canadian resident, about the fact I was applying to bring her to Canada, even about just how nervous I was about everything. Sarah didn't tell me I was making another crazy, impetuous mistake, didn't promise to fix it by putting her immigration lawyer guy on the case, didn't even ask if I'd at least renovated the house, as she'd suggested many times already, in preparation for my bride's arrival. Instead, she said, "I wished I'd been there. For the wedding, I mean. It sounds like it must have been fun." It was. Should I have invited her?

"I'm so happy you're happy," she said after a long silence. "Perhaps it's a zero-sum game," she mused, "or maybe family happiness is serial. I was happy for thirty-three years. Now it's your turn...."

"I don't think it works like that," I said. "You'll be fine. We'll be fine."

"I hope so. I may have lost a husband, but I've gained a niece and a great-nephew. And a sister-in-law. I want to meet them all."

"You will," I said. "You will."

* * * *

Mariela held the flowers in her hand now, read and re-read Sarah's words on the card.

"She sounds so nice," she said. "I can't wait to meet her."

I couldn't wait to meet *that* Sarah either.

"You will," I said. "You will."

I really should call the office. I did. We hadn't won the contract with Emera. I was off the hook.

2

"**U**MBERTO FOUND IT REALLY DIFFICULT AT FIRST," LILY TOLD ME, WARNING me about adjustment issues for Mariela. "No family, no friends, no job to go to. For the first few months, he just sat in front of the TV and channel surfed—the news, old movie channels, monster truck shows, *The Bachelorette*, even *Say Yes to the Dress*.... I'm not sure he understood what they were saying."

"What happened?"

"Luckily, I remembered Umberto had studied painting in Cuba. So I turned the guest room into a studio, enrolled him in painting classes at the art college."

"And...."

"He's happy now."

I wasn't so sure. Mariela and I now socialized exclusively—past the point of tedium—with Lily and Umberto. Pub nights, dinner parties, even a full month binge-watching all five seasons of *The Wire*. Umberto, whose English was, after five years in Canada, still rudimentary at best, routinely fell asleep in the middle of shows, not to mention at our dinner parties, even occasionally during pub nights, snoring loudly while the rest of us pretended not to notice.

Umberto only seemed to come to life whenever he and Mariela reminisced in Spanish about their lives back in Cuba. I was slowly mastering my own halting variation of Spanish. I forced myself to spend at least a couple of hours a week with my Rosetta Stone CDs, but I had long since resigned myself to the reality I would never be able to follow a conversation between two speed-talking Cubans, which sounded in my head like a Spanish LP played at 78 rpm.

"Speak English," Lily would instruct Umberto. "Remember what we talked about." To me. "He needs to practise his English."

Mariela certainly didn't need to practise her English. But what did she need? I'd bought her an Apple laptop computer and an iPhone, set her up with her own Gmail address and shown her how to communicate with her friends back in Havana. I promised to buy her one of the new iPads.

"What does it do?" she asked.

"I'm not sure," I said, "but everyone wants one."

"Why would I want one?"

I wasn't sure.

She seemed to be always forgetting her iPhone somewhere. At Tim Hortons, at the library, at Lily's. Thank god for Apple's Find My Phone app. I also added her name to my bank and credit card accounts. I thought it would make her feel more independent. Little did I know. I offered to pay for driving lessons—one of us should know how, I joked—with the promise I'd buy us a car if she got her licence. I even asked her if there was a university course or other class she'd always wanted to take but had never had the chance. Now was her chance. I wasn't really sure she was allowed to do that on her visitor's visa, but school turned out to be a bridge I didn't have to cross.

"No," she said. "I'm fine."

So every day I went off to work to a job that bored and now sometimes annoyed me, for both its big-picture irrelevance to real life and also for the small-picture inconvenience that being at work meant I couldn't be with Mariela all the time. I'd have quit if I didn't know how important having a job was. Once Mariela got permanent residency, I'd quit. And do? I'd figure that out when the time came.

How did Mariela spend her days? I no longer knew. I knew about her nights. Sort of. She often woke with a scream or a shout in the middle of the night. A nightmare, she would tell me. What about, I would ask? Nothing, she would reply. Or, I don't remember. She would slowly fall back to sleep entangled in me. In the morning,

I'd have to disentangle, trying not to wake her. She would still be asleep when I left for work. So what did she do after that? At first, she would tell me about her adventures. About the day she'd spent at the Maritime Museum of the Atlantic, for example, learning about the infamous Halifax Explosion, which had flattened much of the city way back in 1917.

"Right where we're standing," she marvelled. "The biggest man-made explosion before the atomic bomb," she quoted from the brochure like the tour guide she had been. "We would have been killed." About her afternoon adventure walking the aisles at our local Superstore, counting the different brands of toilet paper. "Why so many different kinds of everything?"

"Wait until I take you to Costco," I said. I'd never been, but I'd read about it. If I remembered correctly, you had to be a member to shop there. And besides, we'd need a car. We never went. We did take a bus to Value Village once. Mariela created spiffy new wardrobes for both of us for almost no money in just an hour of rummaging through the racks of used clothing. She would have looked good in anything, of course, but even I began to get compliments from the women at work.

One night, I arrived home from work to find all the downstairs furniture rearranged. "Do you like it?" she asked. I didn't. I thought the couch had looked perfectly fine, perfect in fact, in front of the large living room bay window where it had sat since I was a child. Mariela had relocated it to a side wall and replaced it with two wing-back chairs facing each other from either side of the window.

"It blocked the view," she said of the couch. "Now we can sit after dinner and talk and have our coffee and watch the world go by. Do you like it?"

I still didn't. I didn't say that, of course. I didn't say anything, which Mariela rightly took as disapproval. That was the beginning of our first fight as a married couple. It wasn't a fight exactly. Neither of us was good at fighting. We stewed, we simmered. We didn't talk to one another for a week. I knew I should tell her I was sorry, that what she had done with the furniture improved both the look and also the functionality of the living room, which it did, and why the fuck should I care anyway, and I would try to be more open in the future because my house really was her house, and blah blah bah.

I was not good at saying I was sorry. Living alone—or with my demented father—I'd never had to utter the words aloud. So I decided to wait Mariela out. I would not apologize, but I would not escalate either. Pretend nothing had changed. A few nights into our radio-silence non-communication, I happened to mention that *Glee*—a TV series, a musical comedy about an American high school choir full of singing, dancing, and social issues—which I knew Mariela liked was airing that evening. "Want to watch it with me," I said. We did. But we didn't talk, just watched, companionably.

The next day, Mariela told me David had emailed her and asked to be remembered to me.

"Tell him 'Hi' back," I responded.

And so it went, chipping away at the silences, talking about nothing and then something, and then something else, none of which had anything to with the furniture, which was now just there. One night, after dinner, I sat in the wingback chair, looking out at the street. Mariela brought me coffee, sat opposite me, stared out the window. Our first official married fight was over.

Looking back, however, I think that was when she stopped telling me about her days.

* * * *

Lily called while Mariela and I were in the middle of dinner. "I need to talk to you," she said. "Just you. Not her." Not *her*? When I arrived at Lily's house, Umberto was not there.

"Gone out," Lily said flatly, handing me a glass of white wine and filling her own, which, I gathered from the slur in her voice, was not her first, nor even perhaps her second.

"Did you know?"

"Know what?"

"What was going on with them? Between them?"

"What do you mean?"

"What do I mean, 'what do you mean'? You know what I mean." I didn't. "Between Umberto and your little *chica*."

Umberto? Mariela? I tried to knit all the fragments of my own unanswered questions and disconnected, disconcerting thoughts into a single, logical fact-string, allow the spinning tumblers of my doubts to lock into place. They didn't. Or did they? These days, whenever I asked Mariela what she'd been up to, she played blasé. Or perhaps evasive? "The usual." "Nothing much." "What I told you yesterday." "Why do you keep asking when you already know the answer is still nothing?"

Because I love you and want to know about everything you do every day. I did not say that. I did not say anything. Fact. I did not know if I still loved Mariela, or if I loved her in the way I'd loved her back in Havana. Totally, unconditionally. Love was harder than I'd ever imagined, and I wasn't sure it was worth it.

I had discovered to my surprise Mariela was not perfect, not even physically. There was a small mole on her left cheek. It had been there as long as I had known her, of course. At first, I thought of it as a beauty mark, but now, occasionally, when she forgot to pluck it, I could see a single hair rising from its volcano. It was not her only facial hair. There was a wispy shadow moustache above her lip whenever she perspired, or if she failed to shave for a few days. And the fine sideburn hairs that seemed to matt to her skin in the heat? Who would have guessed she would sweat as much as she did? Even in Nova Scotia? Not me. But she did.

And then, too, still, always, there was the jealousy. I will confess I did worry where she really went every day, with whom she went, and what she might be doing with whomever she went wherever with. How could I not? She was young and beautiful—my newfound pickiness notwithstanding—and I was old and not. One morning before she woke up, I had searched through the emails on her computer, scanned the text messages on her phone. Looking, I suppose, for proof of her secret life. But, with my limited Spanish, nothing seemed untoward. There were emails from David that seemed to be about the latest tribulations in his relationship with his Italian lover, and one from Silvia asking how Mariela liked Canada—"Very much. The people here are so friendly." There were texts from Lío (from my phone?) relaying messages from regular clients who missed Mariela and just wanted to say hi and wish her well in Canada. I even surveyed the "Recents" on her phone log. It contained mostly Cuban numbers, along with one or two calls to an area code I didn't recognize but then forgot to check out—a mistake I would only discover later. There were a few calls to me, and some calls to and from Lily's number. That hadn't struck me as strange. She and Lily would often make the arrangements for the four of us to get together for dinner, or a movie. I hadn't imagined Umberto and Mariela might be calling each other, let alone having an affair. Mariela had always made it plain she considered Umberto *no muy brillante*. Whenever the four of us got together, I couldn't help but note the two of them indulging in backs-and-forths about Cuba, but that was only natural. Spanish was their shared language, Cuba their shared home.

"How do you know?" I finally asked Lily, hoping she didn't. "About Umberto and Mariela?"

"I'll show you," she said. Before she did, she poured us each another full-to-the-lip glass of wine and led me into the spare bedroom she had converted into Umberto's painting studio. "There," she said, pointing to a large canvas perched on an easel in the corner of the room. Staring back was a perfect likeness of Mariela. Umberto had captured her luminous, penetrating, laser green eyes, focused at that moment on something, or someone, beyond the frame. Her raven hair, loosed from the ponytail in which she most often wore it these days, framed her face. It was tousled, as if she'd just woken up. There was the hint of a smile playing at her lips. Was it lascivious? I willed myself to keep my eyes focused on her eyes, her face, her smile—no, not lascivious—but I sensed there was more. My gaze slid down past her long, delicate neck to the tawny bare skin of her chest down to just above her nipples. You couldn't actually see them or anything else. Mariela sat astride a wooden chair whose solid back hid the rest of her breasts and feminine charms from prying eyes. But you knew she was naked. Her legs were splayed out from the sides of the chair, the sides of her haunches visible, more than hinting at what could not be seen.

"So..." Lily said.

"So," I repeated dumbly.

She began to cry. "My friends warned me, told me it would never last, that I was being an old fool. And I was...we were. Both of us—you, me—fools!"

Were we? I'd always thought of Umberto—with a mantle of condescension I had no right to don—as poor old Lily's pool-boy boy-toy. So what did that make me? Poor old Eli? Was that why I had never invited Mariela to C3's regular Friday Night Frivols, Steve's weekly steam-blowing-off staff social events in the firm's board room? "You really should join us," Steve had said more than once, "and bring along that mysterious woman of yours we're all dying to meet." I never did, and I only attended myself on a couple of occasions, all before Mariela arrived. Would they have judged me as I would have judged me?

At this moment, I did not like being lumped in with Lily's lament.

"Have you talked to him about...about...?" I asked, not able to find my way to the end of my thought.

"He says it was nothing, just an assignment for one of his art college courses. 'A life study,' he told me. He said he needed a model, and Mariela volunteered. I'll just bet she did! If that was really all it was, just an assignment, why didn't he paint me? And what happens now? To them? To us? We're responsible, you know. They can do whatever they want—shack up together, go on welfare—and we'll have to pay for it."

I tried to remember the forms I'd signed, what Vince said they meant. I thought Lily's assessment was probably spot on.

"What will you do?" she asked. *Do?* "I told Umberto I'd buy him a ticket home," she said, "but he says he doesn't want to leave. Surprise, surprise. He says I'm being too harsh. Am I? What will you do?"

"Talk to her, hear her side, I suppose." I didn't want to talk to Mariela, not about this. It was unfair, of course, but I felt more bubbling, unfocused anger at Lily for forcing me to confront Mariela's behaviour than I did with Mariela for doing whatever she had done. What had she done? "I should go," I said.

"Yes, you should," Lily said. I sensed she was angrier with me too. "We were fine until *she* came along, until you brought her into our lives. You ruined everything. And I don't think we should be seeing each other anymore."

Amen to that.

* * * *

When I returned from Lily's, Mariela was sitting in the wingback chair in the living room, reading. I had been tempted to wait, confront her later when I'd sorted out my own conflicted emotions, thought it all through. But I knew me too well. If I didn't raise it now, I never would. In for one semi-nude painting, I decided, in for the full emotional pounding.

Mariela denied nothing. And everything. She acknowledged—how could she not?—she'd posed for Umberto, but insisted there'd been no affair. "He had this assignment and everyone in his class was pairing off, but he was too shy and his English not good enough to ask anyone else, so he asked me." Besides, she said, she wasn't really naked. She'd worn a bra and a thong. Umberto had simply replaced the straps and the tops of her bra cups, as well as her panty waistband with imagined, painted skin to make her appear naked. "It was better for his assignment." That made me feel much better.

"What about all those phone calls to Lily's number?" I said, upping the ante. "Were you really talking to Umberto?"

"How would you know about that?" she demanded, eyes flashing. "Are you spying on me now?"

"No." Yes. "I just happened to see.... Were you? Talking to Umberto, I mean?"

"Sometimes. He was lonely. And Lily barely speaks any Spanish, so we talked. It made him feel better."

"Just talked?"

"Yes. Just talked. I can't believe you're jealous, Mr. Eli Cooper. How many times have I told you, Umberto is not a very smart person. He is not my type."

Did that mean I was smart, that I was her type? Had she ever actually said Umberto was not her type before?

"Do you want to send me back to Cuba?" she asked finally, her voice rising to a controlled shout. "Because if you do, all you have to do is say it and I will be gone."

The gauntlet had been tossed, the glove dropped.

"No," I said quickly. "That's not what I want." Was I too hasty? What did I want? "I just...I just...I don't want to be surprised like that. Especially not by Lily."

"*Es fea*," Mariela spat. I had no idea what she said, but I could guess what she meant. "You wouldn't believe the things she makes him do."

I didn't want to know, and I didn't want to know how she knew, but I was grateful we'd found something we could agree on.

"Look," I said, "I still love you. I want us to be together, but I have to know I can trust you."

"I'm sorry," she said, her eyes welling up. She was better at I'm-sorry than I would ever be. But was she? Really? Sorry? "I love you too," she said, standing up, running toward me, arms open, collapsing into my chest. I wrapped my arms around her, felt her heart. "I know I should have told you. But I was afraid you would be angry. And nothing happened, really, nothing. I love you."

We stood there for a long time, holding each other, slowing down time, speeding up the blood coursing now through our bodies. And then we made love. It was the best love we'd made since that night in Havana on the bed beneath Lío's mirrored ceiling, the night I'd proposed to Mariela. But then the lovemaking was over. As our breathing slowed to normal, I stared at the ceiling that was not mirrored, and willed myself to believe we had just jumped another relationship hurdle, that things could only get better now.

"It's too bad you didn't get to meet Arty, dear," Aunt Abigail said to Mariela, then fumbled. "Before he...." Before he died? Before he cracked up? Before he went off to war and won a medal he didn't want and came back damaged goods?

Bringing Mariela to the old folks' home to meet Aunt Abigail in advance of our family gathering had been Sarah's idea. "So Mariela isn't overwhelmed all at once with all these new people she's never met."

The family gathering had been Sarah's idea too. It had begun with talk—Sarah talk—that Mariela and I should get married again in Halifax, "so your family can attend and celebrate with you this time." That idea had eventually been folded—and then disappeared—into the more inclusive and generic notion of a family gathering featuring a final goodbye to dear old Dad. Sarah called it the First Ever Cooper Family Reunion, but since there'd never been a previous gathering to make this a reunion, I called it a union.

The day before the official events, I took Mariela to meet my aunt for the first time. I'd been reluctant to introduce them because I worried Abigail might blurt some casual comment about Mariela's brown skin or about the obvious age difference between us. I need not have worried. Abigail was just happy to have visitors to show off to her fellow residents and so she invited us to lunch, introducing us to everyone at every table in the entire dining room. "Meet my nephew, Elijah, and his beautiful wife, Mary. Isn't she a doll?"

Aunt Abigail seemed less interested in learning anything about Mariela, including her actual name or the story of Mariela and me, than in corralling a fresh audience for her own old stories, most of which seemed to revolve around her long-estranged, now-dead brother from a time before he became my father.

Although I had told Mariela about the circumstances in which my father died, as I now decorously phrased it, I'd never explained about Dad's medal, about how he had come to send it back, about how I had inadvertently celebrated his private shame in his public obituary.

After revisiting my death-notice *faux pas* for the edification of my wife, my "late" Aunt Abigail did her best to rehabilitate my father's reputation, if not my own.

"Arty really was a hero," she told Mariela. "He saw this U-boat on his radar, and he..." and she proceeded to unfold the story she'd told Sarah and me in the funeral home, the one I now revisit nightly in the nightmare movies that play on an endless loop in my own head.

It had happened on the Irish Sea in the dying-ember days of World War Two aboard a destroyer assigned to convoy protection duties. Dad, having only recently joined the navy, was a junior radar operator. At some point in the middle of one night, he'd spotted what he thought was the exhaust snorkel of a lurking German submarine on his screen. He alerted a senior officer. The officer noted nothing untoward. "Your mind's playing tricks, son." But my father refused to concede—he must have been a stubborn bastard, even then—and went to the captain, insisting the blip came from an enemy U-boat. The captain ordered the destroyer back toward whatever my father had seen. My father had been right. By the time the skirmish was over, the submarine had been sunk and the convoy—along with its hundreds of sailors and soldiers—saved.

"BOOM!! BOOM!! WHOOSH!! WHOOSH!!" Aunt Abigail shouted, simulating what she imagined were the sounds of depth charges exploding underwater and sending gushers of bomb-roiled water skyward. "And everybody cheered! Arty saved them all!"

THE SWEETNESS IN THE LIME

Sometimes, in my own mind's movie, I am my father basking in the warm glow of the cheering until I suddenly notice all the bodies flying out of, and then falling back into the sea. In other variations of the same dream, it is the next morning, and I stand on the deck staring into a sea filled with bobbing dead bodies. I know these are the bodies of young Germans the same age as my father was then, but all the dead faces that stare back at me are Dad's bloated, mottled, and blue-ish face, covered with a light dusting of snow.

"Arty couldn't stop crying after that," Abigail explained to Mariela, who looked stricken. I reached over, placed my hand on hers. She looked at Abigail, then at me, then at her lap. What was she thinking? I had no clue then how painful this story must have been for her. Abigail continued, relentlessly. "He kept repeating he'd killed them all, that he was a murderer. Everybody told him it wasn't his fault, that if it hadn't been for him, they'd be the ones floating dead in the water. But it didn't help. I think it became worse for him because the war ended right after that. It made their deaths even more pointless."

Abigail is looking at me now. "Your mother and I were invited to the ceremony where they gave him his medal, you know. There was a navy band. Some admiral came from Ottawa, made a big speech about what a hero Arty was. I was so proud of him. I remember seeing the tears rolling down Arty's cheeks, but I didn't understand why he was crying. The next day, he applied for a discharge, and sent the medal back. And that was the end of it."

Noticing Mariela's unease, I made a show of looking at my watch. "We have to go," I announced to Mariela's relief. "My daughter and her son are due at our house at any moment."

"You sure you can't stay?" Aunt Abigail suddenly seemed desperate, and desperately lonely. "It's Friday and we're having fish sticks for dinner. They're very good."

I needed to visit her more often. "We'll pick you up tomorrow," I said.

I stood up then, reached deep into my pocket, felt for the metal disk, rubbed it between my fingers.

* * * *

Kim's pre-gathering visit went much better—and much worse.

In the months since we'd discovered our own disconnected connection, Kim and I had spent hours on the phone—I finally bought a new cordless model with its own answering machine—spilling out our life's stories to each other. I told her truths I rarely told myself. That I'd lied to everyone when I claimed I was supposed to be in the car with Donnie, for instance, and that that inadvertently (perhaps advertently) enabled me to insinuate myself into Eleanor's life. I told her about the pregnancy and Eleanor's sudden disappearance and my failure to figure out where she'd gone or to find her. I even confessed my decades-long obsession with the Illusion of Eleanor and how I had allowed that to affect my own life and my lack of love life. The most embarrassing, painful-to-acknowledge reality was that I had actually thought very little (to nothing) about the fact there might be a real child until the night I picked up the phone and heard her voice. Luckily, Kim seemed happier to finally hear my stories than to judge them—or me.

Of course, I'd told her about Mariela too, and about my hopes and new-found dreams. She listened more like the psychologist she'd studied to be—"and how did that make you feel?"—than the daughter of the mother whose long shadow I was finally abandoning. "You've waited too long," she said. "You deserve happiness. I hope you will find it." I did too.

In the months since Mariela and I had had our last disagreement, and our makeup moment, I had tried to be a better husband, a more social, giving, trusting person. I'd begun inviting Mariela to Steve's Friday Frivols. She was, as I knew she would be, the star attraction—beautiful, exotic, mysterious. No one questioned—not to my face at any rate—how such a woman could end up with me. The women especially—Steve's staff consisted mostly of young women in their late twenties or early thirties—seemed drawn to Mariela. They invited her to join them for their regular girls' night out, which gave Mariela a semi-independent social life and me the opportunity to practise not being jealous. I mostly succeeded.

Now we—me, Mariela, Sarah, Kim, her little boy—were together at last. While Kim and Sarah made so-pleased-to-meet-you small talk over drinks, Mariela ignored all of us, got down on the floor of our living room, and played with Little Eli. His full name was Donald Elijah. Kim called him Donnie. I was the only one—and only in my head—who referred to him as Little Eli.

Mariela had made a big production of presenting her step-grandchild with a gift she'd bought, a small stuffed doll. She lay down on her stomach on the floor, held the doll in one hand and made it dance in the air in front of the baby. He would reach for it. Mariela would snatch it away. Reach, snatch, reach, repeat. He laughed with giddy open-mouthed excitement. After a while, Mariela sat up, opened up her arms, and Eli melted into them. She held him close, savoured the sweet baby smell of him. She seemed transformed, transported.

I thought I understood. Mariela was still young enough to want a child of her own. We had never discussed having children. She had never brought it up, and I had avoided even thinking about such a possibility. I was pushing past my middle fifties. I couldn't picture myself as a doting father, couldn't imagine changing diapers, surviving the terrible twos, navigating the teenage tortures, attending various graduations in my walker, the wedding in a wheelchair, greeting my first grandchild on my way to the grave.

I assumed this floor play was all for my benefit, and that it was all about Mariela's desire to have a child. I was wrong about that. As I would soon discover.

"T O FAMILY," SARAH DECLARED, RAISING HER CHAMPAGNE FLUTE. "To family," we all chanted back, raising our flutes in response. We had gathered at Jane's on the Common—again—and sat together around a large table in the restaurant's small, semi-private anteroom.

On this occasion, our "family" consisted of me and Mariela, Sarah (Saul was long gone if not forgotten or forgiven), Sarah's two grown children, Jacob and Amy, Amy's lover, Jane Gerstein (who had the modest plus for Sarah of being Jewish to offset her major minus of being more than thirty years older than Amy, which, of course, made her more OK with me), Aunt Abigail, and my daughter, Kimberly, and grandson, Little Eli.

There was much to celebrate, including my marriage, my newly discovered multi-generational family, even what Sarah now decorously referred to as Amy's "new life direction." And, of course, being together as one happy family, now and forever more. Amen.

There had been remembrance too. Sarah had borrowed her friend Arthur the Architect's cabin cruiser for the day so we could motor out to just beyond the harbour mouth and scatter my father's ashes into the sea. "I promise not to get in the way," Arthur had said, though he seemed to spend an inordinate amount of time commiserating with, or perhaps chatting up, Sarah as he stood at the wheel, maneuvering his way from his yacht club mooring to the open ocean.

Or perhaps it was Sarah who chose to spend an inordinate amount of time with Arthur. Who was I to judge?

I still wasn't sure I'd come to terms with who my father was and what his life had meant to me. I had only recently begun to acknowledge how alike we were, and not just physically, although there was that too. I'd be shaving and glance at the mirror, only to see my father's eyes staring back at me or hear some long-ago memory of him in my own laughter. Then too there was the fact of how insular and solitary, how closed off from the world, we both were. Had there been some Eleanor at some point in my father's life? Was she among the unidentified in the old photos in our family album, perhaps that "fucking cunt" of "We'll Meet Again" fame? Had my mother been his Mariela, saving him from his first-love obsession? I was probably imposing too much personal parallelism on his life story. It seemed more likely his wartime experiences had pushed him over the edge and into his own abyss without the need for a woman to do the job. Or—and this was more to the frightening point for me—maybe my father's aloneness was congenital, passed down through the generations from him to me.

Arthur finally cut the engine and retreated to the cabin below "so you folks can have your time together." To do what? We had not thought this through, or at least I hadn't. Was there some sort of formal ceremony involved? Sarah, as she so often did, took charge. She stood on the deck near one side of the vessel, holding the urn with our father's ashes in her hands, beckoning us to gather round. The boat bobbed in the waves, silent except for the light slapping of water on hull. An intense, Havana-like midsummer sun bounced off the water, glared back at us, stung my eyes.

"Not all of you knew our father when he was alive," Sarah began, "but we are all part of him now. By birth, by marriage, by lineage, by love..." she said, casting a meaningful glance at Amy and Jane, who held hands. "He was not always an easy man to know." She smiled. "As Eli can attest." I nodded. "But I believe he loved us, especially Eli who cared for him when he could no longer look after himself.... Thank you, Eli." Mariela wrapped her arm around my back, hugged me closer. "We chose this location, here beyond the mouth of the harbour, to scatter our father's ashes, because this was an important place for him, an important moment in his life." Was it? "As a young man, he left the safety of his home to sail across the ocean to serve his country. As some of you know—" she looked at her children, to whom she must have told at least some version of this story—"he was a hero during World War Two, saving the lives of many of his comrades. It wasn't easy for him. He saw things a young man should not see. It is probably fair to say he never recovered." Sarah stopped then, trying to recover herself. She looked over at Aunt Abigail, whose perpetually watery eyes seemed even wetter than usual and whose hands were cupped over her mouth, as if to stifle a scream. Sarah finally found her voice again. "We cannot change the past. We cannot undo what has been done. But we, all of us, have a chance now to shape our future, the future of our family. Together. Building on the past, on the lives of those who went before us. So...thank you...Daddy...I miss you." She wiped a tear from her face. "Let us take a moment, a moment of silence, to remember."

Finally, Sarah spoke again, her voice lighter, as if grateful she'd made it this far. "Thank you, everyone," she said, opening the top of the urn. "Before we say our last goodbyes to our father, I wanted to recite a poem by Alfred Lord Tennyson. It's about dying, about the sea. I hope you like it, Daddy." I was astonished. Another revealing, previously unrevealed side of my sister. She spoke clearly, and with conviction.

> Sunset and evening star,
> And one clear call for me!
> And may there be no moaning of the bar,
> When I put out to sea.

Sarah finished, paused, a second moment of silence none of us seemed ready to break until Sarah herself did so. "Now it's time for us to scatter Arthur Cooper's ashes." She reached in, grabbed a handful. "I hope you will each join me by taking some of his ashes and scattering them in the sea." She passed me the urn. I scooped out some of the ashes in my right hand. His bits were coarser than

I'd expected, grainier. I handed the urn to Mariela, who spilled some in her hand, and passed it on.

Finally, when we each held our handful, Sarah spoke again. "I'd like us to scatter the ashes together. Think a beautiful thought and then, on the count of three, let us join my father with the ocean. One...two...three!"

We all tossed my father into the air. It did not go as planned. There was a sudden gust of wind and my father's million little pieces flew back toward the boat and into us. He was in my mouth, my hair, my eyes. Perhaps there was symbolism in that. I had not experienced any beautiful thoughts. But I did manage to surreptitiously reach into my pants pocket and retrieve that small round disk while Sarah counted down. As I tossed my father's ashes into the air with my right hand, I furtively dropped the object in my left over the side of Arthur's boat and into the water, where I watched it disappear forever, swallowed up by the sea. It was my father's Distinguished Service Medal. Gone.

"Rest in peace," I whispered.

* * * *

Dinner was finally over, the toasts had all been toasted. Jacob had commandeered Sarah's rented car to ferry Aunt Abigail back to her nursing home and take Kim and her baby to the downtown hotel where Sarah had booked rooms for all the out-of-town guests. Amy and Jane announced they would walk back to the hotel. Mariela and I sat with Sarah while she settled the bill.

"I think that went well," Sarah said, handing the credit card reader back to our server, who smiled in surprise at the size of the tip. "Worth every penny," Sarah told her as she put the receipt in her purse. "Worth every penny."

"So," she mused after our server had departed, "is this an ending, or a new beginning? So many crossroads to be crossed. For all of us." She took a sip of her decaf cappuccino. "I'm meeting with my divorce lawyer on Monday. He says Saul will have no choice but to offer up a big guilt-settlement, big enough for a fresh start." She paused, as if lost in a thought she'd already fully formed. "There's a teaching job opening up at the law school here. What would you two think if I moved back to Halifax?"

"That would be lovely," Mariela chimed in, "to have my sister-in-law in the same city as me."

"Yes," I added, less certainly, "that would be...lovely."

"Arthur and I have been talking about spending more time together, just to see what happens between us. Perhaps we will go into the renovation business together, perhaps...something more."

She put her cup down, looked directly at me. "You're now officially my inspiration," she said.

"I am?"

"You are. When Saul left, I was sure my life was over. But then I thought about you. And how you'd found happiness after so many years. And I thought, 'Why not me too?' Why not?"

Sarah stopped for a few moments then, burrowing back again inside her own head. None of us spoke, and then Sarah reached out, put her hands over Mariela's on the table, held them tight. "I saw you with the baby yesterday, Mariela, saw how you looked," Sarah said. "You want to be a mother, Mariela. I can see that." Mariela flushed. Then Sarah turned to me. "I think you'd be an amazing father, Eli. Even now, at your age. I know you would." My turn to redden. "You could have a baby and I could be the aunty who spoils him. And we'd all live happily ever after."

Part of me wanted to believe in Sarah's happily ever after. Amen. And part of me did believe. All of the tumblers of my existence—my new life with Mariela, my discovery of Kim and my grandson, my new and improved relationship to Sarah—had all magically clicked into place, unlocking the possibility of a future I could not have imagined before. Today's family gathering had seemed like a turning point, steering us into that future. And yet, there was that other part of me, the part that knew nothing good could come of anything that seemed so good.

5

A FEW WEEKS AFTER THE FAMILY PARTY ENDED AND EVERYONE HAD GONE their separate ways, this letter sat, lying in wait for me on the kitchen table when I came down for breakfast.

> My darling Eli,
>
> You see, I can call you by your right name! Without spelling it all out, or reducing you to just *tu apellido*, though I am still very fond of that name, Cooper, my love. I am finally learning your Canadian ways, my very darling Eli.
>
> I wish I could continue in this vein, make light of everything. But I can't. There are things I must tell you. I hope you will understand. I know I should tell you in person but, as I have explained, I find it easier to express my thoughts in English by writing them out.
>
> By the time you read this, I will be gone. You should not try to find me.
>
> I have not lied to you, but I have not told you the truth either, not all of it. I need to go back, tell you now, without all my dangling threads—what you once called my hiccups—so you will understand how the threads come together, even if you cannot forgive me when you know.
>
> I told you about Alex and me, and all of that is true, but it isn't all. Alex and I have a child, a son who was born on March 2, 2001. His name is Antonio. I call him Tonito. When he was three, Alex took him on the raft to Florida.

You will think you know what that means—that he must be dead. Everyone tells me that. Everyone says I must get on with my life. But he is my life.

I have dreams. You know about my crazy dreams, but you don't know, not really. I told you I could not remember what my dreams were about. They are about Tonito. They are signs. I was am certain Tonito is still alive. I believe he is with a family, a Cuban American family, a good Cuban American family, somewhere in Florida. They rescued him at sea, or maybe on a beach, and took him into their home and raised him as their own until they could find a way to return him to me. They did not tell anyone because they knew what happened with Elián. They want to return him quietly to his family in Cuba, but they don't know how.

So I must find them instead.

You entered my life after the Americans refused me the visa. At first, I tried to convince myself I would never consider what I knew I was already considering—using you to get to the United States to find him. I didn't. Not then. But then the hurricanes happened, and you were so kind—and I took advantage.

What am I saying? That I did not love you at all? No. What is that American song about loving you in my fashion? I do, my darling, and perhaps, if not for Tonito, I could love you in your fashion too. I know I have been happier in my life since I met you. I am happier than I ever was with Alex. I feel so comfortable with you, especially when it is the two of us.

So why am I leaving you now? Because I never intended to stay. That may sound cruel—and it is—but I knew from the beginning that whatever happened between us could never be enough to dissuade me from what I must do, the answers I must find.

I don't expect you to forgive me. What I have done is unforgivable.

Please do not try to find me or follow me.

I hope you find happiness.

I must go now, before I can't.

All my love,

Mariela

IT DIDN'T TAKE THE SKILL SET OF A COLUMBO TO FIGURE OUT WHERE MARIELA was headed. Her letter left little doubt about either her general direction or her eventual destination. But she'd also inadvertently left behind a trail of boulder-sized, flashing electronic bread crumbs to make it easy for me to discover all the gory how-I'd deceived-myself details too.

Mariela had taken her cellphone, the one registered in my name, whose bill came to me and whose calling details were available to me online anytime anywhere. But her device was also digitally tethered to my own Find My Phone tracker because Mariela could never find hers. And, though she'd taken her phone, Mariela had conveniently left behind the laptop I'd also bought for her. Her Wi-Fi-connected laptop contained some of the same applications as the ones on her phone—mail, messaging—and they were conveniently synchronized with her phone so I could now monitor her continuing electronic life in real time. So far, she wasn't emailing, or messaging.

Because I'd put the credit card I'd arranged for Mariela in both our names—so the bill would come to me to pay—a record of all of her purchases was now also conveniently available in updated electronic form for my viewing with just a few computer strokes.

What did I learn? Well, for starters, I discovered Mariela had been planning this for some time. Retracing the steps in her browser history, I realized she'd begun researching various combinations of "rafters," "Florida," "coast guard," "May 2004," "2004," "Alejandro Jones," "Alex Jones," "Antonio Jones Pérez," and "Tonito," within weeks of arriving in Halifax. She'd scoured the Miami *Herald*'s online archives for May 2004. She'd even purchased one article, "Four Cuban Rafters Die at Sea in Attempt to Leave Country." I found the article in a Desktop folder labelled "Untitled Folder" (all the folders were untitled since, apparently, I hadn't taught her how to change folder names), but the article turned out to be about unrelated dead Cuban rafters. I tried to imagine how difficult it must have been for Mariela to order a copy of that article, and the relief she must have felt when she read it. Relief coupled with...I stopped trying to imagine.

I'd taught her to use Google Alerts. "Let's plug in Cuba," I suggested. I thought it would be a good way for her to keep up with news from her homeland, though almost all the sources Google chose turned out to be American, and all the stories anti-Castro, which she didn't want to read. Later, Mariela plugged in her own alert using Tonito's full name and "Cuba." But there had never been, so far as I could tell, a single story in all of Google News matching her search terms.

Mariela also began bookmarking links in her browser for "Cheap Hotels Miami," and "Cheap Flights Halifax Miami." She discovered the unfettered, un-Cuban joys of Expedia and Tripadvisor. Cross-checking with her Gmail history and then retrieving the online records for her credit card purchases, I realized she'd booked her ticket from Halifax to Miami via Toronto more than six weeks before...before our family gathering! It was a one-way ticket, and it had departed at 6:30 this morning. During the same Expedia session, Mariela also booked a week in a very cheap hostel in Miami Beach called the Sand Castle, saving herself—me—close to twenty per cent by booking flight and hotel together.

The Find My Phone app now reported her cellphone—and presumably Mariela—was at the Toronto International Airport. Her flight to Miami wasn't scheduled to take off for another hour. Should I call? I should. I needed to talk to her, tell her I love her and convince her to come home.... No, I shouldn't. She'd made her decision and I should get on with my life. Shouldn't didn't stand a chance. I called. She didn't answer. Damn Caller ID.

Which gave me the opportunity to reconsider. What would I have said anyway? And what would I have really meant to say? Mariela had gifted me an unanticipated opportunity to jump off this out-of-my-control Tilt-a-Whirl. Who knew relationships could be so difficult, so mind-mashing, so all-time consuming?

I had managed to live most of my first five-and-a-half decades— give or take those few bad, late teenaged years—without the need of anyone else to accommodate, bargain with, bow to, be jealous of, obsess about, love. And I had been happy. In *my* fashion.

I checked Find My Phone again. Where had the time gone? Mariela was now in Miami, comfortably ensconced in Room 107 at the Sand Castle on Miami Beach. Based on Google Street View, as well as its 1.8 rating on Tripadvisor, the hostel appeared to be a dive.

Now, where was I? Oh, yes. The question was not really whether I should walk away while I had the chance—I should—but how would I explain this life-turn of events to everyone? To Sarah? To the people at work? To myself? *Mariela left me.* There would be tut-tuts, of course, and unspoken—spoken too, probably—I-told-you-so's, accompanied by knowing nods. Perhaps there would even be the occasional supportive "that bitch." Worse would be the dollops of pity, served with a shovel. "Poor Eli." People would try to be kind, invite me for drinks, or to dinner parties where I could be the obvious uncoupled guest, a dangler for the divorcées and recently widowed. Everyone could watch, without watching, the petri dish of our coming together to see if the experiment would take.

Who was I kidding? There were not that many among my acquaintances who would self-identify as a friend, and most of those were situational, work friends like Steve and the women at C3, who would miss me for a week before forgetting to remember my name. Most of my former colleagues at the *Tribune* already had. As I had forgotten theirs. None of them would care enough to invite me out to commiserate, let alone set me up with someone else.

Sarah would have eagerly taken on that role if, that is, she wasn't so pretzel-twisted-up in her own many and various family-related psychodramas. My relationship, or non-relationship, with Mariela could now never be more than a minor, digressionary subplot in the complicated drama of her current life. How had Sarah and I reached the late middle of our lives, an age when we should be settling into the smug, comfortable contentment of pre-retirement years, only to find ourselves trapped again in the throes of our own teenaged angst?

My own teenaged angst seemed all too grown up. My wife had—has—a child I never knew existed because she never told me. She told me she loved me when she didn't, when all the time she was planning to leave me. And now—like Eleanor—she had left, disappeared. There was a pattern here I had obviously missed. Maybe it did all fit together. Donnie loved Eleanor. Mariela loved her son. Who loved me? Anger welled up in me. Anger at anyone, everyone who might conceivably be responsible for whatever this had become. Starting with the bellhop at the resort who had arranged my ride to Havana with Uncle Lío and his niece. Fucking Reynaldo! I did remember his name.

Mariela had gone dark. She hadn't sent one email or made a single cellphone call since she'd left Halifax...how long ago? Forty-two hours. I hadn't slept. I couldn't. I wanted—needed—to turn away, to turn off my computer, to forget everything that had happened, was happening, would happen. I couldn't.

I obsessively checked, re-checked Find My Phone. The morning after she'd landed in Miami, Mariela left the hostel, took what I guessed, by the swiftness of the beacon's movements, must have been a bus into downtown Miami. Then she proceeded slowly—walking?—up 8th Street Southwest. I soon discovered—Wikipedia knows all—the street was better known as Calle Ocho, the heart of Miami's Little Havana Cuban exile neighbourhood. Mariela stopped occasionally and had appeared to linger for a few hours around Máximo Gómez Park, which Wikipedia informed me was a popular gathering spot where Cuban exiles played dominoes and chatted over old times. Was Mariela chatting up the exiles, asking if they'd seen Tonito? The domino park, I also learned, was near the Latin American Walk of Fame where Latin American pop culture icons were immortalized with their own pink marble stars embedded into the sidewalk. Willy

Chirino, I discovered, had a star there. Had Mariela stopped at his star, perhaps even chuckled, remembering my Chorizo mispronunciation from a few lifetimes ago?

Find My Phone didn't answer that question. It did tell me Mariela had then walked ten minutes north to 1st Street SW and spent an hour in Miami Dade's Hispanic Library. After that, she appeared to walk in circles for several blocks—was she lost?—before finally heading west for close to an hour back into the heart of downtown Miami. According to the beacon, she'd ended her journey at the Intercontinental Hotel. The Intercontinental Hotel? But then the beacon shifted slightly across the street—recalibrating?—to Bay Front Park, where Mariela's phone seemed not to move for the next two hours. It took me a while, but I finally figured out that Bay Front Park housed a statue known as the Liberty Column, a round white marble column, which, according to my Google Images search, reached skyward from two outstretched hopeful hands to "commemorate the journey and suffering of Cuban rafters...."

In that moment, I wanted nothing more than to be there in that park with Mariela, my arm around her shoulders, her tears soaking my shirt, sharing her agony.

What was I thinking? I was not thinking, not rationally. If I let her go now, this will not end well for her. I will be searching for her, just as she is searching for Tonito. I remembered I had allowed Eleanor to disappear from my life long ago. That had not ended well. It seemed nothing ended well, so perhaps I should not let it end at all.

I checked the beacon one more time. The cellphone had returned to the hostel. I did not call Mariela's cellphone this time. Instead, I looked up the Sand Castle's website, found the number for registration.

"Thank you for calling *your* Sand Castle," chirped a female voice that could have been recorded but clearly wasn't, given the crazy cacophony of surfing music and shouting revellers in the background. "How may I direct your call?"

"Mariela Pérez, please?"

"Mariela, Mariela, Mariela...Pérez, Pérez—here we are." Cheerful, chipper, spaced out. "One moment please."

Sudden silence. Then the sound of ringing. One ring...two... three. Maybe she wasn't even—

"Yes...." Mariela. Tentative. Who'd be calling her here now?

"Mariela. It's me, Eli." Silence. "Don't hang up, please. I just wanted to say—" What did I want to say?—"I just wanted to say I want to help. No strings, no expectations. I just want to help you find Tonito. Will you let me?"

Silence. And then a heavy sigh filled with un-shed tears.

"Yes...please come."

MY BLANK PAGES

HAVANA, 2017

I**T'S CLOSE TO MIDNIGHT WHEN** I **HEAR A FAINT KNOCKING ON THE DOOR TO** our family quarters.

I had long since retired back to my windowless room in our un-air-conditioned apartment in the casa. I keep cool here on hot nights by dressing down to my boxers and T-shirt and directing the fan, high speed, toward my face. Tonight, as usual, I'd poured myself a glass of rum, settled into my rickety wooden chair, propped my feet on my battered desk, and stared into the abyss of the empty first page of the reporter's steno pad on my lap. I'd brought a dozen notebooks with me from Canada because I planned to write my way to some understanding of all that has happened to me. Tonight, as usual, the page is still blank. It doesn't matter.

I throw on a robe and snake my way past the room where Mariela and Tony are sleeping and open the door. It's Charles and Sandra, the carpenter from Bayonne and his wife. "I'm sorry," Charles stage-whispers. "We didn't mean to wake you." I can see he's tipsy. "But we'll be leaving first thing in the morning and we just had to thank you."

"That restaurant you suggested was just so great," gushes Sandra, who extends her arm for me to admire. "Carlos gave me this!" She's wearing an antique-looking silver costume-jewelry bracelet on her wrist. I knew Carlos—Carlos Cristóbal Márquez

Valdés—San Cristóbal's chef-owner, often visits diners at the end of their meals, pouring each one free snifters of aged rum and offering small gifts—Cuban cigars for the men, costume jewelry for the ladies—as a thank you for their patronage. I had known that when I suggested Charles and Sandra eat there.

"This is such a wonderful city," Charles says. "Such wonderful people."

"I think so," I tell him. And I do.

After Charles and Sandra make their farewells—"We'll be back," she tells me earnestly—and retire to their room, I tiptoe to the open doorway of the bedroom next to mine, the one Mariela now shares with Tony. That had not been the plan, at least not mine. But life intervened, Tony mostly. He had been a colicky baby and a fitful sleeper. During his terrible twos, he would wake up screaming almost every night. At first, Mariela tried to comfort him back to sleep in his own bedroom. After a while, when she couldn't settle him there, she would bring him to sleep in our bed. Later, I began sleeping in Tony's single bed so Mariela and Tony could have the bigger bed, and I could get some rest. It wasn't supposed to be a permanent arrangement, but it is. And I'm OK with that. I am.

I remember the last time Mariela and I made love. It happened four years ago, the night we finally bid adieu to our contractor and claimed the renovated casa as our own. We made warm, languorous, unhurried love in the largest guest room while the air conditioner conditioned the room and Tony slept beside us in a crib.

The time before that? I remember that too. We were in Key West in a hotel near the bus terminal. Our lovemaking that night had been different...slow, intense, then cathartic. That was the night that changed the course of the rest of my life. And I'm OK with that too. More than OK.

IN
THIS MOMENT

1

"**Y**OU *ARE* KIDDING ME? RIGHT?" JONATHAN GRAVENOR EYED ME incredulously as he glanced up, oh so briefly, from the half-finished plate of Paella Valenciana in front of him, his mouth still semi-stuffed with a semi-masticated mess of lobster, squid, chicken, and rice. His eyes skipped dismissively over the photos and documents Mariela had scattered on the table in front of him.

"We're not even in needle in a haystack territory here," he said. "More like a grain of sand in an ocean's worth of shitstorm." He swallowed and then scooped, without pause for breath, another mouthful into his oversized maw.

So why the fuck did you agree to meet with us, I wanted to scream. And why the fuck did you order the most expensive item on the menu, a dish that not only took the chef forty-five minutes to prepare—more than enough time for you to slosh down three Yankee-dollar mojitos that were not nearly as good as Esteban's—but, worse, order the only item on the menu that just happened to require a "two-person minimum," forcing me to order it too? We hadn't discussed the details, but I already knew I was paying for Jonathan's ("call me Juany") meal and his drinks. Which might have been OK if...I turned to look at Mariela, who had ordered but not yet tasted the mixed salad, the cheapest item on the Versailles' menu. She had seemed so hopeful when we first sat down. Now, she looked stricken.

Juany was not at all the person I'd expected, or the person I'd led Mariela to expect. But he had been my last resort. His website said he was an award-winning freelance journalist who'd written a number of what appeared to be thoughtful, balanced articles for *Miami New Times* about the local Cuban exile community, including its raft refugees. He'd sounded reasonable enough on the telephone when I explained, cryptically, why I was calling. He hadn't said, "You *are* kidding me?" He'd said, "Sure. I think I might be able to help you with that. Why don't we meet at the Versailles? We can have some lunch and I can give you some direction."

I had vague recollections of the Versailles. The restaurant's name popped up in the news during American presidential campaigns when politicians visited Little Havana to court the Cuban American vote. According to its website, the Versailles was "a neighbourhood restaurant founded to feed and assuage the nostalgia of a people...where exiles gather to plot against and to topple Fidel Castro (at least with words), or so the urban legend goes."

But the bustling real-life restaurant where we sat on this humid late afternoon more resembled a popular, high-end truck stop than some mysterious den filled with cigar-smoking exiles hatching regime-change schemes. The establishment, which sat on a site that seemed to occupy most of a city block off Calle Ocho, boasted plenty of parking. Inside, its rabbit warren of large and small dining rooms, each framed by space-expanding floor-to-ceiling mirrors (its homage to Versailles?), filled and emptied like the tide with endlessly configurable tables and endlessly changing configurations of customers. Most of them, it seemed to me from their accents or from the unfamiliar languages they spoke, were probably package-bus-tour tourists boisterously enjoying their all-inclusive taste of Cuba in the middle of Miami before heading off to whatever was their next cultural culinary sampler.

I wouldn't have chosen this as a place to meet—I could barely hear Juany over the din, or through his chewing—but what choice did we have? We'd been in Miami for almost a week and I was no closer to helping Mariela find Tonito, or—more likely—discovering his sad, final fate. I was, my fantasies notwithstanding, not a reporter. Over my years of randomly fact-checking the reporting of others, I'd developed what I thought of as superior internet skills. But those were no match for my current challenge. I needed to find a real reporter who could help. I found Juany on the internet.

"Why 'Juany'?" I asked during the small talk between mojitos after I'd exhausted the rest of my repertoire of inconsequential chat. He did not look Hispanic. "I mean, why not Jonathan, or John, or even Johnny?"

"My mother was an *exiliada*," he explained, "one of the non-criminal, non-crazy Cubans who fled here during Mariel back in '80. The Cubans who came to Miami during that boat lift had a bad rep with the locals, mostly deserved, so she did her best not to acknowledge she was even Cuban. Must have worked. She married my father. He was a banker from New York who somehow ended up in Pensacola. He got caught up in the cocaine business in the nineties. Not sure where he is now, or if he is. The feds were after him, the dealers were after him.... Anyway, my teenaged rebellion was to resurrect a Cuban heritage I didn't really have—mostly by calling myself Juan instead of Jonathan. My Spanish is still the shits. Jonathan Gravenor looks better as a byline, but Juany gets me contacts in the community. And those contacts are what gets me my stories." He extended his glass in the direction of a waiter. "*Uno... más...por...favor*," he said, emphasizing each word as if pronouncing it for the first time. "And for my friends too."

"No, no thanks," I said, waving off the waiter. Juany's community contacts were all that interested me. I was looking for someone—anyone—in Miami who cared enough about the fate of Cuban rafters to keep detailed records of their arrivals and current whereabouts.

"We'll find him," I'd gallantly reassured Mariela, Superman to the rescue, after I'd arrived at her door at the Sand Castle late on the afternoon of the day after I'd called. "*I'll* find him." She'd clung to me for what seemed like hours, kissing my neck, leaning back to stare into my face, pressing her face against my chest. Kissing… leaning back…pressing…repeat. And again.

Mariela's effusive welcome may have had something to do with her faith in my reassurances. But more likely, Mariela's own first few days in Miami had mirrored, at least emotionally, my own initial forlorn experiences in Havana. "I felt so alone, so helpless," she confided.

"It's OK," I whispered in her ear during one chest press. "I'm here now. We'll find Tonito together." What was I saying? What was I thinking? What was I doing here at all?

Before I'd left Halifax, I called C3 and left a message for Steve. "I need some personal time so I won't be in for a few days," I explained as neutrally as I could muster to Alana, Steve's executive assistant.

"Steve isn't going to like that," Alana said. "We just landed that big national tourism account, you know, the one he's been after for months, so it's all hands on deck."

"Sorry," I said. I wasn't. "Just tell him something urgent has come up and I have to go away for a few days. I'm at the airport now, just about to board."

I wasn't. Not then. I was at home waiting for the limo, but I didn't want to have to talk to Steve, to invent the lie that could explain my absence without explaining that my much younger Cuban wife had suddenly and unsurprisingly left me, not for another man but for a child who was almost certainly dead, and so I needed to go find her, and him.

"I'll email him when I land."

I didn't have to. Steve emailed me while I was in the air between Toronto and Miami. Steve wrote that he was "so very disappointed" in his "Writer Man." I had "let down" the entire C3 team. "Is this how you repay my trust in you?" he demanded, not bothering to explain why his trust in me had not included an actual salaried position with benefits, or even the prospect of severance after having given the company more than a year of loyal service in support of whatever dubious corporate causes paid us to sing their tunes. As it transpired, the question of severance was now no longer moot. "Since I clearly can no longer depend on your loyalty," Steve finished with a flourish, "I have no choice but to immediately terminate your contract with Coastal Communications Consultancy." Ever the PR man, however, he immediately added, without a smidgeon of irony, "Thank you for your service. I wish you the best of luck in your future endeavours."

I would not have been unhappy, except for one obvious consequence. I could no longer claim the existence of even a precarious contract position in my application to sponsor Mariela. Would I have to update the form? I would need to check with Vince to see—Really? Who was I kidding? Mariela had voluntarily left Canada after having been granted an oh-so-convenient visitor's visa. She'd landed on American soil and so her lack of Canadian sponsorship didn't matter. She could stay in the US, become a citizen. She wasn't coming back to Canada, or to me...or was she? Who knew? Not me. I didn't ask, and Mariela didn't volunteer. We had seemingly decided, mutually and without consciously acquiescing, not to discuss her letter, or our relationship, or our future.

My first order of business had been to relocate us to slightly more upscale accommodation. Even before I left Halifax, I'd Expedia-booked us into the Hacienda Carmelita, a low-slung, lime-green stucco motor hotel off Calle Ocho. It was almost as grungy and almost as cheap as the Sand Castle but—bonus—too far from the beach to attract the surfers and college-kid partiers, or the actual rats Mariela warned me rambled like royalty through the Castle's rooms at night. Better, the Carmelita was within walking distance of the centre of Little Havana, which Mariela had correctly concluded was the logical place to begin searching for a missing Cuban child. Best—which I'd only taken note after Steve's email eliminating my job—the Carmelita offered free daily "continental breakfast" in the lobby (mostly just black coffee and dry Cheerios, since neither the toaster nor the bar fridge functioned, "not since last year," the attendant told me without apology), as well as free Wi-Fi.

Of course, there was nothing I could have *not* discovered using the motel's somnolent Wi-Fi that I couldn't *not* have managed easier and faster at home. So, while Mariela anxiously paced the worn plush carpet in our lime-green-with-white-trim room (the owners must have settled on a theme, or at least found a spectacular sale on lime-green paint), I sat on a lumpy twin bed, hovering earnestly over the laptop balanced on my knees. That gave me the false sense I was on an important assignment in a foreign land, being the journalist I wasn't.

Despite days of internet sleuthing, in fact, I had not uncovered one single snippet about Tonito's life or—though I never allowed for this in my earnest we-can-do-this conversations with Mariela—his almost certain death. Perhaps it really was possible for a Cuban to dissolve into the melting pot of the United States, or—again more likely—disappear without trace into the Straits of Florida.

By chance, I did find a couple of glowing references to Mariela's ex-husband Alex popping up randomly in the middle of Tripadvisor recommendations about the resort where he'd worked. "Remember the name Alex Jones," wrote one obviously satisfied customer, a woman from Germany, who gushed "Al has the voice of an angel. The world will be hearing about this very hot Cuban entertainer soon." I did not share this woman's recommendation with Mariela.

One night, after Mariela had gone to sleep, I surfed over to an obituaries' website called tributes.com and plugged in the full names of each of the Cubans rafters, using the same selected parameters—"2000 to present," "Florida," including and not including "notables." Would being a dead rafter qualify one as a notable in Miami? Not that it mattered. There was only one exact match for the name Alexander Jones. I'd decided to try, among other possibilities, the formal version of the anglicized name he'd used at the resort. But that Alexander Jones had been eighty-three when he "joined God's choir of angels" back in 2005.

There should have been an easy way to match the identities of those who'd departed from Cuba with those who'd arrived in the United States but, thanks to the state of un-relations between the United States and Cuba, no such online database existed. I assumed the United States Coast Guard kept detailed records of the rafters they'd actually rescued at sea. I considered filing a freedom of information request, knowing I would eventually learn the coast guard had no records "responsive to your request." But that might take a year, or more. Mariela and I were in Miami now.

The newspaper websites proved no more fruitful. With rare exceptions, like the Elián González affair, Cuban state media largely ignored the existence of the rafters. That unacknowledged stigma, of course, made it less likely that Cubans would officially report their loved ones as missing. Mariela told me she hadn't bothered to file a missing persons' report about Alex and Tonito. "What would they do?" she asked sagely enough.

On the other side of the Straits, the arrival of yet another boat-load of rafters seemed to have become so ho-hum the Florida news-papers rarely reported on them anymore, unless as part of a hector-ing lecture on the abysmal conditions Cubans still faced in Castro's repressive police state, leading to their desperation to escape their oppression, "even at the risk of their own lives. For many, death in the Florida Straits is preferable to life in Castro's Cuba." Really?

I couldn't find a single website offering dependable, exact—or even approximate but agreed upon—statistics showing how many Cubans had attempted the perilous ninety-mile sea crossing from their homeland to the United States. Or how many had died in the attempt. Four out of every ten, declared one site. Seven out of ten, claimed another. In any case, even the most conservative estimates suggested there were thousands—tens of thousands, even hundreds of thousands—of Cubans who'd left Cuba but never arrived at their destination. How could I discover the fate of just one grain of sand among all those grains in that ocean of a shitstorm?

One night early on, while randomly searching "Cuba," "rafters," "statistics," "Florida," "Straits," "rescue," "death," I came across a *Miami New Times* article on Cuban rafters by one Jonathan Gravenor. It wasn't at all what I'd been looking for. The story focused on the rafters' successes in integrating into the Miami community, and the only statistics he quoted had to do with all the new businesses these entrepreneurial newcomers had started. Still, it was an interest-ing story, quoting lots of rafters, including several who'd arrived in 2004. I bookmarked the story, initially thinking I might try to track a few of them down later, if nothing else panned out.

Nothing else did.

Mariela and I even spent a futile day walking up and down Calle Ocho showing random passersby photos of Tonito, Alex, Delfín, and Roberto. The fact Mariela had carried all of their photos—along with copies of each of their birth certificates and even a snapshot Roberto's mother had taken of the raft in the garage—from Cuba to Canada, and then to Miami made it obvious, even to my most trusting, ever hopeful self, that Mariela had calculated and orchestrated every step of her journey. I also had to acknowledge to myself, if not Mariela, just how pop-star handsome young Alex appeared to be in the photos. I did gush over Tonito. "Such a beautiful boy! He looks just like his mother," I said. Not that he did, not really, not to me at least. Mariela blushed and held the photo close to her chest, smiled to herself, if only for a moment. Mission accomplished.

That night, back in the hotel room, I'd looked up Jonathan Gravenor's website. There were links to a number of other stories he'd written about Cuban exiles, as well as about changing Cuban American attitudes toward US-Cuba relations. I tracked down a phone number and called him. On the telephone, Jonathan had sounded considerably older and significantly wiser than the schlubby, late-twentysomething Juany who now sat across from us at the Versailles, scarfing his way through his paella and ordering guava cheesecake (also the most expensive item on the menu) for dessert.

I hadn't told him much on the phone—asking for a friend... Cuban woman looking for family members...rafters...came to Florida in 2004...disappeared...wants to reunite. Perhaps he assumed we knew they'd actually made it to Florida. Likely, he saw a poignant, happy-ending family reunion tale in it all. And now he was as disappointed with me as I was with him.

"This," he said, pointing at the photos and birth certificates, "is all you have to go on?"

"I know it's not much," I began, apologetic, "but—"

Mariela cut me off. It was the first time she'd spoken since we introduced ourselves while we waited to be seated. "I have more," she said, taking a notebook out of her purse. "I know the exact hour of the day when they left, the hour-by-hour weather for the week after that, the currents in the Straits of Florida at that time of year—"

"OK, OK." Juany held up his hands in a gesture that looked remarkably like a benediction but was really surrender. "I get where you're coming from." Caught in the searchlight of Mariela's green eyes, perhaps recognizing for the first time the unplumbable depths of her pain and eagerness, Juany seemed to connect Mariela with someone else, perhaps to his own rafter mother. His "been there, done that" tone lost its brittle edge, and his features rearranged themselves into an expression approaching empathy.

"Let me think," he said finally. He swallowed his food, put down his fork. "I may know someone..." he began. "I don't know *him* exactly, but I have contacts with people who know him. He's this old guy, a *brigadista,* was involved in all the plots to overthrow Castro, may still be for all I know. But he kept—keeps—records of everything that happens that has to do with Cuba. Everything. If anyone knows—"

"Will you?" Mariela cut him off, urgent now. "Please."

"I can try," Juany replied, adding for Mariela's benefit. "I *will* try. But there are no guarantees. He lives alone. No phone. So it will take me a few days. But I'll be in touch, one way or the other."

He took a sip of his *cafecito,* turned to me, morphing suddenly back into his cocky, journalist persona. "And hey, if we do find the kid, I get first dibs on the story. OK?"

2

MARIELA AND I LOOKED AT ONE ANOTHER, GIGGLING LIKE SCHOOLKIDS AT the back of the bus pulling a naughty on the teacher during a school excursion. "One...two..." I whispered as we scrunched down in our seats, out of view of the man with the microphone standing at the front, swaying to the bus's motion. "Three!"

When the man with the mic intoned, one more time, in his heavily German-accented English, "so many riches and famous people living here," we mouthed along in sync, doing our best to stifle our laughter, failing, then doing our best to appear duly chastened in the face of the disapproving stares from the other tourists seated around us, failing at that as well, and then doing our best one more time to ignore all of them while we snuggled deeper into the seat, into each other, finally succeeding at that.

It felt good to play tourist, to forget for a moment why we were here and where all of whatever this was, or was not, might eventually lead for Mariela, for me, for both of us, together or apart. The Best of Miami Bus Tour had been my idea. Since Juany told us it might take him a few days to track down his brigadista and since we had run out of ideas for finding the unfindable, I suggested we pretend to be tourists for the day instead. Mariela eagerly agreed, seeming as relieved as I was to let Juany's brigadista serve as our beacon of faint hope, at least for the day.

I'd assumed the tour would showcase Miami's history and culture while helping me finally situate myself geographically in this city of towers and turnpikes, but it turned out to be a guided tour—in rotating English, Spanish, and German—of the homes of all the "riches and famous people" who live, or once lived, in Miami.

"Over here on your left you can see Fisher Island, man-made, the richest zip code in all the United States," our guide gushed as the bus lumbered across the MacArthur Causeway. "One-hundred-and-fifty families from forty nations...Steffi Graff, Oprah, Boris Becker, and so many riches and famous businessmens from all over the world.... On your right is Star Island, one of the most exclusive communities in all Florida...Elizabeth Taylor, Shaq, Ricky Martin, Carmen Electra, Julio Iglesias, Sean Combs...so many, many riches and famous people have called this island home.... And see...Palm Island just beyond that...Paris Hilton has a house here. And the gangster Al Capone, he once lived in a wonderful house at 93 Palm Avenue...That house," our guide chuckled, "could be yours, ladies and gentlemen. All you need is $6.8 million, and you too could be one of Miami's—" wait for it—"riches and most famous peoples."

During the course of our two-hour tour, there also seemed to be more ambivalent references to cocaine and the wealth it had brought to Miami in the eighties and nineties than to the Cuban exiles who'd helped define the city for previous generations of Americans. But we did pass the Versailles ("famous Cuban restaurant, many famous peoples eat there") and the gates of the Woodlawn cemetery ("the final resting place for two former presidents from Cuba, three former presidents of Nicaragua...and so many other riches and famous dead people") on our rumbling ride through Little Havana. I wondered, but only briefly, if four un-riches, un-famous Cubans might be buried there now too.

"We stop here," our guide said as the bus made a brief stretch-and-spend stop on Calle Ocho. "It mean 8 Street in Spanish language," he helpfully explained, adding that the Cubans, who'd arrived on the street beginning in the sixties and bought houses from Jews moving to Miami Beach, had now themselves mostly moved on. "Not so many Cubans as before because so many peoples from Central and Latin America here now," he explained, quickly moving on to more riches and famous. "On this street, you will see stars on the sidewalk like in Hollywood and California, singers and many other riches and famous peoples from Latin America, Spain, Cuba...you can make some pictures."

Mariela and I decided to stay in the air-conditioned bus, snuggle, pretend we were teenagers, or tourists, or anyone we were not.

When we arrived back at the Carmelita, there was a message on the phone from Juany. "He says he'll talk to you, but no phones, no recorders, and no guns," Juany explained when I returned his call. "OK?" OK.

"I told him all about the specific dates and stuff your lady showed me. And the photos. He's really keen to see the raft photo. Says it might help. So bring it, OK?"

PACO DID NOT TELL US HIS LAST NAME, IF INDEED THE NAME PACO BORE ANY relationship to an actual nickname, or first name. Everything about Paco oozed unreal-surreal. While he would never have made the Best of Miami Bus Tour's list of the city's "riches and most famous," he already topped my own list of Miami's weirdest.

Paco lived in a rundown pastel pink bungalow on a large property on the fringes of the city, surrounded by a thick pink, taller-than-me concrete wall studded at the top with broken glass and razor wire. You had to buzz and identify yourself and your business to an unseen camera in order to get through the wrought-iron gate, and then do it all again in order to pass through the steel door that served as the entrance to Paco's lair.

Paco was in his eighties, short and frail with lank greasy grey hair. He was also skinny as the toothpick that dangled from his lips. Despite the heat, he wore a too-roomy flannel lumberjack shirt unfashionably tucked into a pair of better-days blue jeans, held up by a too-big belt that could have wrapped twice around his waist. A portable oxygen tank helped to keep him wheeze-breathing. Despite all that, Paco projected an intimidating, dangerous presence. Perhaps it was the fact the walls of his kitchen—the only room we were permitted to enter—seemed to double as a weapons depot, filled to bursting with an army-sized arsenal of rifles, guns and assorted weaponry, all intended for mass destruction and all organized by make and model.

"In case," he explained cryptically. And then he pulled up his shirt to show us the faded red-raw puckers where bullets had once entered his abdomen, his chest, and his shoulder. "Feel," he invited Mariela, though not Juany or me. She gently ran her fingers over the ridges, pulled them back. "Castro," he said simply. "Sixty-one."

Juany, appearing to realize we were heading for an extended history lesson, did his best to cut it short. "I think Fernando told you on the phone what these folks are looking for," he said to Paco.

"Pictures," Paco answered enigmatically. "Show me."

Mariela took the photos from her purse, handed the pile off to Juany who passed them, in turn, to Paco, who dismissively riffled through her collection of pictures of Alex, Roberto, Delfín, and Tonito, one after another in quick succession, dropping each one on the kitchen table. Paco stopped, however, when he came to the snapshot Roberto's mother had taken of the raft her son and his friends had been building to ferry them to America. He carefully studied it for what seemed like minutes, moved the image around in his hands, as if approaching it from a different angle might produce the information he was looking for. Finally, he looked up at Juany.

"Bottom cupboard on your right," he instructed. Juany opened a kitchen cupboard, which was bereft of pots or pans, but filled from top to bottom with piles of what looked like random file folders. They were not random. "Third pile on your right, fourth folder from the top," he pointed.

"The old guy's a crackpot, but an organized, obsessive crackpot," Juany had explained on the drive to Paco's house. "My guy knows him from the brigades. They fought together at the Bay of Pigs, spent time in prison in Cuba. Apparently, Paco hasn't been any good for regular work since then—war wounds, PTSD, I don't know what...so he lives in his pink fortress—on a pension, maybe some help from the rich brigadistas, who knows—and he collects. And collects. Apparently, at some point, maybe after Elián, he began collecting information about every rafter, every raft, that came from Cuba. Somehow people in the exile community heard about what he was doing—who knows how—and began sending him news stories, photos, notes. My guy says if anyone knows anything about your rafters, it would be Paco."

Juany retrieved the folder, handed it to Paco. In the notch of the folder, I could see a meticulously handwritten subject line. "MAY 16, 2004—Stock Island, Key West." Paco opened the folder, removed an eight-by-ten black-and-white photo, studied it, picked up Mariela's photo, examined them side by side, handed them both to Juany, who considered them, and then passed them on to Mariela. I looked over her shoulder as her eyes darted from one image to the other, then back again.

"One and the same," Paco pronounced with satisfied finality. "Doesn't look it from the second picture, course, but whoever built it musta done a good job...travel all that way and not a piece fall off. They done good work."

"Where did—"

"Who found—"

Juany and I stepped over one another, trying to get Paco to answer our standard-issue journalist's questions. Mariela said nothing. She stared instead, agape, at something in Paco's black-and-white photo that the rest of us had missed. I looked again, more carefully this time. And then I saw it. Sticking out from beneath the planking of the raft, there was an arm—not a human arm, but one belonging to a small doll.

Bob turned out to be a grandfatherly, salt-of-the-water fisherman
from Stock Island, a spit of a place just past the Boca Chica Naval
Air Station on the Florida's Overseas Highway and just before end-
of-the-keys, end-of-the-highway Key West.

Juany had an interview scheduled for his next magazine piece
in Miami that day, which he luckily couldn't change, so Mariela and
I had taken the endless three-and-a-half-hour Greyhound bus trek
from Miami to Key West on our own. We didn't talk. Mariela seemed
lost inside her own thoughts, I lost myself thinking about what she
must be thinking.

Bob met us at the station in his pickup truck and drove us to his
home, a hurricane-ready raised bungalow on concrete posts near a
trailer park. He'd been apologetic when I called the day before. "I'm
real sorry, but that raft, or whatever you call it, is long gone. I kept
it for a month or so. Just in case somebody claimed it. Nobody did.
My wife said it was an eyesore she didn't want around. So I broke
it up, saved a few boards and a couple of oil drums that didn't leak,
then dropped the rest off at the dump." Bob told us he didn't know
anything more about the raft that was worth knowing, but he had
eventually, reluctantly agreed to meet with us anyway.

In person, he was far more personable. He led us up his home's
outside staircase and into a small, tidy kitchen where he introduced
us to his wife, Maudie, a cheerful, squat woman in her sixties, who
offered us tea and cookies. "Store-bought, I'm sorry to say."

"Not to worry," I said. "Store-bought's fine." And they were. Better than fine. We hadn't eaten since Miami.

"And I hope you don't mind kids," Maudie said. "We got the grandkids for the weekend. Not sure where they are now, but I do know they'll be back. And then we'll all know it."

"I love children," Mariela said, sharply enough that Bob and Maudie both turned to look at her. "I just mean," she said, recovering quickly, "I don't mind having children around."

"So," Bob said, looking at me, friendly-wary. *Who was I and what was this all about anyway?* "You said on the telephone you were interested in that old raft I found. Not sure what I can tell you. I don't remember so good these days. But why don't you ask away."

Bob was looking at me. I looked at Mariela. She looked back. She wanted me to take the lead. After her off-kilter I-love-children outburst, she seemed fearful of the way words might come out of her mouth.

"Oh, and before you ask your questions...." Bob stepped on the silence. "I guess I have a few of my own. First of all, what's your interest in all this anyway? And why after all these years?"

I looked again at Mariela. She nodded. "My wife is from Cuba," I began, "and she believes she might know"—not 'have known.' I'd become more adept at the delicate phrasing required to traverse these shoals—"the people on that raft."

"No people!" Bob's response was swift, almost angry. "There were no people on board when I found her. No people at all."

"No, I understand," I said. I did. Or thought I did. "We're just trying to find out whatever we can. For their families back in Cuba," I lied.

"And how'd you know to find me?" Why did he sound so suspicious? And how could he not have known about Paco and the photo already?

"Uh, it's a long story," I responded, off balance now, no longer sure what or how much I should say. "There's a guy in Miami we met, a Cuban. His hobby is collecting information about all the rafts that came this way—"

"Must have been Arturo," Bob said to his wife, relaxing slightly. Then to us, "Cuban guy used to work for me on the boat sometimes. He was real interested when I brought the raft ashore. Wanted to know where I found it, and when. Took a bunch of pictures. He's gone now. Couple years. Maybe to Miami. Maybe he's the one you were talking to."

"Maybe," I said. No need to tell him about Paco. "Anyway," I continued, brushing past the truth nettles in my path, "if you could just tell us a little bit more about where and when you found it, the circumstances, that sort of thing."

Bob took a breath, calm now, began. "Sure. Well, it was a long time ago and, like I said, my memory...but I believe it happened sometime in the spring of zero-four—"

"May 16?" I cut in, remembering the date on Paco's file folder. "Could it have been then?"

"Could have been. Makes sense. I know it was right after stone crab season. I was supposed to have a charter that day, some guy from up north wanted to go marlin fishing, but then he cancelled on me at the last minute." Bob's memory seemed to be better than he'd let on. "So I figured I'd just take the boat out for a little exercise, you know, get a little sun." He looked shyly, slyly at his wife. "A little nap, maybe a little nip."

"I know what you do out there," Maudie chided indulgently, then looked over at us. "No secrets after thirty years." She smiled. "No secrets at all." I wondered if that could ever be true.

"So," I said, trying to keep our conversation from veering too far off course, "what do you remember about the raft? Where were you when you found it? What time of day?" I wasn't sure why I'd even asked that last question, except I remembered Mariela telling Juany she'd studied the tides and currents, knew the hour-by-hour weather in the Strait. Maybe—

"Bob, honey, why don't you just take them out there, show them?" Maudie again. "'Sides, it'd be a beautiful afternoon on the water."

"It would that," Bob responded, relieved, it seemed, to escape the confines of the kitchen, perhaps the presence of Maudie.

In short order, we drove to the marina where Bob kept the twenty-five-foot Parker Pilothouse Sport cabin cruiser he called *Baudie* (a clever play on Bob and Maudie, don't you know), which boasted dependable, fully refurbished Yamaha F300 engines. I could not have told you any of that on my own, but Bob seemed eager to share in the sporty man-to-man kind of way some men have, even if the man he was talking to had no idea what he was talking about.

"The real money's in charters these days," Bob explained to me as we motored into open ocean. "Fishing's OK, but it mostly just fills in the gaps between the charters."

Mariela said nothing. She stood outside the *Baudie*'s cockpit near the stern, staring out into the vast nothingness of ocean. Staring. Imagining…imagining what?

Finally, Bob checked his GPS coordinates, cut the engine. A sudden, deafening silence filled the spaces where the thrum of the engines had been.

"It was right around here," Bob said. "Two-and-a-half, three miles southwest of Taylor State Park. Late afternoon, the sun hanging on in the west over there. I was just tootling around, enjoying the breeze, like I said, enjoying a little nip…" He reached down, opened a small box at his feet, lifted out a bottle of Bacardi white, a rum I might have enjoyed before I knew its history. He took a long swig as if recreating the events of that day, passed the bottle to me. I took a swig—when in Rome—and turned toward the stern. Mariela must have slipped into the cabin after Bob turned off the engine. I extended the bottle. She shook her head. I passed it back to Bob.

"Saw it off in the distance, that direction," he said, pointing to the south, "maybe two hundred yards or so. I knew what it was right away. Not the first raft I've seen in these waters, that's for sure. I couldn't see any sign of life aboard, but it was hard to know at that distance, and my eyes aren't that good with the distance anymore, so I decided to steer closer. Thought if there was anyone aboard I could maybe point them in the right direction toward Key West. Easy enough to get disoriented out here. Especially with no GPS. Most rafts don't have GPS," he said, chuckling at his own joke. "But there wasn't anybody. So then I looked closer. The raft was in surprisingly good shape. I thought, well, why not, I could use it for a barge, maybe do a little towing, but—"

"And you didn't see anyone on board, in the water around—"

"No!" he snapped. "I already told you...no people!"

I backed off. "OK." Changed course. "So what did you do then? Call the coast guard?"

Bob seemed to eye me even more suspiciously now. What had I said? I could sense his mind working, but I had no clue what neural pathways he was navigating, or in what direction, or for what purpose.

"There wasn't any point," he said softly after a minute. "What would they have done? I mean it was just one more empty raft. If the coast guard chased after every empty raft in the Straits of Florida, they'd never have any time to do anything else, now would they?"

I looked over at Mariela who stood, listening. What was she thinking? That Bob hadn't seen anyone, so they must have already died? Or that Bob hadn't seen anyone, so they must have been picked up already by another vessel, or maybe they swam to shore, or?... I needed to push harder. "So, you're absolutely sure. You didn't see anyone, any sign of life, any—"

Bob was angry now. "Why the fuck do you keep asking me that? I already told you. There was nobody. I didn't see anybody, I—"

"My son was on that raft." We both turned to look at Mariela, Bob suddenly stunned silent, staring now, waiting, expectant. "His name is Tonito and he was three years old then." She spoke in an even, unemotional voice, though I could see the wetness clouding her eyes. "I am trying to find my son." Mariela reached into her purse then, removed the photo of Tonito, shoved it toward Bob, who grasped it, reluctantly, at its edge between his thumb and forefinger, as if the image itself could do him harm. He did hazard one fleeting glance at Tonito's smiling face, saw more than he could cope with, pushed the photo back into Mariela's hands, and then rushed out the cockpit door. Leaning as far as he could manage out over the side of the *Baudie*, Bob gagged, vomited, gagged, vomited until he had nothing left inside to throw up.

I tried to make sense of what had just happened. The ocean was flat, wave-less. Bob had taken no more than a few swigs from the rum bottle, and none of us had eaten more than a few bites of Maudie's store-bought cookies. While Mariela and I stood frozen in our odd tableau, staring, trying not to stare, Bob wiped his mouth with his forearm, then wiped his arm on his jeans, then used his balled-up fist to wipe the tears out of his eyes, and, finally, stood up.

"I know," he said after he stumbled back into the cockpit, looking directly into Mariela's eyes. I had no idea what he meant. Then he turned to me. "I figured that's why you called the other night. All this time, I been waiting for somebody to call. And then, you know, I almost told you not to come. Wasn't sure I could tell you what I had to tell you. Do you ever feel like that? You know you need to tell, but you're so afraid of telling...."

I had felt that. He turned back to Mariela, beseeching in his eyes now. "I saw your boy, ma'am. I saw them all. They was still on the raft, four of them, laying there on the decking, twisted together, the men almost in a circle around the boy. He was in the middle, all curled up. They were all dead. They'd been dead for a while, bloated, purple. The maggots had been at them." He stopped, looked at Mariela. "Sorry. The birds were hovering too, waiting for me to leave so they could come back."

Mariela cried without sound, tears rolling down her cheeks. I wanted to go to her, wrap her in my arms, hold her. I couldn't move.

Bob let out a long, snuffly sigh that began deep in his gut. "I know I should have called the coast guard. I thought about it. I did. But then I thought, you know, god forgive me, all the waiting around for them to arrive, and all the questions, and all the paperwork...." He paused, waiting for his breathing to slow. "And I'd been drinking too. All afternoon. I didn't need to get charged just for doing the right thing...so I never called." Paused again. Looked at us, one to the other. Tried to read our reactions. We were unreadable. "I'm sorry," he said finally, "so sorry."

I guessed I knew but knew I didn't. Not for sure. "What did you do then?" I asked.

"I came alongside," Bob answered simply, "attached a tow line, and then I went aboard. The smell was something awful...sorry, ma'am, but it was. I don't know now what I thought I was going to do. Probably I didn't think...otherwise, I wouldn't have...or I don't believe I would have...the idea just came to me, sudden, some lines in my head...." He was reciting now, words I recognized. "But such a tide as moving seems asleep/Too full for sound and foam/When that which drew from out the boundless deep/Turns again home." Bob saw my reaction. "You know the one I mean. We buried my daddy out here years ago. He was a fisherman too. Gave him a big send off. The minister read that whole poem. I was so taken with it, I remember, I memorized it. Word for word. So then I decided that's what I'd do. I'd bury them at sea, let them go home again.... I knelt down beside those people, spoke those words...." Bob's voice faltered for a long moment. "And then I rolled them over the side and into the ocean, watched them all disappear." He had to stop again. He looked now at Mariela. "That little boy, your boy? I could swear he had a smile on his face." There seemed to be nothing left to say.

We stood in awkward, isolated silence for what seemed like forever. Finally, Mariela took Bob's hand and then mine, and walked us to the stern of the boat. We each looked off into the nothing between here and Cuba. Mariela began,

> Sunset and evening star,
> And one clear call for me!
> And may there be no moaning of the bar,
> When I put out to sea...

I couldn't help but marvel. Had Mariela learned that poem growing up in Cuba? When she studied English? Or had she—like Bob with his own father's pastor—been so moved by Sarah's reading of it at my father's memorial she'd memorized it too. There was no point in puzzling this out. As she continued, I added my voice. Bob joined in too. I couldn't have told you where the words came from. It didn't matter.

***

Despite Maudie's entreaties, we didn't stay for dinner. "Thanks, really, thank you, but we should get the bus back to Miami tonight," I said, though we didn't. We checked into a hotel near the bus terminal. Bob and Maudie's grandchildren had returned from wherever they'd been, and the small bungalow had filled with the childish sounds of shouts and laughter. I wasn't sure Mariela could cope with that now. I wasn't sure I could either.

"I'll drive them back to the station," Bob said, relieved. To Maudie, "I won't be long." At the bottom of the outside staircase, Bob directed us to wait by the truck. "I'll be right there." He walked over to a shed near the rear of the yard, opened the door, went in, turned on a light. A few minutes later, he returned. "I found this. On the raft," he said simply, handing Mariela a small, stuffed, handmade doll. "I'm not sure why I kept it," he said, almost to himself. "Maybe I knew you'd come someday."

Mariela was still clutching Mi Toni to her chest when we checked into the hotel. It sat, watchful, at the head of one of the room's double beds while we ate our room service meal in silence.

"I knew," Mariela said finally, her voice as flat as the afternoon's ocean. "I always knew I would find out Tonito was...that Tonito had died. But I had to *know* it. Does that make any sense to you?" It did. "All these years I've kept myself going by pretending I didn't know. And now I know. Now what?"

We made love. It was love of a different order...slow, intense, then cathartic.

Afterward, she said, "I want to go home." It was only later we decided where home would be.

ACKNOWLEDGMENTS

A SPECIAL THANK YOU TO MY WIFE, JEANIE STEINBOCK KIMBER, WHO SET ME off on the decade-long odyssey that became this novel by suggesting, ever so gently, over drinks on a beach at a Cuban holiday resort sometime in the early 2000s, that I set my next book somewhere other than in Nova Scotia. As in all things, she was right. As in many things, I met her halfway.

Thanks, too, to Alejandro Trellis, Cuban tour guide extraordinaire. During the initial research for my novel, I asked Alex to introduce me to the Havana "I wouldn't see as a tourist." He did. But he also, incidentally and coincidentally, derailed my fiction-writing plan for five years by introducing me to the incredible, unbelievable-but-true story of five Cuban intelligence agents then serving unconscionably long sentences in US prisons for trying to prevent terrorism against their country. I thank him for telling me about them. The story of the Cuban Five was one more than worth the learning-writing side-trip.

The years I spent researching their story, in fact, helped deepen my understanding of Cuba and Cubans. That said, for me, Cuba remains endlessly intriguing, always fascinating, occasionally confounding. Which is also part of its charm.

Many people—Cubans and Canadians—educated me along the way. At one time or another, in one way or another, I learned from, among others, Lee Cohen, Elena Díaz González, Brenda Durdle, Dyam Fernandez Perez, Fred Furlong, Dayana Garcia Valdez, René González, Fernando González, Antonio Guerrero, Bill Hackwell,

Gerardo Hernandez, Alicia Jrapko, Emily Kirk, John Kirk, Ramon Labañino, Jesus Magan, Valerie Mansour, Elizabeth Palmeiro, Adriana Pérez, Jesus Rolando Casamayor, Anna Sanchez, and Olga Salanueva. I thank them all.

Sue Ashdown, Karen Dubinsky, Irma González, Michael Kimber, Emily Kirk, John Kirk, Hilary McMahon, Kelly Toughill, and Bill Turpin all generously read drafts of this novel in its various stages of dress and helped save me from many errors I didn't know I was making. Thanks. They are not, of course, responsible for the other mistakes I am sure I made anyway.

I also want to express my thanks to Whitney Moran, the managing editor of Vagrant Press, and editor Elizabeth Eve. Their thoughtful suggestions and encouragement to dig deeper have made this a much better book.

Although this is a work of fiction, I am a journalist and a researcher, and I've borrowed bits and pieces from real life and the internet, then bent and shaped them for my own fictional purposes. The result is a novel and any resemblance to anyone, living or dead, is accidental.

NICOLA DAVISON

Sᴛᴇᴘʜᴇɴ Kɪᴍʙᴇʀ, ᴀɴ ᴀᴡᴀʀᴅ-ᴡɪɴɴɪɴɢ ᴡʀɪᴛᴇʀ, editor, and broadcaster, is the author of ten books, including two novels and eight works of nonfiction. His most recent nonfiction book—*What Lies Across the Water: The Real Story of the Cuban Five*—was longlisted for the Canadian Booksellers Association's Libris Award as Nonfiction Book of the Year, won the 2014 Evelyn Richardson Award for Nonfiction, and the Cuban Institute of the Book's 2016 Reader's Choice Award. A journalist for fifty years, he is a professor in the School of Journalism at the University of King's College in Halifax and co-founder of the King's MFA in Creative Nonfiction program.